Her Guardian Angel

Also from Larissa Ione

Her Guardian Angel
By Larissa Ione

A Demonica Underworld/Masters and Mercenaries Novella

Introduction by Lexi Blake

EVIL EYE
CONCEPTS

Her Guardian Angel
A Demonica Underworld/Masters and Mercenaries Novella
Copyright 2018 Larissa Ione
ISBN: 978-1-945920-84-4

Published by Evil Eye Concepts, Incorporated

This is a work of fiction. Names, places, characters and incidents are the product of the author's imagination and are fictitious. Any resemblance to actual persons, living or dead, events or establishments is solely coincidental.

Sign up for the 1001 Dark Nights Newsletter
and be entered to win a Tiffany Lock necklace.

There's a contest every quarter!

Go to www.1001DarkNights.com to subscribe.

An Introduction to the Lexi Blake Crossover Collection

Who doesn't love a crossover? I know that for me there's always been something magical about two fictional words blending and meeting in a totally unexpected way. For years the only medium that has truly done it well and often is comic books. Superman vs. Batman in a fight to the finish. Marvel's Infinite Universe. There's something about two crazy worlds coming together that almost makes them feel more real. Like there's this brilliant universe filled with fictional characters and they can meet and talk, and sometimes they can fall in love.

I'm a geek. I go a little crazy when Thor meets up with Iron Man or The Flash and Arrow team up.

So why wouldn't we do it in Romanceland?

There are ways out there. A writer can write in another author's world, giving you her take on it. There's some brilliant fanfiction out there, but I wanted something different. I wanted to take my time and gradually introduce these characters from other worlds, bring you in slowly so you don't even realize what I'm doing. So you think this is McKay-Taggart, nothing odd here. Except there is...

Over the course of my last three books—Love Another Day, At Your Service, and Nobody Does It Better—I introduced you to five new characters and five new and brilliant worlds. If I've done my job, you'll know and love these characters—sisters from another mister, brothers from another mother.

So grab a glass of wine and welcome to the Lexi Blake Crossover Collection.

Love,

Lexi

Available now!

Close Cover by Lexi Blake
Her Guardian Angel by Larissa Ione
Justify Me by J. Kenner
Say You Won't Let Go by Corinne Michaels
His to Protect by Carly Phillips
Rescuing Sadie by Susan Stoker

Acknowledgments from the Author

I can't even begin to express how special this book is to me—for a lot of reasons. I can, however, express my thanks to everyone who made it possible, starting with Lexi Blake.

Lexi, thank you for inviting me to play in your world and for trusting me to not unleash an apocalypse in it! Seriously, I'm so honored and humbled by your faith in me. I'm such a huge fan of not only your writing, but of you. I don't know if you realize this, but your invitation to enter into this crossover project helped me solidify the direction I wanted to take this series…it actually shaped the future of the Demonica world and led me to rework Hawkyn to kick off this book…and to kick off what's to come in this series and the next. Much of what happens in upcoming books will stem from the events that took place in Her Guardian Angel, so you have my eternal gratitude and admiration. (And in a show of true respect, I didn't kill you in this story! *g*)

Kim Guidroz, thank you for everything you do! Girl, you are a treasure—like, the rare kind only Wraith could find. I wish we could spend more time together!

And Liz Berry…I'm not even sure where to start. If not for you, none of this would have happened. Not this crossover, and not the Demonica Underworld. There are not enough hugs in the world for that. Thank you from the depths of my heart…and the depths of Sheoul-gra!

Her Guardian Angel also came alive thanks to the heroine's namesake, Suzanne Johnson, who has enriched the Demonica universe in so many ways and more to come. Thank you, Suzanne, for your passion, your generosity, and your delicious recipes!

I also need to send out oodles of thank yous to Kasi Alexander and Fedora Chen for your invaluable contributions and hard work. I'm so happy you're on the Evil Eye team!

Jillian Stein, thank you for…everything. I mean, literally, *everything*. In the Demonica world you'd be, well, you'd be Jillian. But if you weren't *that* character, you'd still be utterly badass, just like in real life.

I couldn't write any acknowledgements without telling Judie Bouldry that she's a big reason I have any writing time at all and she's also why I'm still sane. At least, mostly sane. Judie, thank you for all you do! We *will* take that trip to Europe someday!

And last but not least, I want to thank you, the readers for your continued enthusiasm. We're heading for something bigger in the Demonica world, and I'm very much looking forward to the ride.

Saddle up the hell stallions, everyone, because here we go.

Glossary

The Aegis—Society of human warriors dedicated to protecting the world from evil. Recent dissension among its ranks reduced its numbers and sent The Aegis in a new direction.

Fallen Angel—Believed to be evil by most humans, fallen angels can be grouped into two categories: True Fallen and Unfallen. Unfallen angels have been cast from Heaven and are earthbound, living a life in which they are neither truly good nor truly evil. In this state, they can, rarely, earn their way back into Heaven. Or they can choose to enter Sheoul, the demon realm, in order to complete their fall and become True Fallens.

Harrowgate—Vertical portals, invisible to humans, used to travel between locations on Earth and Sheoul. A very few beings can summon their own personal Harrowgates.

Inner Sanctum—A realm within Sheoul-gra that consists of five Rings, each housing the souls of demons categorized by their level of evil as defined by the Ufelskala. The Inner Sanctum is run by the fallen angel Hades and his staff of wardens, all fallen angels. Access to the Inner Sanctum is strictly limited, as the demons imprisoned within can take advantage of any outside object or living person in order to escape.

Memitim—Earthbound angels assigned to protect important humans called Primori. Memitim remain earthbound until they complete their duties, at which time they Ascend, earning their wings and entry into Heaven.

Primori—Humans and demons whose lives are fated to affect the world in some crucial way.

Sheoul—Demon realm some call Hell. Located on its own plane deep in the bowels of the Earth, accessible to most only by Harrowgates and hellmouths.

Sheoul-gra—A realm that exists independently of Sheoul, it is overseen by Azagoth, also known as the Grim Reaper. Within Sheoul-gra is the Inner Sanctum, where demon souls go to be kept in torturous limbo until they can be reborn.

Shrowd—When angels travel through time, they exist within an impenetrable bubble known as a shrowd. While in the shrowd, angels are invisible and cannot interact with anyone—human, demon, or angel—outside the shrowd. Breaking out of the shrowd is a serious transgression that can, and has, resulted in execution. Also called a quantamun.

Ufelskala—A scoring system for demons, based on their degree of evil. All supernatural creatures and evil humans can be categorized into the five Tiers, with the Fifth Tier comprising the worst of the wicked.

Chapter One

Something out there, in the lengthening evening shadows, was watching him. And seeing how whatever it was made the hair on the back of his neck stand on end and the tattoo on his back sting like some sort of futuristic subdermal warning system, it was probably too much to hope that it was a gorgeous woman who wanted nothing more than a one-night stand.

Declan Burke pushed away from the fifteen-story building that housed his employer's Dallas offices of McKay-Taggart, tossed his coffee cup in the trash, and casually brushed his hand across his holster to loosen his Glock G29 as he moved toward the alley in a loose, easy gait. If someone was spying on him, he wasn't going to let on that he knew it. He was just heading to where he'd parked his Rover on the street this afternoon when he'd come in to grab a few things before he took off on his assignment in South America—

"Hey, Burke!"

Shit. Silent-watcher-slash-one-night-stand forgotten, he inhaled deeply before swinging around to see the big boss, Ian Taggart, sauntering toward him like a man on a mission to sell him something. And Dec knew exactly what that something was. Tag had called last night as Declan was packing his suitcase and asked if he'd rather take another job. His answer had been a hard no. Tag had been persuasive. Dec's answer had then been a fuck no. And finally, a hang-up.

"I already said I'm not taking that job," Declan sighed.

"And you didn't say why."

"Am I required to?"

"You know you're not." Tag stopped in front of him, his blond hair ruffling in the stiflingly hot breeze. "But this is right up your alley. You grew up in D.C. You know the people. You know the politics. You know the money."

Yeah, Declan knew all of that way too intimately. "I said no."

"I wouldn't ask if I didn't think you were the best person for the job."

Swearing silently, Declan looked up at the evening sky until he could reliably talk to his boss without losing his temper.

Finally, he looked back at his boss. "I left that cesspool when I was seventeen, and I haven't looked back. I'm sorry, Ian. I respect the hell out of you, and if you need me for anything else, I'll do it, no questions asked. But not this. Fire me if you need to."

Tag let out an exasperated curse. "You'd seriously rather take the mission in the jungle that'll probably get you killed than work with Senator McRory and his aide on some routine security issues?"

Okay, Tag was exaggerating the risk of the South American job, but even if he weren't... "I can't even count all the ways I could say yes to that."

"Fine," Tag said, "but at least think about it. Your plane doesn't leave until tomorrow night."

"Yeah, sure," Declan offered, knowing he wasn't going to think about it at all. Not for a single second. As far as he was concerned, the topic of the D.C. job was a dead thread.

"Thanks, man." Taggart clapped Declan on the shoulder and headed toward the parking lot.

Declan hung out for another minute, trying to decide what to do now. Going home to an empty, depressing apartment didn't appeal to him, but neither did hitting a noisy club, not when he'd been getting so many headaches in recent months. Besides, he wasn't the most social person on the planet and he hated the bar scene. He only put up with it because lately he'd been restless when he was alone.

Maybe he needed a girlfriend. Or at the very least, he needed to get laid. Of course, meeting someone meant being social. Making small talk. Telling people about his life. What a nightmare.

He was going to die alone, wasn't he?

"Everyone dies alone," his coworker Shane Landon had told him once. "Some sooner than later."

Shane was a real cheery guy sometimes.

Taking a mental coin toss, he settled on grabbing a six-pack of Shiner Bock, heading to his place, and watching a few episodes of season three of *Breaking Bad*. How had he missed the show when it first came out? It was awesome. But hey, now he got to binge watch—

A flash of light blinded him, the intensity making him stumble. Blinking, shielding his eyes, he peered in the direction of the alley he'd been walking toward before Tag stopped him. Bright white light flickered like a florescent bulb between the buildings, and he swore he saw a hulking shadow at the center, something with thick arms and legs...and a massive head with horns.

What the fuck? Suddenly, searing pain ripped through his skull and the tattoo on his back. He heard a scream, his scream, before he fell to his knees, grasping his head in his hands as if that would stop the agony. Through the assault on his senses, he tasted and smelled blood, and as he gasped for air, he swore he saw another shadowy figure join the first, this one smaller, more petite. Even...feminine. And they were fighting.

Even as he moaned in agony, he laughed internally at the absurdity of his thoughts. Shadowy figures battling in the center of a ball of light? Had someone spiked his coffee? Was he really asleep and having a nightmare straight from a comic book?

A lightning strike of pain streaked through him from the top of his skull to the tips of his toes. The world tilted and spun, and he didn't even have the strength to scream again as darkness shrouded his vision and he slid, unconscious, to the ground.

* * * *

Suzanne had never encountered a demon like the one that had just committed some sort of psychic assault on the human she was assigned to protect. And as a Memitim, an earthbound angel charged with protecting people who were important to the fate of humanity, she'd seen a lot of demons. Well, mostly in books, but she'd read a *lot* of books.

The creature was huge, at least twelve feet tall, with horns that extended over three feet from his skull and were as thick as her thigh at the base. But it wasn't his size or his toxic ugliness that was so unique. It was the fact that he was able to affect Declan's body from a distance, without triggering her Primori alarm, that made the demon not only unique, but dangerous as hell.

Spinning, she used a pair of scythes and roundhouse kicks to launch an aggressive attack on the demon. It fell back, but its massive sword forced her to leap backward often, losing momentum with each retreat. Its hooved feet caught her in the ribs a half dozen times, cracking bone and splitting her skin until her blood splashed on her boots. As an angel she healed quickly, but she still felt pain, and she was in agony.

The thing peeled its black, scaly lips back from its shark-like teeth before morphing into human form, becoming an attractive male with short jet-black hair and a goatee, and eyes the color of blue frost.

"Who are you?" he growled in a deep, hell-smoke voice that made the hair on the back of her neck stand up.

"No one important," she said, all cheery and perky to hide the fact that this guy was terrifying and her cracked ribs were making it hard to catch her breath. "Who the hell are *you?*"

He sneered. "Someone who doesn't have time to play with little girls. You can call me Morroc, but get in my way again, and I'll play until you and every one of your kin are nothing but broken flesh dolls."

With that, he disappeared into thin air.

"Thank God," she whispered to herself. Her knees nearly buckled with relief. That was the first demon she'd battled to protect her Primori, and it was one of the most terrifying demons she'd ever seen. She needed to research the sucker, and fast.

With a flick of her wrist, she made her summoned scythes disappear. Several yards away, Declan was lying on the sidewalk and two men were rushing toward him. She wanted to be at his side to reassure herself that he was okay, but the Primori mark, the quarter-sized *heraldi* on her wrist, wasn't burning, which meant he wasn't in danger of dying, so his human friends should be able to help him.

She hoped. The *heraldi* had failed to warn her that Declan was in danger in the first place. If she hadn't popped in to randomly check on him, he'd be dead now.

Declan sat up, waving off help and cursing. Thankful that he seemed to be no worse for wear, she flashed out of there and returned to Sheoul-gra, a prison realm for the souls of demons and evil humans, but also the residence of her father, the Grim Reaper, and hundreds of her brothers and sisters. Dozens of Unfallen angels lived here too, serving at the Grim

Reaper's pleasure in return for a safe place to live and work. As Unfallen, they no longer had wings, powers, or access to Heaven, but they weren't fully fallen, either. Their status left them in a state of limbo and danger, powerless against demons and other fallen angels who made a game out of dragging Unfallen into what demons called Sheoul, AKA Hell to normal people. As her brother Hawkyn's buddy Cipher liked to say, "Gain cool new powers…but lose your soul."

And any shot of redemption.

But some True Fallen angels weren't complete assholes, and a handful worked here in Sheoul-gra, too.

Before she'd come to live here last year she hadn't been able to imagine that her father's domain could be so beautiful, and apparently, that hadn't always been the case. His marriage to a Heavenly angel a few years ago had transformed not just him, but his very realm.

Now, instead of dead, blackened foliage that ate people, there was lush grass and vibrant trees. Instead of fountains that ran with blood, there were clear lakes and streams, and fountains with sparkling water. And instead of soot-covered, dilapidated ruins, there were dormitories and gyms, cafeterias and libraries.

Inhaling air made fragrant by rare giant poppies imported from Sheoul's Horun region, she jogged along a worn path leading to the senior Memitim quarters, hoping to find her brother Hawkyn and Cipher. Hawk had been her mentor since just after she was plucked from her human life a little over fifty years ago, and she trusted him more than anyone. Cipher, as an Unfallen angel, paid for his room and board by providing valuable tech services. Where one was found, the other was usually close by.

Although now that Hawk had a mate and a baby on the way, he spent less time goofing off with Cipher than he used to.

Fortunately, she spotted their blond heads outside in the Commons near the dorms, sitting at one of the big stone table and bench sets. Cipher was hunched over his laptop, his long hair obscuring his handsome face, his fingers tapping on the keyboard with blurring speed, and Hawk was cursing up a storm.

"Hey, guys. What's going on?"

Hawkyn gestured to Cipher. "He's developing a database of all unawakened brothers and sisters so we can start bringing them here in some kind of order."

She remembered her days as an unawakened angel, thinking she was human, living in the human world with a wonderful human family, and her heart thudded fondly. She'd been one of the few, maybe the only, Memitim to have been given a decent life. The rest of her siblings, thousands of them, born over the course of several millennia, had grown up under the worst conditions imaginable. It was by design—angel mothers giving them up to be raised in the human world so they'd understand hardship and humanity.

Suzanne had been lucky, and it warmed her heart to know that, thanks to her father and Hawkyn, all the children currently under the age of twenty who lived in the human world would be brought here, to be raised among their real family.

"Okay," she said, "the database sounds great. So what's the problem?"

Hawkyn growled under his breath. "The Memitim Council, which is supposed to have provided us with the records, hasn't delivered them all. I'd estimate that there are about five hundred missing."

"Out of...?"

"Approximately eleven hundred and sixty-three." Cipher talked as he typed, not looking up from the screen. "There would have been more if Azagoth hadn't started balking about playing baby-daddy a while back. And there are none under the age of four, which coincides with when he married Lilliana."

"Well, let me know when the little ones start arriving. I'll put together some kid-friendly meal plans." She chewed on her lower lip for a second, hesitant to interrupt... But this was important. "Are you guys too busy to help me out for a minute?"

Cipher merely cocked an eyebrow, but in an instant Hawkyn flipped his switch into overprotective brother mode. "'Sup, sis?"

She sank down next to Cipher on the bench before either noticed that her legs were still a little shaky from the encounter with the demon.

"What kind of demon is about twelve feet tall, has horns, hooves, a big mantle of black fur around its shoulders, and attacks with some sort of psychic ability?" Well, the guy had also carried a massive sword with an eight-foot blade. "Oh, and he can take human form."

"I've never seen anything like that," Hawkyn said. "You sure it used a psychic attack? Was your Primori the victim?"

"Yes, to both."

"He's okay, right?" Hawk braced his elbows on the picnic table and leaned toward her. "What's his name? Declan?"

Hawkyn knew Declan's name, but for some reason her brother was constantly trying to distance himself, as if doing so would also distance *her* from Declan. He worried too much.

"He's being tended to. I'll check on him after I'm done here." She turned to Cipher, who was still tapping away on his computer. "Have you heard of a demon like that?"

"No, but I'm checking the angelic and Baradocian databases now." He squinted at the screen. "Did the demon look like a toad with horns?" At her shake of the head, he tried again. "Did it have spines?" Another shake. "Did it spew mucus from a sphincter-looking thing in its chin?"

"Ew, and thankfully, no."

Two birds of prey clashed overhead in the endless blue-gray sky, but Cipher didn't so much as blink. Once he was engaged on the computer, she doubted even a naked female could tear him away. Well, maybe Flail could. The skanky raven-haired True Fallen had been hanging around Sheoul-gra for a few months, running errands for Azagoth. Cipher claimed all they did was "game" together.

Uh-huh. A scantily-clad siren like Flail and a model-hot male like Cipher didn't just sit around and play video games. Suzanne might be a virgin, but she was a seventy-five-year-old one who'd been around the block. Plus, she'd learned a lot from *Cosmopolitan* and *Sex and the City*.

"Was the demon surrounded by light?" Cipher asked.

Finally! She sat up straight. "Yes."

He spun the laptop around. "Is this your demon?"

The picture on the screen, a rough charcoal drawing, was dead on, and she actually shivered. "That's the ugly bastard."

"What is it?" Hawk asked.

Cipher whipped the computer back to him. "According to Baradoc's classification, it's a Siecher." He grimaced. "It's a five on the Ufelskala. Extremely dangerous, impossible to reason with, and carries grudges to the grave. Cross one of these, and it will seek revenge until you and the last of your line is dead. It's a big fan of slaughtering friends and neighbors, as well."

"Yikes." She shuddered, remembering his words to her. *Get in my way again, and I'll play until you and every one of your kin are nothing but broken flesh dolls.* "Do they attack for any reason other than revenge?"

One of Cipher's big shoulders rolled in a lazy shrug. "They're carnivores, but according to this they don't usually prey on humans, and they rarely even leave the demon realm."

If that was true, why would it have attacked Declan? Ugh. Mysteries. She hated them. She'd never been patient enough for that. Which might be why she enjoyed cooking. Recipes rarely made her guess.

"So how do you kill these things?"

Cipher scrolled down the screen and let out a frustrated curse. "It doesn't say. Just that they're hard to injure."

"That's certainly true," she muttered.

"Did you fight it?" Hawkyn's sharp tone meant his overprotective nature had gone into overdrive. Great. He was such a pain in the ass when he went all papa bear. His kid was going to hate life.

"Not for long," she assured him. "I think my presence freaked it out. I certainly didn't hurt it badly."

"Did it use a psychic attack on you?"

"Nope. He used good old-fashioned swords and some serious stomps with his hooves. My ribs are going to hurt for a week." She rubbed said ribs and winced. "Oh, and its psychic attack on Declan didn't trigger my Primori alarm."

"What?" Hawkyn frowned. "That's...bad."

"You think?" Even now she was feeling antsy with the need to check on Declan. If she wasn't getting notice that he was in danger, he could already be dead from another demon attack. "I don't know if that's a result of my *heraldi* being defective or if this particular demon doesn't trigger the alarm."

"Dude." Cipher let out a low whistle. "What are you going to do? Watch him twenty-four seven?"

The idea of spending every waking minute with Declan filled her with a warm, liquid sensation that was, no doubt, forbidden. Memitim were supposed to be emotionless robots who did their jobs and didn't ask questions or get involved with their charges. Straying from that mandate often resulted in punishment in the form of more years of service or even being purged from the Memitim program...which meant that they couldn't Ascend to Heaven to become a full, winged angel.

"I can convene with the Council," Hawkyn said. "Make sure you don't get assigned another Primori until this is handled. Memitim used to get at least a decade with only a single Primori, but the Council fears Memitim shortages in the future until Heavenly angels start giving birth to offspring with our skills and abilities."

Oh, how she loved her brother. Yes, she had thousands of them, all the product of their father, Azagoth's, unions with Heavenly angels for the purpose of creating the Memitim class. Azagoth had stopped making Memitim when he took Lilliana as a mate, so Heaven had decided to allow any angel to give birth to Memitim-class children. Which meant she wouldn't have any more brothers and sisters until Azagoth and Lilliana had children. No big deal; the ones she knew, she loved. Especially Hawk, who had been there for her almost from the moment she'd learned the truth about what she really was. She'd definitely take him up on his offer.

"That would be helpful." It would be just her luck that she'd get assigned a bunch more Primori when she needed to spend all her time on just one. "Do you think they'll go for it?"

"Normally, no. But these are special circumstances."

"Okay, so having Declan as my only charge will make keeping an eye on him easier, but realistically, I can't just hang out in the *shrowd* or at the places he frequents all the time. His coworkers and friends probably already think I'm a stalker. I'm going to need an excuse to be near him."

Cipher looked up from the computer. "What's he do for a living?"

"He's a security expert and bodyguard—" She broke off as the obvious solution popped into her head. Then she grinned. "I'm going to need a D'Angelo house, preferably in Texas where he works, and a story."

"Whoa, now," Hawk said, holding up his hands. "Slow down. I don't know that inserting yourself into Declan's life is a good idea."

But Cipher was already on it, his fingers tapping madly on the keyboard. "There are three D'Angelo houses available in Texas. One is set up like a crack house in Houston, one is in a middle-class neighborhood in Austin, and..." He gave a thumbs-up. "The third is a mansion in Dallas. Perfect for someone who needs to hire a bodyguard."

"Cool." Dallas was spot on, given that Declan lived in the city. "Will you work up my backstory and set the wheels in motion?"

"You got it. Gimme forty-eight hours."

Hawkyn shook his head slowly. "You know Heavenly angels don't like sharing their D'Angelo network with lowly Memitim. They might not let you take over one of their properties or use their cover name for setting up an alias."

"Pfft." Cipher swiped his fingers over the laptop's touchpad. "They don't care. Lets them show lowly Memitim how much better it is to be a real angel."

Hawkyn shot his buddy an annoyed look, but it wasn't clear if he was annoyed that Cipher wasn't helping him win the argument or if he was irked by Cipher's calling Heavenly angels "real" and implying that Memitim were chopped liver. *Fake* chopped liver.

"I don't like this." Hawkyn growled.

Of course he didn't. Hawkyn wouldn't like anything that required her to openly spend time in the human realm. Memitim were supposed to watch their charges from the invisibility and safety of the *shrowd* and interact with humans as little as possible. What she was planning would fully immerse her in the world of not only humans, but her Primori.

"It's the only way I can protect him from the psychic attacks," she pointed out.

"It's also the perfect way for you to get too close to him, Suz. You've already interacted more than you should with the people around him, and you're way more infatuated with him than you should be."

Cipher snorted. "Says the guy who fell in love with the person he was protecting."

"That's different," Hawkyn protested. "Aurora isn't my Primori. She wasn't Primori at all when I met her."

Suzanne rolled her eyes. "Yeah, yeah, whatever. It'll be fine. Besides," she said with a wink that never failed to disarm Hawk, "my favorite brother is on the Memitim Council."

He gave her a you-know-better-than-that look. "I'm not technically on the Council."

"You're the liaison between the Council and the rest of us. I have faith that you can keep me out of trouble."

Hawkyn ran a hand over his face as if trying to scrub away his frustration. "Hey, I have a crazy idea. How about you keep yourself out of trouble? That would be great."

She laughed. She never got into trouble, and he knew it. She could do this job and get out unscathed.

But even as that thought went through her head, a niggle of doubt cast a shadow. Her feelings for Declan were probably already inappropriate for the type of relationship they had—which was none. It was all one-sided because he barely knew she existed. And he believed she was human.

And the thing was, it had to stay that way. Romance between

Memitim and Primori was forbidden. Beyond forbidden. And while, over the course of many thousands of years, several Memitim had failed to protect their very first Primori, none had fallen for them.

Suzanne had already fallen for hers. The question now was what she should do about it.

Chapter Two

"The doctor says I'm fine," Declan growled into the phone for the third time in the three minutes he'd been talking to Tag. "Calling me in this morning to discuss it is bullshit. I could be getting ready for my flight tonight." Actually, he was as prepared as he could be, but Tag didn't need to know that. He pulled his Rover into the parking garage and whipped into a stall. "Look, I'm at the offices. I'll be up in five and you can see for yourself that I'm not on Death's doorstep and that this was a waste of time."

He didn't wait for a reply. He ended the call, shoved the phone into his pocket, and started toward the building. His friend, Steve Barry, held the door open for him, heading out as Declan headed in.

"Good to see you upright," he said, sounding way too amused. "Your face plant on the sidewalk is all the buzz."

Of course it was. "People who work here have been injured having sex, but I'm the topic du jour?"

"It's a sign." Steve's car keys and a string of flash drives and key cards jangled as he twirled them around his finger. As the new guy in the office, he was always taking his work with Hutch in McKay-Taggart's IT department home with him.

"A sign of what?"

"That you need to have more sex. Get injured properly." Steve started out the door but paused. "Speaking of getting injured, are we still on for skydiving next month?"

"Yup. I wouldn't miss watching you piss your pants again for anything."

Steve swore. "It was Mountain Dew, asshole."

Declan laughed. "Yeah, yeah. See you later."

Muttering to himself, Steve took off, and Declan hopped into the elevator. The moment he stepped off on the top floor, Case Taggart and Michael Malone changed course and beelined to him.

Fuck.

"Hey, man," Case said. "Heard you took a header last night. You okay?"

Declan swore. "For a team of professionals, no one here can keep their damned mouths shut."

"Avery says we gossip like a bunch of teenage girls," Liam O'Donnell called out as he walked past, his gaze glued to a stack of papers in his hand.

"That's just great," Declan muttered as he pushed between Case and Michael. "And I'm fine. Little dehydrated."

Case clapped him on the shoulder on the way past. "Glad you're not dead or too brain damaged."

"Thanks, man. You're all heart." Declan escaped the two, fended off two more well-wishers and hecklers, and finally ended up in Tag's office.

Which turned out to be even worse. Tag didn't even say hello. Just launched into a tirade.

"I talked to the doctor," Tag said from where he sat behind his desk. "You're not fine."

"I'm not *not* fine," Declan countered as he took a seat opposite his boss. "The doctor said he couldn't find anything wrong." Of course, Declan hadn't asked the doctor if there was anything wrong with the tattoo. He'd given up trying to get an answer to the question "Why the fuck does this thing feel alive?"

"That doesn't mean there's not a problem. People don't collapse on the sidewalk for no reason."

"Dehydration is a reason."

Tag threw up his hands in frustration. "Not for collapsing. You only have *mild* dehydration."

"So I need to drink more beer. So what?"

Tag mumbled some things under his breath that didn't sound very complimentary. The words "fucking idiot" came up a lot.

"I'm pulling you off the Argentina job."

"What?" Declan surged to his feet. "I said I didn't want to go to D.C.—"

"You're not taking that job either. I think you should take it easy. Stay close to home. Just for a little while."

"This is bullshit," Declan snapped. "I volunteered for the jungle mission because no one else wanted it, and now someone is going to get screwed."

"You know I'm right, Dec," Tag said. "And you'd make the same decision if you were in my shoes."

Yeah, he would. Someone who passed out for no reason—dehydration was a reason—didn't belong in a godforsaken jungle where medical care was sketchy and where he could jeopardize the mission. As a former Air Force Pararescueman, Declan knew more than most about the serious nature of medical issues in the middle of nowhere.

But dammit, Dec liked challenges. He liked being alone, and he liked not answering to anyone. Making the big calls by himself was what he thrived on and what he'd been doing since he was old enough to think through a problem. The only difference was that now his decisions were less self-destructive.

Mostly.

"Look," Tag sighed as he tossed a file on the desk at him. "We're not sidelining you. Just keeping you local."

Declan picked up the file, wondering what kind of lame assignment he was getting. He groaned as he scanned it. Yep, lame.

"So I'm babysitting."

Tag snorted. "You're not babysitting. The client, Suzanne D'Angelo, has a stalker, and she needs a live-in, twenty-four-seven bodyguard for a while."

Declan looked up from the file. "It says she's never gone to the police."

"She doesn't think they'll believe her."

There were red flags all over that shit. "Do you believe her?"

"Doesn't matter. Even if all she wants is a bodyguard to protect her from house flies, as long as she's willing to pay the premium for a single agent, twenty-four-seven, she gets a human flyswatter." He leaned back in his chair. "But for the record, I have no reason to think she's lying to make an ex jealous or some crap."

Declan had been in that situation once. The chick had claimed to have a stalker, but she'd treated him like a male escort until he confronted her. She'd confessed that she only wanted to make her ex jealous, and when he'd asked why she hadn't just hired a male escort instead of a professional bodyguard, she'd claimed to feel "squicky" about hiring someone who dated women for money. And yet, she had been trying to manipulate her ex with a lie.

Funny, he'd found that to be far more "squicky."

He sighed, resigned to babysitting. "When do I start?"

"Tomorrow afternoon. Pack for a month, all scenarios from jeans and a T-shirt casual to ballroom dancing." Tag glanced at his watch. "If you get out of my office in the next ten minutes, you can catch Charlie and she can set up your expense account for this assignment before she leaves for lunch."

Fuck. "How long is the job?"

"It's open-ended. Normally I like to get a time frame from clients, but she's from a very wealthy, powerful family and she's paying extra to have only one person as her guard, so..." He shrugged. "Oh, and I should tell you that she asked for you specifically."

He frowned and scanned her name and info again. Didn't recognize any of it. Well, he knew the D'Angelo name. Who didn't? The reclusive family and their massive wealth were the subject of a lot of crackpot conspiracy theories. According to a lot of the weirder rags, the D'Angelos had their fingers in government politics around the world, they might be aliens, and it was entirely possible that they were immortal.

People were crazy.

"Why me?"

"I don't know." He spun his laptop around and pushed a button to start a video from the office security cameras. "This is her."

Instant recognition.

Declan inhaled slowly, as if he could take in the warm brown sugar scent he'd associated with the wavy-haired beauty since the first time he'd bumped into her.

"She's a regular at Top and the coffee shop down the street. She seems to know Jules pretty well. I've seen them talking a lot at the restaurant."

"How well do you know her?"

"The most intimate thing I know about her is that she likes iced coconut milk mocha macchiatos. Venti. Double shot. And scones. She can eat like, five of them. She can't weigh more than a hundred and ten pounds. Damnedest thing I ever saw."

Oh, and she smelled edible. Very, very edible.

Tag's eyebrows climbed. "That's a lotta detail to say she likes frou-frou coffee and eats like a horse. Or like Boomer."

"I notice shit," Declan said, daring Tag to claim otherwise. Dec had an eye for detail and a brain that recorded and filed away minutiae with the efficiency of a computer, and Tag knew it. It was why he'd hired him. Well, that and the fact that Dec had a military background and was no slouch in a fight.

But there was no way Declan was going to admit that, in this case, Tag's suspicious instincts were on point. Declan had intentionally memorized everything about Suzanne, from her mane of thick, dark curls she'd worn in a ponytail twice, pulled back in barrettes once, and left loose to swing around her shoulders about a million times, to her curvy, toned physique and bed-me-baby brown eyes.

"So?" Tag drawled. "You on board?"

Watching over a rich heiress was never going to give him the satisfaction he'd probably find in Argentina, and it would most likely be a thousand times more frustrating. But if he didn't take the job, Tag would put him on some super-boring administrative detail until he was sure Declan wouldn't keel over in the middle of a jungle.

"Yeah," he groused. "I'll do it. But there had better be a stalker."

Tag grinned. "If it'll make you feel any better, just think of it this way. Dallas this time of year might as well be the jungle."

Somehow, that did not make Declan feel better.

At all.

* * * *

Suzanne was running late. As usual.

But this time it wasn't her fault. She bounced impatiently on her toes and glanced at her watch. She was taking possession of the angel house tonight, which would give her just eighteen hours to inspect the layout, learn how all the security features worked, and basically make the place look like she actually lived there.

Instead, here she was wasting time in Sheoul-gra, gathered with her fellow Memitim as they waited for Azagoth to finish talking. Yes, what their father was planning was important, but she had a job to do.

"Tomorrow we will welcome the first group of Memitim children.

We're bringing in the oldest ones first. Cipher and his team will assign each one to a mentor, and those mentors will help settle them in. If you volunteered, you'll need to see..."

Azagoth droned on, but she really needed to get out of there. She checked her watch again. Shit.

"Suzanne?" Her father's soft voice, deceptively quiet, called out with so much authority that everything, including the insects and birds, went silent. "Am I boring you?"

"Of course not," she said hastily. "I, ah..." She trailed off as her sister Temperance materialized on the landing pad a few yards away, her clothing stained with blood, her face swollen, one leg twisted at an impossible angle.

Before Suzanne could react, before *anyone* could react, Azagoth moved in a bolt of lightning, sweeping her into his arms as she collapsed.

"It's Meera," she moaned. "She's...dead. Her Primori too. I-I tried to help, but there were so many of them... I'm sorry...so sorry..." She sagged against Azagoth's broad chest, her broken body going limp. The only sound breaking the oppressive silence was the rattle of her struggling, shallow breaths.

Suzanne stood there, stunned and overwhelmed, unable to process this. Meera had been an amazing warrior with no Primori losses on her record. She'd been crass, brash, and horny as a succubus. She used to say that her pent-up sexual energy made her a killing machine. At over twelve hundred years old, Meera was sure she was due for Ascension, and she couldn't wait. The first thing she'd do, she'd tell anyone who listened, was lose her virginity. The second thing would be to lose it again, just to be sure.

She'd been so full of life.

How could she be dead?

Suzanne blinked back tears as she watched Azagoth cradle Temperance close, eyes closed, his forehead resting against hers. Suzanne didn't know her father well, had only known him for a couple of years, but she knew he wasn't one to show emotion. Well, he showed his anger pretty freely, but nothing else.

For the first time, she saw *him*. Saw the angel he'd been before he voluntarily lost his wings to create the demon prison known as Sheoul-gra. Evil had darkened his soul, but Lilliana, his angel mate, had brought him from the brink, smoothing his rough edges and soothing the beast within. It was thanks to Lilliana, Suz was sure, that any of them were able to witness the raw grief in his expression and the tenderness in the way he held his daughter.

As the shock wore off in the crowd, a low buzz rose up, and then Darien, their resident healer, shoved his way to the front and jogged over to Azagoth.

"Father," he said in a gentle but trembling voice one might use while attempting to take away a steak from a hellhound, "I'll take her."

Nodding numbly, Azagoth handed her over, and as Darien took off for his little clinic, Azagoth turned back to the group.

"We'll finish this later." He strode toward his mansion, a shadowy cloak surrounding him like a shroud.

Hawkyn appeared at Suzanne's side, joined by a dark-haired half-brother, Journey. "Damn," Hawk breathed. "I can't believe it. I thought Meera was invincible."

Suzanne swallowed tightly. "Me too."

Journey fidgeted with one of the plugs in his earlobes. "She was so close to Ascension. I didn't know her well, but she was always cool to me."

Meera was always just...cool. About everything. But she'd grown antsy lately, tired of the restrictive rules on Memitim, wanting to experience all the things they were forbidden to do. Now she'd never experience them.

"Hawk?"

"Yeah?"

Suzanne dashed away a tear. "How does the Council know if we've broken rules or done something bad?"

"Why?" He narrowed his eyes at her. "What did you do?"

"Nothing," she said quickly. "I swear."

He exhaled slowly, as if trying to decide how much to tell her. "Memitim aren't watched. Not usually, anyway. If the Council finds out about something we did, it's probably because one of our brothers or sisters ratted us out." That last part came out on a growl because being ratted out was exactly what had happened to Hawk recently. "We're also expected to confess our sins before the Council when we Ascend. Why do you ask?"

Because Suz didn't want to end up like Meera, dead before she'd experienced life.

"I just remember Meera being tempted to break rules, but she was paranoid about being watched. I figured that since you're now part of the Council you'd know if her paranoia was justified." She shook her head. "I hate that Meera died just as some of the restrictions have been loosened."

Some, but not all. And those *some* were thanks to Azagoth's recent demands and Hawkyn's influence as the liaison between the earthbound Memitim and the Council.

Hawkyn eyed her skeptically. "Don't do anything dumb, sis."

"*Moi?*" She batted her eyes at him in mock innocence. "Never."

"I mean it. You're setting yourself up for a lot of temptation by moving your Primori under the same roof with you."

"She's *what?*" Journey asked.

She waved her hand in dismissal. "It's nothing, guys. Just doing my job."

"Suzanne," Hawkyn said in a low voice that dripped with warning. "Be careful. I'll be checking on you."

"Ugh." His kid wasn't just going to hate life; it was going to spend its childhood looking over its shoulder for its helicopter dad. "Why couldn't you have Ascended like a normal Memitim does when their time here is up?"

She was kidding, and Hawk knew it. Ascension was the goal of every Memitim, but it came at a cost; after you got your wings, you weren't allowed to see your earthbound siblings until they Ascended as well. So no, she was glad Hawkyn had been elevated to a liaison position instead, not quite a fully feathered angel, but no longer earthbound, either.

"Because they knew someone needed to keep an eye on you, you pain in the ass." He was joking too, but she had to admit she really was a pain in the ass. "You need to listen to me. Stay away from Declan."

On that, he wasn't kidding.

And she wasn't going to listen.

Chapter Three

Suzanne D'Angelo's mansion was exactly what Declan expected after researching the extensive holdings of the massive D'Angelo family. The place was obnoxiously huge, with well-kept landscaping visible between the sections of iron fencing and brick walls. Acres of lush lawn extended all around it, and he'd bet his left nut that there'd be a guest house and pool in the back. Hell, he wouldn't be surprised to see a helipad either.

It looked like every rich person's house looked. His grandfather's house. His father's house. Not that he'd seen his old man's place often. One couldn't have his illegitimate, inconvenient son over unless the wife and legitimate kids were gone, after all.

Declan stopped his Rover just short of the gate, his gut churning, his hands not as steady as he'd like. Jesus. He'd been away from this kind of life for thirteen years and he still couldn't shake the bad memories or the feelings of shame and inadequacy that came over him when he found himself in the presence of great wealth. It wasn't that he was ashamed of not being a billionaire and living in a mansion. No, what took root in the pit of his belly was rejection. Humiliation. The feeling of being told you were nothing if you didn't have money, breeding, and an Ivy League education.

Logically, Declan knew he wasn't nothing. He'd been through one of the toughest, most demanding military training programs in the country. He'd saved lives. He was determined, resourceful, and capable. He was more than ready to handle anything from a plane crash to a catastrophic natural disaster. He'd like to see any of those Ivy League fucks survive a zombie apocalypse. Or even a day in a jungle.

So no, Dec wasn't nothing. But childhood memories were a bitch, so etched in the soul that they were impossible to scour away even with better memories.

This job was going to suck.

He looked beyond the gate, wondering if Ms. D'Angelo had dogs. He liked dogs. But he hadn't liked his father's Dobermans, who he'd sicced on Declan once. Dec had been twelve, alone on Thanksgiving because his mother had been attending some political event, his maternal grandparents couldn't be bothered to fly their illegitimate grandson out to the Hamptons, and all he'd wanted was to see how his father's family celebrated. He'd never found out, because the dogs had been set on him before he'd gone halfway across the yard.

To this day his mauled right ankle bothered him when it rained.

Cursing at his pointless reminiscing, he checked his surroundings out of habit and then dialed Jules.

"Hey," he said when she answered. "It's Declan again."

"Hi, Dec. What can I do for you?"

"I just wanted to see if you remembered anything else about Suzanne that could be helpful." Jules shouted something about carrots and onions at someone nearby, and Declan winced. "Sorry. I didn't know you were at the restaurant today."

"No worries," she said. "We're doing prep work, and we're ahead of schedule." She sighed. "Okay, Suzanne... Like I said, she's really nice. Just odd sometimes."

Wasn't everyone? Still, specifics might be nice.

"Odd?" he asked. "How?"

"She has a way of getting you to talk, and sometimes she seems a lot older than she is. And she asks a lot of personal questions." She paused. "But I don't think it's because she's nosy. I think she just likes to help people. It's going to drive you crazy."

Yeah, it was. Declan was very private, and the last thing he wanted to do was answer a bunch of intrusive queries about his life. When he was with anyone—a client, a date, a coworker, he liked to keep things light and impersonal. Not even Steve, who was his best friend, really knew anything about him.

"Oh, and Declan?"

"Yeah?"

Jules hesitated. "Just...be nice."

Be nice? "What the hell do you think I'm going to do to her?"

She laughed a little. "Hon, you can be a bit intimidating. I know you're a good guy, but Suzanne has a stalker, which means she's probably already feeling vulnerable. Don't scare her."

Okay, sure, he got that. But he also got that Suzanne was lucky she had the money to protect herself from creeps. Most women didn't have that luxury, so he wasn't going to cry too hard over her circumstances.

"One more thing," Jules said. "One of our waitresses asked if you're single. I wasn't sure what to tell her."

He had a feeling he knew who it was. "Kelly? The brunette who flirts with me when I come in?"

"That's the one. She undresses you with her eyes every time she sees you. She'd love to undress you with her hands."

As tempting as it was to hook up with Kelly, he knew that's all it would be—a hookup, and he'd long ago learned not to love and leave anyone who would be handling your food. Or your assignments. Or anything at all in your life.

"Tell her I'm not on the market right now."

"You got it. Call if you need anything else."

"Thanks," he said. "But I'd better stop calling or Javier is going to kick my ass."

She laughed. "I can handle Javi. You just take care of yourself and Suzanne. She eats her weight in desserts every time she comes in and we can't afford to lose her business."

It was Dec's turn to laugh. He'd seen Suzanne put away food, and it was a sight to behold. Especially when her tongue slipped between her full lips to catch a dribble of strawberry juice or a thread of caramel sauce.

"Thanks, Jules. I got it covered. See ya."

He hung up and put the Rover in gear.

* * * *

Suzanne couldn't remember the last time she was this nervous. Not even battling demons was as nerve-racking as pretending to be someone you weren't in a house that wasn't yours while waiting to formally meet the man you hired to protect you, when really it was the other way around.

Throw in the fact that she was a little infatuated with the man, and she was shaking like she'd consumed a few dozen iced coconut milk mocha macchiatos in a matter of minutes.

That Meera had died just twenty-four hours ago wasn't helping, either. Making matters worse, Journey had called this morning to tell her that Meera and her Primori were killed by fallen angels...just like what had happened to their brother Maximus a month ago and their brother Gregorio two months before that.

It was starting to look like someone was hunting either Memitim, or Primori, or both.

"Declan is driving through the gate."

Thankful for the distraction from her depressing thoughts, Suzanne turned to another sister, Sechseyna, who had volunteered to act as a housekeeper. Several of their Memitim siblings were taking on roles for this job, anxious to do anything besides train in Sheoul-gra when they weren't actively protecting their Primoris. She had a feeling, however, that Hawkyn had told them to keep an eye on *her*, as well.

As if Suzanne couldn't take care of herself. She was seventy-five freaking years old, she'd killed several demons—supervised, during training sessions—and she'd trained nonstop for over fifty of those years. She didn't need any damned nannies.

Even Cipher had stuck up for her when she told Hawkyn that exact thing. Then Cipher had given her the most insulting backstory and personal history ever. But she could work with it. She'd always been a social butterfly, so pretending to be a vapid socialite in the sprawling and insanely wealthy D'Angelo family with nothing to do but manage her inherited estate wouldn't be that difficult to pull off.

She'd practiced earlier today while she'd been clothes shopping in the most upscale shops she could find in Chicago, Paris, Milan, and Los Angeles, thanks to the D'Angelo network's limitless expense account. Memitim had access to a generous stipend if they needed it, but there'd be a lot of questions if she started spending thousands of dollars on clothing and jewelry.

"He should be at the door any second," Suzanne said, sounding a little breathless even to her own ears.

Her sister clucked her tongue. "I still think you should at least be wearing clothes. What kind of impression are you trying to make wearing...that?"

A seductive one. In all the times she'd seen Declan at Top or the coffee shop, he'd barely acknowledged her existence. Granted, she'd mostly watched him from afar to comply with Memitim rules. Hell, she'd spent almost her entire life being inconspicuous to humans, and she was tired of it. He was going to notice her, dammit.

"It's called a swimsuit," Suzanne huffed.

"Some people would call it lingerie."

"Yeah? Well, those some people were clearly born hundreds of years ago, when women couldn't so much as show their ankles."

Sechseyna sniffed and tucked a strand of escaped blond hair back into its neat bun. "There's something to be said for leaving some things for the imagination." She raked Suzanne with her disapproving gaze, her blue-violet eyes glinting behind the big, glamorous glasses she'd insisted on wearing as part of her costume, which Suzanne would describe as "pent-up lab assistant." "You've left nothing. And how can that bikini bottom even be comfortable? Is the back made with floss?"

"I *am* wearing a cover-up."

Her sister gave her a flat look. "It's so transparent I can see your ovaries."

Suzanne looked down at the gauzy gold-trimmed green robe that barely reached mid-thigh. "It's called sheer. And it matches the swimsuit. And you *do* have X-ray vision. Now, if you'll just—"

The doorbell rang, and Suzanne nearly jumped out of her skin—and out of the super skimpy bikini, which would surely get reported back to Hawkyn. Whatever. She was playing a role, and a young, rich socialite would totally wear this.

Totally, she mentally added again, keeping in character, of course.

Sechseyna opened the door. "Hello, Mr. Burke." She made a "come-in" gesture with an exaggerated flourish, playing maid to the hilt. "Miss Suzanne has been waiting for you."

He filled the doorway, his expression hard and professional, but Suzanne got a little thrill at the way his sharp gaze lingered, just for a fraction of a second, on the deep cleavage enhanced by her swimsuit.

"Ms. D'Angelo," he drawled in that rich, honeyed voice she'd been obsessed with since the day he was assigned to her last year.

Her tongue was so dry it stuck to the roof of her mouth and she couldn't speak for a few awkward seconds.

Finally, she managed a sad little, "Please, call me Suzanne." She gestured to her sister, suddenly anxious to get away from him so she could regain her composure. "Sexy will show you to your room and get you settled in."

"Excuse me?" He glanced at Sechseyna. "What was your name again?"

"You heard it right," Sexy said with a grin. "It's short for Sechseyna."

Suzanne nodded. "It was a popular name when she was born."

"*When* she was born?"

Oops. "I meant where," she said with a dismissive flick of the wrist. "Anyway, make yourself comfortable. Put on a swimsuit if you want and join me at the pool."

A startled look crossed his face but was gone in an instant, deftly hidden behind a business-like mask of indifference. "If it's all the same to you, ma'am, I think I'd rather get right to work. We have a lot of things to talk about."

Good grief. He sounded like Hawkyn. All work and no play. "Like what?"

"I'm going to want to go over what you expect of me, and I'll need details about your stalker, your schedule, and I need to look into your security measures, including video cameras, alarms, points of entry, vulnerable sections of your fence...things like that."

He was so serious and professional, and she had no doubt he was capable of protecting regular humans from other regular humans. That wasn't why he was truly here, but she had to play the game, so she smiled and nodded.

"I'll call my personal assistant to help you with the security stuff," she said. "Hawkyn should be here by the time you come back downstairs."

Sexy cocked an eyebrow at that. No doubt Hawk was going to be super annoyed to be cast as her personal assistant. He'd be even more annoyed when Suzanne teased him about it.

Declan's mouth, set in a hardass line, turned up in a polite, if impersonal, smile. "I look forward to meeting him and to working with you."

With that, he followed Sechseyna up the grand staircase that led to Suzanne's bedroom to the left, and to a mansion wing she hadn't even explored yet on the right. This place was enormous, in keeping with the massive "D'Angelo family" wealth and extravagance that served as a cover for angels who operated on Earth to influence human government, entertainment...basically anything they felt like manipulating.

She watched Declan's fine ass, encased in faded jeans, as he ascended the stairs, and then, with a satisfied sigh, she went out to the pool.

Hawkyn arrived just as she sank down on a lounge chair.

"Don't worry," he said before she could ask, "I didn't flash in. I walked in through the gate and front door. Figured your human was here."

Her human. She couldn't help but like the sound of that.

"And what in all that's sleazy and unholy are you wearing?"

Geez, her siblings were prudes. "As I explained to Sexy, it's a swimsuit. I realize they didn't have these outfits meant for swimming back when you were born, but they're pretty handy." She shifted one shoulder strap that was digging in. Apparently, sexy swimsuits weren't comfortable. "Unless you'd prefer I swim naked?"

"You're playing with fire, sister," he ground out.

She could only hope. "It'll be fine. Declan is very professional." Too professional, really.

Hawkyn cursed under his breath. "Where is he?"

"He's settling into his room." She adjusted her cover-up with a self-conscious tug. "He wants to talk to you about security and stuff."

"Why me?"

"I told him you were my personal assistant."

He shot her a glare. "Suz, I told you I didn't want to be involved."

"Oh, that's a laugh. You have your nose in my business all the time. You're already involved. This will give you an excuse."

"You could just tell him I'm your brother."

She took a sip of the virgin piña colada she'd whipped up at the pool bar before Declan arrived.

"Doesn't fit with the background story Cipher came up with." She shooed him away with her hand. "Now go talk to Declan about all the crap I shouldn't know anything about. I *am* a bubble-headed heiress, after all."

"Like I said earlier, what you are is a pain in the ass," he muttered just as Declan stepped outside.

"Oh, hey," Hawkyn said. "You must be Declan. I'm Suzanne's...assistant." The last word was gritted out between clenched teeth, and she had to hide a smile in her glass.

Declan offered Hawkyn his hand and the two males shook. It didn't escape her notice that Declan, a mere human, wasn't diminished at all by Hawkyn's powerful presence. That was one of the reasons she'd been attracted to him from the beginning. In some ways, he transcended humanity. There was just something...larger than life about him, an intensity and inner strength combined with confidence that so many were missing.

Some woman was going to be real lucky someday, and it gave Suzanne heartburn to think about. But that was a trauma for later. Right now she had to keep him safe so he could make a woman lucky.

I want to be that woman.

She couldn't be, and she knew it. She'd been born into service to humanity, and she had a destiny to fulfill.

But maybe, just maybe, Declan could be hers for a night. Smiling, she lifted her piña colada into the air. *To you, Meera. This will be for both of us.*

Chapter Four

Declan couldn't believe that Suzanne didn't have a security staff for this gigantic place. Granted, the fence was more than enough to keep out all but the most determined intruders, and there were external cameras everywhere. Plus a state-of-the-art security system with alarms, automatic door locks, and windows that could be shuttered for extra protection.

He did note that there were no dogs. His ankle was happy to hear that.

Her assistant, Hawkyn, was helpful when it came to security features and showing him around the place, but for someone who was supposed to know her well, he didn't have many details about her schedule, her daily routine, or her stalker. He just kept telling Dec to ask her.

So now, with Hawkyn gone, Declan was headed to the pool to do just that.

He stepped out into the meticulously landscaped backyard, where the infinity pool, complete with a freaking waterfall and a slide, took center stage. Well, it would have if one of the most eye-catching women he'd ever seen wasn't lounging next to it. No, she was the focal point, and his gaze lingered on her ample curves and bare skin for far longer than it should have.

"Hawkyn?" she called out. "Is that you?"

How had she heard him? "No, ma'am," he said, moving toward her. "It's Declan."

One graceful hand came up to remove her sunglasses as she turned toward him. "It's Suzanne. Not ma'am or Ms. D'Angelo." Her full lips curved into a stunning smile any man would kill to have aimed his way. "You should put on a swimsuit. Or shorts at the very least."

"I'll change into something cooler later," he said. "Right now I'd like to go over some things with you."

She rolled her eyes. "Ugh. So serious."

"Stalkers are serious, and you know that, or you wouldn't have hired me."

"Of course. Sorry. You're just trying to do the job I hired you for." She gestured to the deck chair next to her. "Have a seat."

He'd been hoping she'd come inside, but hey, who didn't love sitting in the full Texas sun while wearing jeans, boots, and a black polo shirt? Should have taken her up on the offer to change clothes. At least he had his sunglasses.

He sank down in the chair and slipped the shades over his eyes. She was still sexy as hell through the dark lenses. Not that he'd expected anything else, but at least this way she wouldn't know when he was admiring the deep cleavage between the swells of her magnificent breasts. Or her flat, muscular stomach. Or her legs, which went on forever and were probably as firm as his. Her tone was incredible, as if she spent hours per day working out. And maybe she did. He had no idea what her life was like, which was why they needed to talk.

"I hope your room is adequate," she said, bringing her glass to lips that glistened with a sheer pink gloss.

"Room? It's a suite with a closet bigger than my entire apartment bedroom. Hell, the bathroom is bigger than my apartment's kitchen and living room combined. I'd say it's more than adequate." He'd grown up around diplomats, political royalty, and some of the wealthiest people in the world, and he'd never been given a suite like that before. "Is it near yours?"

She jerked a little. "Why?"

Had she thought he was being inappropriate? Remembering what Jules had said, he shifted slightly, putting more room between them in case she felt uncomfortable.

"I'd like to be within earshot in case you need me," he explained. "But if that makes you uneasy, it's not necessary. Your house and property have multiple layers of security."

"Oh, I see. And yes, it's close. Just down the hall."

"Good. Be sure to let me know if you have any...guests."

Her dark eyebrows lifted in perplexed little arches over the rim of her sunglasses. "Guests?"

"Of the romantic overnight persuasion. I'd hate to hear screaming and bust in on anything that'll embarrass us both." *Did* she scream in bed?

"Oh." Pink bloomed in her cheeks. "Ah, no, there won't be any guests like that."

It was stupid and strange, but he was actually pleased by her answer. "Okay, then. Why don't you tell me about this stalker of yours? In the file my boss gave me, it says his name is Adam Painter, age thirty. I did a cursory internet search and found a lot of men fitting that description. I don't suppose you have a photo?"

"No, sorry. I never thought about taking a picture of him." She looked down at her drink. "And honestly, I don't think that's his real name. It's just what he told me."

"Where did you meet him?"

She hesitated, and he wondered if this was painful to talk about. "Hold on." She took off her sunglasses, reached into the bag next to her chair, and pulled out her phone. Her painted nails clicked on the screen as she tapped a few things, and then she read silently for a moment before finally nodding to herself. "I do this YouTube cooking show, *Angel in the Kitchen*. It's kind of niche, so it attracts some crackpots. He started leaving comments a few months ago, and he seemed nice enough at the time. But then he started showing up at some of my live, on-location tapings."

"Where do you do those?"

She pulled one shapely leg up and propped her arm on her knee. "I did one episode about camp grilling, so I went to a campsite near Abilene. And I did a beach cookout one at, you know, a beach. I tell my viewers ahead of time where I'll be in case they want to come hang out."

"That seems safe." It probably wasn't wise to pop off with sarcasm within minutes of meeting his employer, but he'd never been good at self-censorship.

"I can take care of myself," she said in an irked huff. "And besides, I usually have Cipher with me."

"Cipher?" The people around her had the oddest names.

Her chocolate eyes flared, but only for a second. "It's a nickname. He's my agent-slash-tech guy. Anyway, Adam showed up to both, and he was very pushy."

"And what made you decide you needed a bodyguard?"

"He started sending me progressively weirder emails. It was like he thought we were dating. He knew things he shouldn't know. Where I'd been that day. Who I'd seen. He started threatening the people around me, and then a couple of weeks ago he threatened me if I didn't start acting like a proper girlfriend. I can show you the emails. I mean, I have proof."

What an odd way to phrase that. Did she think he wouldn't believe her? Tag had mentioned she hadn't been to the police for that reason.

"Thanks, I'd like to see them. I might be able to trace a location with the metadata."

She waved her hand. "Cipher already tried. If he can't do it, no one can."

Declan didn't know Cipher—what a fucking moronic name—but he did know guys at McKay-Taggart who were good enough to work for freaking S.H.I.E.L.D...if the fictional espionage, counter-terrorism, special law enforcement agency existed outside of the Marvel universe, anyway.

"You never know," he said simply. "Does he know where you live?"

She pulled her other leg up and wrapped her arms around both knees. "Last week he was standing down the street when I came home from shopping." She glanced down at her painted toes. "I bought the cutest gold Jimmy Choos."

Of course she had. And her legs probably looked amazing in those shoes. "Did he try to make contact?"

"He just stood there. I pretended I didn't see him. I came right inside and locked the gate. Then I decided to hire you."

"Where do you usually do your cooking show?"

"In my kitchen. My old kitchen," she added quickly. "I just moved into this house and haven't done an episode from here yet."

"Okay. Is that all you do?"

"What do you mean, *is that all I do*?" She studied the multitude of bejeweled rings on her fingers. "I'm very rich. I do lots of stuff. Like get pedicures. And shop. Isn't that what rich people do?"

"I wouldn't know."

Actually, he did know. And she was right. When vastly wealthy people weren't putting their money into politicians who would keep them rich, they were taking vacations, buying shit, killing shit, or chairing boards that either made them look good or gave them a voice in policies that benefitted them.

God, he hated rich people.

What was strange was that Suzanne, despite sitting in all the trappings of wealth, didn't seem rich. Like it wasn't what she was. More like it was something she had to live with.

The patio door opened, and Sexy stepped out. Her name was bizarre too, but he had to admit that it fit her. He wondered if she was single. His buddy Steve would love her. He'd always had a thing for platinum blondes and glasses.

"Suz," she called out, "you got a message from Cipher. He wants you to flash—call! I mean, *call* in as soon as you can." She offered a brief smile and made a hasty retreat back inside.

"Go ahead," he said. "I have some exploring to do. Hawkyn showed me around, but he didn't seem to know much about the place."

She rolled to her side to fetch the cover-up she'd tossed over the table beside her, and he nearly swallowed his tongue at the sight of her perfect ass, round and hard as a peach, just an arm's length away. His groin tightened and his mouth watered, and damn, he could spoon against that fine backside all fucking night.

"Is there something specific you want to know?" she asked as she rolled back toward him.

"Actually, yes." He shifted to make room in his jeans for the semi-erection trying to become a fully engorged, embarrassing hard-on. "There's a doorway beneath the grand staircase. Where does it go? It was locked when I tried it."

"Hmm. I'm not sure. Show me what you're talking about." She rose to her feet in a graceful surge that he couldn't help but appreciate. A lot. Feeling like a gawker, he averted his gaze as she threw on her shimmering cover-up that did very little to actually cover her. Which he knew because he only had enough discipline to avert his gaze for a few seconds.

Those legs. That ass.

Declan had spent time with some of the most beautiful and pampered women in the world thanks to both his upbringing and his job with McKay-Taggart, but there was something about Suzanne that blew them all out of the water. Yes, she was gorgeous. Yes, she was physically fit to the point of perfection. But there was something else. A quality he couldn't quite define. Like maybe she should be surrounded in a golden glow. Whatever it was, it drew him with an almost physical pull, and it had since the day he'd first seen her at the coffee shop.

He followed her inside, proud of the way he only fantasized about gripping her ass during sex once during the walk, and then he led her to the door he'd mentioned.

"Huh." She frowned at the door. "I've never even seen this before."

He snorted, but quickly realized she was serious. "How long have you lived here?"

"Not long. A couple of months."

She'd lived here for months and hadn't noticed the freaking door under the stairway? He tugged on said door, but it wouldn't budge any more than when he'd tried it earlier.

"Here, let me try." Her slender fingers wrapped around the doorknob, and the thing swung open with no effort at all.

"I must have loosened it," he muttered, and she looked at him like he was a dumbass. That was fair.

She flicked on the light and gasped.

Declan wasn't a man who was easily surprised, but damn if his jaw didn't hit the floor. The *rubber* floor.

"What...is this?" She stepped inside, her eyes wide with curiosity as she took in the dungeon decor.

Stepping in with her, he catalogued the room from top to bottom. "It looks like a play room."

"Play? What kind of play?" She sounded horrified. "There are restraints. And there's torture equipment."

"Well, yeah. There are clubs dedicated to this kind of thing." He knew because he'd spent time at a BDSM club called Sanctum, where his coworkers liked to let off steam. He didn't belong to the club, didn't belong in that lifestyle, had merely been there as part of the security team, but he definitely understood the draw.

"Do people really play with saws and hammers?"

Frowning, he followed her gaze to a tray she'd pulled out of a drawer on the far wall, and a chill went up his spine. She was right. The restraints were commonly found in BDSM play, but some of the equipment went beyond "play."

Whoever set up this room was into blood or fear or serial killing.

Not cool.

He ran his finger over a set of cuffs with sharp metal spines on the inside. Jesus. This was disturbing. "Who did you buy this place from?"

"I didn't. It's part of the family holdings. I think they rented it out."

"To who?" he wondered out loud. "Fans of *Hostel?*"

"*Hostel?*"

"It's a horror movie where rich people get their rocks off by torturing and killing people."

She spun around and offered him a shaky smile. "Well, I don't get off on that, so what do you say we lock this sucker up and forget it exists?"

Declan seriously doubted he'd forget that there was a room in the house that could have been designed by Jack the Ripper, but hell, he'd give it a shot.

"Sounds like a plan." He ushered her out and closed the door behind him, noting that she looked a little unsettled, which likely meant she truly hadn't known about the room.

She didn't meet his gaze as she pulled the skimpy cover-up tightly around her. "I'm going to shower. Dinner is at six."

She didn't even wait for a response before she was taking the stairs two at a time.

He had the strangest urge to follow her and stand outside her bedroom door so he could protect her from anything that tried to get to her. Yes, that was his job, but he could do it perfectly well from anywhere on the grounds. So why did he want to be that close?

Man, he should have taken the fucking admin job.

His pocket vibrated, and he checked his phone, smiling when he saw Ian's number flash on the screen. The boss was checking in, and for once, Declan was grateful because that meant he didn't have to analyze his desire to stand outside Suzanne's bedroom like a dog waiting for scraps from its master.

And yet, as he gazed up the staircase after Suzanne, two words came to mind.

Woof. Woof.

* * * *

The savory scent of bacon, sautéed shallots, and garlic filled the kitchen, putting Suzanne in her happy place. At least, she was in her happy place until the phone rang and Cipher's number popped up on the Caller ID.

She didn't even bother with hello. "Okay, Cipher, what kind of house did you arrange for me?"

His deep voice rolled like thunder over the airwaves. "What are you talking about?"

"Don't play dumb." Propping the phone between her shoulder and ear so she had the use of both hands, she dumped a big can of tomatoes into the shallot and garlic mixture she'd sautéed in bacon drippings. "There's a room here. It's a damned torture chamber."

"Oh, that." He took a drink of something. Probably wine. He loved his dry merlot. "Yeah."

"Dammit, I splattered tomato juice on my pants." The flowing cream muslin pants were her favorites, and they looked fabulous with the loose teal and cream lace top she'd managed to *not* spill anything on. Yet. "And what do you mean, *yeah?*"

She could practically hear him shrug. "All of the houses in the angelic network have some sort of room where demons can be held. Or interrogated. If you were a full angel you would have been able to see the protective and restraining symbols painted on the floor, ceiling, and walls."

"Well, thanks for the warning," she said, not bothering to hide her sarcasm. "My human 'bodyguard' saw it and probably thinks I'm a sadist."

"You let him inside the room?"

"I didn't know what it was." She dumped several slices of crispy bacon on a cutting board and started chopping. "You know, because you didn't tell me about it."

"Ah, right." Cipher didn't sound chagrined at all. Amused, yes. There was lots of that. "How did you explain it?"

Her face heated because she hadn't known how to explain it. She'd never seen anything like it.

"He thinks it's some sort of sex room, but I told him it was here when I moved into the house." Cipher laughed. Harder than he should have, the bastard. "Yeah, yeah, it's hilarious. Bite me."

He laughed harder, so she did the mature thing and hung up on him. But she had to admit it was pretty funny. Or it would be if she wasn't the one with the sex room/torture chamber in her house. Hell, she'd laugh until she choked if Cipher were in her situation. But then, he deserved it.

Footsteps, as lightly laid as a cat's, echoed through the hallway, easily picked up by Suzanne's heightened senses. Declan, definitely. Her brothers and sisters could move silently, although she had to admit that Declan was super quiet for a human. Especially for such a big human.

When he stepped inside the kitchen, his presence sucked all the air from her lungs. Damn, he was fine. Freshly showered, he was dressed in

BDU-style khakis, an untucked, white linen button-down shirt, and leather flip-flops.

He must have caught her looking at his feet, because he wiggled his toes and said gruffly, "Don't worry. In the event of an emergency, I'll kick them off. I'm more than capable in bare feet."

As a fan of bare feet, she loved that. She poked her shoeless foot around the side of the island and wiggled her blueberry-lacquered toes.

"I get it. I have much better balance and body awareness without shoes. Depending on the situation, that can be a huge advantage."

He cocked a blond eyebrow. "Yeah? Like what?"

"Gymnastics," she said as she checked the pot of water she'd started for the pasta. Almost boiling. "Dancing. Fighting. Sex."

She wasn't sure why she said that last thing, given that she'd never had sex. But she wanted to. Soon.

Another eyebrow joined the first. "You need an advantage for sex?"

"You know what I mean." Somehow, she resisted the temptation to eat half the chopped bacon as she scraped it in with the tomatoes. "We're not conscious of it, but sensory input can help—and hinder—us in more ways than we can list."

There was a pause. And then a murmured, "You surprise me."

"Why's that?"

"You're not what I expected." Before she could ask what he expected, he gestured to the boiling pot. Time for the pasta. "What are you doing?"

"Isn't it obvious? I'm cooking dinner."

"Don't you have servants for that?"

She shrugged. "Yes, but I like to cook. You?"

"I grill a life-altering steak. I mean, the grill is totally my bitch. But in the kitchen? Nah." He propped his hip against the counter and looked at her like she was crazy. "You really like cooking?"

"For the longest time I wanted to make it my career. Plus, it reminds me of my childhood."

Most Memitim had awful childhoods by design. The idea behind leaving a baby with shitty parents or in shitty situations was to make Memitim tough. But she'd somehow escaped that fate and had grown up in a loving, happy human family. A family she missed, a family she'd broken rules to see while they were still alive. They'd believed she was dead, gone missing while at college. Suzanne suffered almost crippling guilt when she thought about how her parents had died believing she'd been abducted and, most likely, murdered. But five years ago, when her sister, Elizabeth, was in her final days in a nursing home, she'd seen through Suzanne's invisibility *shroud*.

"Suzanne," she'd whispered, looking at the corner from where Suzanne had been watching over her, "is it really you?"

Suzanne had stepped out of the *shroud* and into the room, clear as day, and held her sister's hand while they talked about the past and the future her sister was about to have in Heaven. Suzanne had confessed everything to her dying sister, and to this day, it was the most soul-cleansing thing she'd ever done.

"Wait, you *wanted* to make it your career? As in, this was in the past?"

She sighed. All these years later and she still missed that life. She had power and eternal youth and as much money as she wanted, but she also had massive responsibility, dangerous assignments, and very little freedom.

"It was a long time ago."

He snorted. "Because you're so ancient."

Funny. She was actually a baby angel in comparison to most of her siblings. "It's because I wasn't meant for it."

No, cooking was merely a hobby, but one she loved.

He looked amused, his steel gray eyes glinting with humor. "And what were you meant for?"

"Service to others."

Now he just looked confused. "What kind of service?"

Oh, the kind that saves lives and preserves history. But really, why had she said she was meant for service? What kind of services did rich people do for others? Donate money? Sure, that sounded good.

"I do a lot of charity work." She didn't want to see his reaction to her lame answer, so she concentrated on digging a serving dish from the cupboard. "I even donated to this year's McKay-Taggart fundraiser for after-school enrichment programs. Your employers seem pretty cool."

"They are," he agreed. "They also said you asked for me specifically. Why?"

Still avoiding his gaze, she stirred the pasta sauce. "Because I knew you."

"You didn't *know* me. You bumped into me now and then in the coffee shop and at Top."

"We did more than bump," she pointed out, a little hurt even though she had no right to be. Had she expected him to obsess about her since the first day he'd seen her, the way she'd obsessed about him? "We talked."

He snorted. "About coffee. It wasn't like we were engaged in deep conversation."

She looked at him from over her shoulder. "You flirted with me."

"Well, you *are* an attractive woman."

Hurt forgotten, she felt heat creep into her cheeks at the compliment. She wasn't used to them. She'd spent most of her life in the company of other Memitim, and the Unfallen and True Fallen in Sheoul-gra didn't dare make moves on her for fear that her father would turn them inside out. Literally.

"I...I don't know what to say."

"You can say why you hired me."

He was back to being all business, which she should appreciate. But she really wanted to hear more about how he thought she was attractive.

"Like I said. I knew you. Call it what you want, you were the only McKay-Taggart employee I'd met, so you weren't a complete stranger like everyone else."

She got on her tiptoes to reach for a can of non-stick cooking spray. Her fingers brushed the can, but she couldn't quite reach.

"Here," he said. "Let me get that for you." Suddenly he was behind her, his hip brushing hers, his chest pressed lightly against her shoulder. God, he smelled good, like soap and suede, and a hint of earth. A shiver of desire coursed through her, shocking in its intensity.

Too soon he stepped back and handed her the can. Which, for the life of her, she couldn't remember why she needed.

"Thank you," she said breathlessly.

Geez, here she was all hot and bothered and practically panting, and he looked as cool as ever, with those flat gray eyes and his stony expression, and maybe she really didn't have a shot at getting him into bed.

Disappointment turned out to be more effective than a cold shower at dispelling lust.

She pivoted around him, set the can on the counter, and pulled the garlic bread from the oven.

"You said you haven't been here long," he said. "Where did you live before?"

She eyed him askance as she put the tray of bread on the counter. "Do you really expect me to believe you didn't run through every bit of my background you could find before coming over?"

"I did," he admitted, watching her test a noodle. "But for an heiress, you've got a practically non-existent digital fingerprint. All I could find was that you grew up with your hotel magnate parents in South Africa until you were eighteen, when they were killed in a plane crash. After that, you moved to the United States. Atlanta. Until a couple of months ago when you moved here. Why is that?"

She took the pot of pasta off the stove and dumped it into a strainer, as much because she didn't want him to see her face while she lied her ass off as because the spaghetti was perfectly al dente.

"Money draws attention, and the D'Angelo name is big in Georgia. So I moved here."

Man, she hated lying. She'd never even been to South Africa, her parents hadn't died in a plane crash, and she hadn't lived in Atlanta. Well, not really. She'd grown up outside of Atlanta with her human parents, and she figured Cipher had included Atlanta in her backstory to at least keep some elements of truth in her story.

"You use a different last name for your cooking show. Why is that? I'd think that the D'Angelo name would be an asset."

The D'Angelo name was the one most angels took by default, but she hadn't wanted her cooking show to catch too much attention from the Heavenly sort who frowned on Memitim being in the public eye or worse, famous.

Not that she was famous, of course. But her cooking show had gained something of a cult following...among both demons and humans.

"I want to do this on my own. Running a D'Angelo TV show doesn't exactly work with my life goals."

"And what you want to do with your life is what...charity work?"

Okay, that was as stupid as it sounded. Cipher had left some holes in her backstory, and she'd been dumb enough to not fill in the gaps. Unless the subject was food, she really didn't think well on her feet, and she never had.

"Yes," she said hastily, her mind working overtime to spin this into a potential career. "I was thinking of starting a foundation. For orphans." Oh, geez, could she dig any deeper? Time to change the subject. She gestured at the glass double doors that led to the backyard. "The table is set outside, so why don't you head out and pour the wine and I'll be there with dinner in a moment."

He frowned. "You really didn't need to go to any trouble—"

"No trouble," she interrupted, her panic making her snappish. She just needed him out of the kitchen to give her a second to breathe and regroup. "I enjoy cooking, and I'm new to the area so I don't know many people, and it'll be nice to have someone to dine with."

For some reason, he looked uneasy, but he didn't argue.

Still, he didn't strike her as the type to let anything go, and if he ever found a crack in her story, he'd break it open like a fragile egg.

Well, now she just had to hope she could dazzle him with good food. And maybe a skimpy outfit wouldn't hurt. In any case, it was time to turn up the heat, and as she reached for the red pepper flakes, she knew exactly how to do that.

Chapter Five

When Declan saw the table out by the pool, set up for a decadent meal, he knew he was in trouble. Soft music played in the background, wine had been opened and left to breathe, and the lights from the pool and the string overhead bathed the area in a romantic glow.

This was so above his pay grade.

What did Suzanne expect of him? Flashbacks to the time he'd been used by a client to make an ex jealous popped into his head, but he was hungry, and whatever Suzanne had been cooking smelled like heaven, so hey, he could pour wine and see what kind of expectations he could extract from her after a couple of glasses. He'd planned to probe a little more into her life anyway because something seemed off. It wasn't just that she didn't seem like someone who had grown up dining on gold plates. Her story also didn't sit right with him. She couldn't have a career as a chef because she was destined for service? What did that mean? All of her time was being taken up by how much money she had to give away?

Declan sucked at math, but even he knew something wasn't adding up.

Shaking his head, he poured the wine, a rich, fragrant Chianti that glinted in the soft light.

Suzanne emerged from inside, and he had to force himself not to stare. She was gorgeous tonight, her silky teal tank flowing over her breasts and swinging loosely at her hips with every step. A chunky, beaded necklace and matching earrings and bracelet added elegance to her otherwise casual outfit. Her bare feet slapped on the pool deck as she carried a basket of bread in one hand and a dish of pasta in the other.

"I hope you're hungry," she said with the slightest Southern accent. It seemed odd that she'd grown up in South Africa and didn't have an accent, and yet she'd picked up a Georgia lilt in just a few years. "I hope you forgive me for not making salad. I forgot to have Sexy pick up lettuce when she went shopping earlier."

"Honestly, I didn't expect dinner at all." He took the pasta from her and set it on the table. "Usually I just run out and get a burger or order pizza when I'm on a job."

"That won't happen while you're working for me," she promised. "I have a fully stocked kitchen—unless you want a salad, obviously—and you're welcome to anything in it. I also plan to cook a lot." He pulled a chair out for her and scooted it forward as she sat down, gracing him with a smile. "Thank you."

"I should be the one thanking you." He gestured to the food as he took a seat. "But again, you really didn't need to go to all this trouble."

"Like I said, I enjoy cooking, and dining outside is always a pleasure."

"Always? Ever eaten an MRE outside in a jungle?" He grimaced. "Not a pleasure."

Her laughter rang like a clear, perfect bell in the evening air. "I take it back. Humidity and insects suck. We're lucky to have a relatively dry evening tonight." She tilted her head toward the pasta. "I hope you like it."

He filled his plate with the spaghetti and a couple of slices of garlic bread. The first spicy, smoky bite made him moan. "This is incredible. What is it?"

"It's my take on Spaghetti all'Amatriciana." She took a sip of her wine. "It's my favorite. It's so easy and quick, but it tastes like you've been cooking all day."

"I could *eat* this all day."

"Well, there's plenty, so have as much as you want."

She wore her hair down tonight, the curls flowing over her slender, bare shoulders, and when she reached up to tuck a strand behind her ear, his breath caught. How had he not noticed the mark on her arm? It appeared to be a brand, about the size of a quarter, on the inside of her wrist.

Gently, he reached out and took her hand, turning it to expose the mark. "What is this?" Eyes wide, Suzanne tried to pull away, but he tightened his grip, being careful not to hurt her. "Suzanne?"

"It's nothing," she said, a little too forcefully. Beneath his fingertips, her pulse picked up, tapping out an anxious rhythm that furthered his suspicion that it was more than *nothing*. "It was a stupid drunken thing to do where I grew up. Some, uh, friends and I wanted to get matching tattoos, but we were afraid our parents would freak out, so we did that branding thing instead."

Ouch. Declan had a tattoo, one he regretted with every fiber of his being, but he didn't remember it hurting. Maybe because he'd been shitfaced. But he was pretty damned sure he could never be too drunk to not feel a red-hot element searing his skin.

"And you thought they'd be okay with scarring yourself permanently?"

She shrugged. "Well, the lines aren't as noticeable, and I wore a lot of bracelets to cover it up."

"What's the symbol mean?" He ran his thumb over the raised, flesh-colored lines, his curiosity engaged at the wavy pattern inside the circle.

"It means 'commitment to one's duty.'"

He blinked. "Seems like an odd thing for a group of young friends to get."

She took a sizable drink of her wine, and he got the impression she was buying time before she answered. But why?

"It can also be considered commitment to one's friendship." She put down her glass, her gaze falling to where he held her wrist in his hand. "But since my friends and I have lost track of each other, I've adopted the duty meaning."

Clearing her throat awkwardly, she smiled and looked up, a hint of wine glistening on her lips. Was it crazy that he wanted to taste it? He also didn't want to release her hand, but at some point, he'd stopped being interested in her brand and had become fascinated by how soft and smooth her skin was. How her pulse pounded beneath his fingertips. How those burgundy-painted nails would feel digging into his shoulders during sex.

Fuck.

Reluctantly, he released her and shoved a piece of garlic bread in his mouth like she was a vampire and he needed protection.

"So," she said, tucking her hand in her lap. "Enough about me. Tell me about you."

Not a subject he wanted to talk about. But he supposed he owed her a little information.

"What do you want to know?"

"How long have you been with McKay-Taggart?"

Easy enough. "A few years. Before that I was a PJ in the Air Force."

Her fork clinked against her plate as she twirled it in the pasta. "What's a PJ?"

"Pararescue jumper. Special ops. Basically, a combat search and rescue paramedic." He shrugged. "Means I'm as good at causing injuries as I am at fixing them."

She studied him for a second and then nodded. "Hmm...makes sense."

"What makes sense?"

"You." She gestured with her garlic bread. "Nine months ago, you saved a lady who fell and hit her head at the coffee shop. She was confused and slurring her words, and you knew she was having a stroke when everyone around her thought her behavior was the result of a concussion from the fall."

He stared in surprise, his pause giving her time to take her first bite of pasta. "How did you know about that?"

"I saw it happen."

"You were there? I don't remember that." And he would have.

"I was there, but there was a lot of commotion, so you probably didn't see me." She dabbed her mouth with a napkin. "So why did you choose that job in the military?"

He shrugged. "I've always had kind of a savior complex. Ever since I was nine and saved a dog from a bunch of kids that were abusing it." He'd kept the dog, a husky mix, until it died six years later. It had been his constant companion at a time when he'd needed it, and he'd been a dog lover ever since. With the exception of Dobermans. "The kids beat the shit out of me, but it was worth it. Gave me the incentive to get involved in martial arts, and I got a cool dog."

"Do you miss the Air Force?"

No one had ever asked him that, and he had to think about it for a second. Ultimately, the answer was pretty clear. "I miss the job. I don't miss the life."

"Is that why you left? Because you didn't like military life?"

She has a way of getting you to talk. Jules's words from earlier echoed in his head, and damn if she hadn't been right. *It's going to drive you crazy.* Yeah, she was right about that too.

"I had reasons," he said, and Suzanne's eyes flared at his abrupt reply, which sounded harsher than he'd intended. But he really didn't like talking about his time in the military...or about his past in general, and Suzanne had somehow gotten him to reveal too much already. "Anyway, I joined McKay-Taggart until I'm ready to do something else."

They both paused to eat, with Declan practically shoveling the food into his mouth. He loved Italian, and this was one of the best spaghetti dishes he'd ever had.

"Something else?" she asked as he swallowed his last bite. "Like what?"

"I've got a standing offer to join FEMA." He filled his plate again, and so did Suzanne. He'd bet she could keep up with him, bite for bite. "It's tempting, but I need a break from government employment for a while."

Mainly, he needed to keep his father's influence out of his life, and since his father was a U.S. senator, his reach was extensive. And maybe, despite the fact that FEMA would give him the kind of work that would address his desire to help people, he was putting off accepting the job because he'd miss the element of danger he craved.

"So you get hired out as a bodyguard," she mused. "I'll bet you have a lot of stories."

He smirked and reached for his ice water. "You wouldn't believe half of them."

"Oh, you'd be surprised," she said softly. "Tell me the craziest."

He had several to choose from, and after rejecting most of them for various reasons, he settled on the one that had come up in Taggart's office earlier in the day.

"Once," he began, "a lady hired me to make an ex jealous. I didn't know the truth at the time; she claimed to have a stalker and needed a bodyguard, but when we were in public she climbed all over me. Freaked me out at first."

"At first?"

"Yeah. She said she thought it would discourage her stalker if he thought I was her boyfriend. Made sense." She'd been an octopus, but hey, some jobs required sacrifice. "Eventually I figured out that whenever she was being flirty, the same guy would be nearby. I thought it was her stalker, but it turned out that it was her ex. She didn't have a stalker. *She* was the stalker. Oh, and they were swingers. So she took me to a fucking sex party."

Suzanne laughed. "Was her ex there?"

"Yup. She was trying to hook up with him by getting his date to hook up with me."

Suzanne's eyes glittered with curiosity, and paired with her reaction to the sex play room that might also be a serial killer workstation, he got the impression she wasn't very experienced in bed. "Did you do it?"

He winced. "It wasn't one of my finer moments. But she was hot and I hadn't been laid in almost a year."

"A year? Seriously?"

"Why so surprised?"

Avoiding his gaze, she absently circled the rim of her wine glass with one shiny fingernail. "I don't know. You hang out with people who belong to a sex club. And Top has a designated sex closet."

"Sanctum is a BDSM club, and how do you know about the sex closet?"

She shrugged. "I've spent a lot of time at the restaurant. I hear things."

The way she said it, almost shyly but with curiosity, continued to surprise him. In his experience, those with a lot of money were naïve about how normal people lived, but sex was not one of those things. There was something very...off about Suzanne. She was clearly worldly, smart, and wealthy, but there was an underlying genuineness and innocence that didn't line up with what was on the surface.

He reached for his wine, but just as his fingers brushed the glass, someone drove a nail through his brain. That was the only explanation for the sharp, searing pain that streaked from the top of his skull to the base. He managed to not grab his head and fall out of his chair, and if Suzanne noticed, she didn't show it. In fact, she was suddenly alert and looking out over the property grounds.

"I need to check on dessert," she said, bounding to her feet. "I'll be right back."

She took off in a rush, leaving him to cradle his skull and just try to breathe.

Chapter Six

Suzanne was freaking the hell out.

The wing anchors, the marks on her shoulder blades from which her wings would sprout from once she Ascended, itched with the presence of evil. Declan's *heraldi* didn't burn, which, under normal circumstances, would mean he probably wasn't in danger. But the demon stalking him wasn't normal. None of this was normal.

"Sexy!" she shouted as she darted through the kitchen. "Sexy!"

Her sister was running down the grand staircase, her eyes wild. "I sense evil."

Suzanne nodded. "Stay with Declan. Get him to come inside if you can."

"Wait!" Sexy flashed down the stairs, blocking Suzanne's path. "You stay with Declan. I'll go after the demon."

"It's *my* job."

"I have four hundred years of experience you don't have, Suzanne. Don't be an idiot."

Suzanne hated being reminded that she was practically an infant in the angel world, and she especially hated being called an idiot.

"This is my show," she snapped. "My Primori, my duty. *I'm* in charge, and you'll do what I say."

Sexy bared her fangs—fangs Suzanne hadn't inherited from their fallen angel father. "You're a foolish little girl sometimes, sister." She brushed past Suzanne with enough force to knock her into the wall as Sexy left to tend to Declan.

Suzanne cursed softly and flashed herself outside the security fence, assuming that the malevolent being couldn't cross the angelic threshold.

But she'd only taken a few steps along the perimeter when the evil vibration faded. Dammit. A car cruised past, its lights blinding her momentarily as she pondered her next move.

Check on Declan.

Unsure where he might be, she re-entered the property through the gate so she wouldn't flash inside and materialize in front of Declan or something.

She hurried through the house to the backyard, but Declan was gone. Panic fluttered in the pit of her stomach, turning her dinner sour. He wasn't in the kitchen, the den, or the family room, and just as she started to call out for him, Sexy rounded the corner.

"He's in his bedroom," she said, as if she hadn't just called Suzanne an idiot. "He's got a pretty bad headache. I gave him a couple aspirin."

Suzanne froze. "A headache? And you left him alone?"

"It's just a headache."

"It's not just a headache! That's how this demon attacks." She darted to the kitchen, Sexy on her heels. "I'm going to call Cipher and find out why the demon could affect Declan through the angelic veil around the house. Will you stay with him for a few minutes?"

"Of course." Sexy hurried toward the staircase as Suzanne located her cell phone.

Cipher was on speed dial, and she had him on the line in under five seconds. "Talk to me, baby angel."

"Stop calling me that," she sighed, knowing it was pointless to protest. He'd been calling her that since the day he'd shown up in Sheoul-gra, dragged there in chains by Hawkyn. Worse, it had caught on and several of her brothers and sisters called her that now.

"Sure thing," he said, just like every time she protested. "Whatcha need?"

"I need to know why the demon that's after Declan was able to affect him from outside the mansion's perimeter."

There was a slight pause. "That shouldn't happen. Hold on." The sound of clacking keyboard keys and cell phone alerts filled her ear for what seemed like hours but was probably only a couple of minutes. Finally, Cipher came back on the line. "Okay, it looks like the enchantment that was installed stops most remote attacks, but with others it merely filters out the worst of it. Is Declan all right?"

"I think so. I just wish we knew why the demon is after him."

"Do you think it knows he's Primori? Maybe it's hunting them specifically."

She thought about that for a minute. "I don't think so. When we fought, Morroc seemed surprised by my presence. If he knew Declan was Primori, he'd know about Memitim."

It would be helpful to know why Declan was Primori, too, but Memitim were never given that information. They were important enough to merit angelic guardians, and yet their guardians were forced to do their jobs with one wing tied behind their backs.

Assuming they had wings.

"Where is Declan now?" Cipher asked.

"In his room with Sexy. I'm about to go check on him."

"Cool," he said. "Let me know if you need anything else. I'll be here kicking zombie ass."

Suzanne said good-bye to the video-game loving fallen angel and hung up. She started for Declan's room, but she didn't want to appear too concerned, so she reversed course, went to the kitchen and loaded a tray with dessert.

Sexy was just coming out of his room as Suzanne approached. "He's fine," Sexy said in a low voice. "The headache is gone. But he's grumpy as hell. Doesn't like being fussed over."

"You fussed over him?" Suzanne hoped the sudden sting of jealousy didn't make its way into her voice. "You, who once told our brother Maddox to stop whining over a broken leg?"

Sexy huffed. "We heal quickly. And he was whining." She eyed the tray in Suzanne's hands. "Only two dishes? Guess I don't count?"

"There's more in the fridge, and aren't you leaving anyway?"

Another huff. "Yes. But you know how much I love your desserts. And having you serve me them." Sexy gave Suzanne a mischievous wink. "I'll come by tomorrow after my Primori rounds. See ya."

She grinned and dematerialized, which she knew she wasn't supposed to do with Declan in the house unless there was an emergency. What if he'd opened the bedroom door just then and saw her disappear? It was a good thing there were no cameras inside the house. For some reason, angels were only worried about the outside. They probably couldn't comprehend of a situation in which something could get past their security measures to get inside.

In any case, Suzanne was going to give her sister a serious dressing down tomorrow, which would probably go about as well as it had when she'd put her foot down tonight.

Shifting the tray into one hand, she rapped lightly on Declan's door, and at his shout of "Come in," she entered.

He was lounging on the couch in the sitting area, his long legs draped over one armrest, his head propped up on the other. When he saw her, he sat up and swung his feet onto the floor.

"Hey." He raked his hand through his hair, leaving it delightfully mussed. "Sorry I bailed on dinner. I swear it wasn't a statement about your cooking."

"I know," she said, closing the door behind her. "Sexy said you got a sudden headache. Are you okay?"

"Yeah." He blew out an exasperated breath. "I've been getting them a lot lately. Doctor says they're cluster headaches, but the weird thing is that they only last a few minutes. Sometimes just a few seconds. I'm starting to think I have a brain tumor."

"Well, I have something that's guaranteed to make you feel better." She put down the tray on the coffee table next to a pile of comic books. She'd seen several boxes of the things when she'd checked out his apartment once, but she'd assumed they were a childhood keepsake. Apparently not. "Do you like strawberries?"

"They're my favorite fruit."

"Then you're going to love this." She handed him a glass dish piled high with strawberries in a black pepper and balsamic vinegar reduction.

"Looks fancy."

"It's another one of my favorites. Simple, but tastes like it took a long time to make."

She watched him take a spoonful of the sliced fruit and plenty of sauce. He moaned, closed his eyes, and his expression of pure male ecstasy made her breasts tingle and her panties grow damp. Oh, to see that same look on his face during sex...she shivered with female appreciation.

"Damn, this is good," he purred. "Do you make these dishes on your cooking show?"

"I did the spaghetti and strawberry dessert three shows ago." She grinned. "I always tell viewers that if they cook the dishes while they're watching my video, they'll get the effect from the food that I intend."

One blond eyebrow climbed up his forehead. "Effect?"

She nodded. "Every episode has a theme. Last month, the theme was mood enhancing meals that fight depression. I had nearly a hundred emails from people who made my Chicken Angel Alfredo while they watched the show, and they said that when they ate it, even as leftovers, they experienced amazing positive feelings that lasted an entire day."

The skepticism in his expression didn't bother her at all. She knew what she was saying sounded loony, but she really could transmit her energy through the food and the video. It was one of her special angel talents, and it was one of the reasons angels weren't supposed to be filmed or recorded speaking without a damned good reason. Heavenly influence on large populations was usually forbidden, although it had been used not long ago on a worldwide scale in order to convince humans that the recent near-apocalypse was caused by a virus, terrorism, and human panic rather than demons.

Declan finished his strawberries and set the dish down. "And what theme did you use for the Spaghetti all'Amatriciana and balsamic strawberries episode?"

She hoped she wasn't blushing, but she could definitely feel a tingle of heat in her cheeks. "Spice and sensuality. I told viewers that if they made the dishes while watching my show, they'd experience the most amazing physical reactions."

"Sexual reactions?" The way he said it, low and smoky, hit her right in the ovaries.

"For some." Somehow she managed to not sound breathless. "Others will merely feel warm and fuzzy."

Amusement curved the corners of his mouth. "Sexy food. I like it." He stretched out his long legs and shifted to get more comfortable. "So what happens when *you* make the dishes?"

When she cooked, her mood infused the food with energy, which was why she never cooked for others when she was angry or sad. One time she'd made the mistake of baking cookies for the Memitim cafeteria in Sheoul-gra when she was furious, and the result was a full day of fistfights. On another occasion when she'd held a pity party for herself, she'd made brownie trifle, Trefoil cheesecake bites, and pecan pie but forgot to warn others not to eat it. As a result, nearly two dozen of her brothers and sisters spent hours broken down in tears.

Since then, she'd only prepared food when she was feeling upbeat, which was almost always. She was, by nature, a positive person, and it took a lot to bring her down.

"When I cook, people can taste the love I put into it," she said simply. It was something her human grandmother used to say, and Suzanne had always believed she could taste her grandma's love in every bite. She eyed him as he watched her. "So you know one of my passions. Tell me one of yours."

There was a naughty glint in the steel gray of his eyes that made her breath catch as he slowly leaned toward her. His gaze held hers, keeping her utterly frozen in place. When those firm, full lips opened to speak, she dug her fingernails into her palms in hopes that the pain would prevent her from doing something stupid, like kissing him.

His voice was rich, dark, and as silky as an angel's feathers. "One of my greatest passions is between your legs."

Suzanne nearly choked on her own spit. "W-what?"

His gaze dropped to her thighs, and she looked down...to see that she'd sat on one of his comic books.

"Seriously?" She pulled the comic book out from under her. "These are your passion?"

"Some people cook," he said with a shrug, "and some people relax with comic books and graphic novels."

She scowled at the cover of the book in her hand. *The Flash*. The top comic in the stack on the coffee table was *Nightwing*. Now the decor in his apartment made sense. She'd popped in a time or two, telling herself it was to learn everything she could about her Primori, but aside from a bunch of action figures and military artwork, his place had been starkly minimalist. But he did have a *lot* of those superhero figures and boxes of comics.

"There's something for everyone." He ruffled through the stack and tossed some, one by one, onto the couch next to her. "*Transformers, The Walking Dead, Star Trek, Suicide Squad, Demonica, The Avengers.*"

Hawkyn would love the *Star Trek* ones. Wait...had he said *Demonica*? Curious, she sifted through the comics and plucked a *Demonica* from the pile. Every angel in existence was aware of this particular series, and most of them wanted to put those responsible in chains. Or worse.

Fortunately for those responsible, their identities hadn't yet become known. The most popular theory involved angels, but almost as popular was the idea that at least one of the authors was a human demon slayer.

Suzanne had yet to form an opinion, but if the *Demonica* authors were angels, she had to admire their audacity. They were putting Heavenly and demonic secrets out there on display for humans to see, and if their identities ever got out, they could face imprisonment, torture, and maybe even lose their wings.

"That's a good one." Declan gestured to the *Demonica* comic in her hand. "It's set in an alternate reality in which demons exist, but most humans don't know about them. And there's an international agency called The Aegis that hunts demons. They're the good guys. Mostly. You should give it a try. There are angels, were creatures, vampires... There's even a hospital that treats demons."

"This is crazy," she said as she flipped through the colorful pages.

"Well, it *is* fiction. But if it's too much, you could try a classic, like *Superman* or *Wonder Woman*."

"No, it's not that. I'd actually like to read some of these *Demonica* ones. It's just crazy how far comics have come. I grew up with *Archie* and *Alley Oop*."

"*Alley Oop?*" He whistled under his breath. "You didn't grow up in Africa. You grew up in a time warp."

Crap. She really had to be more careful about the things she said. "What can I say? They didn't have a lot of comic book stores where I lived."

"If you want I can take you to one so you can pick up some back issues of *Demonica*."

"I'd like that." She set the comic down. "Tomorrow?"

"Whenever you want. You're the client."

She smiled, but she didn't like the reminder that she was deceiving him. Yes, it was for his own good, but she'd never liked lying to people she cared about. And she did care about him. Too much.

She gathered the dessert dishes on the tray and stood. "Well, I'd better let you rest. How's your head feeling?"

"It's all better." He gave her a sexy, playful smile that made her want to find an excuse to stay. "Must have been your spicy strawberries."

If anything, her strawberries would make him feel upbeat and maybe a little amorous—things she'd felt while cooking.

"I don't think so, but you just gave me the idea to do a 'healing foods' episode for one of my upcoming shows."

"Glad to help."

She headed toward the doorway. "I'll see you in the morning."

He beat her to the door and held it open for her. "Thank you again for dinner."

"Of course."

As she brushed past him, relishing the feel of his skin on hers, he cleared his throat. "If you hear noises in the middle of the night, don't panic. It's just me patrolling."

She nearly dropped the tray despite his warning about not panicking. "You don't need to do that," she said hastily. The last thing she wanted him to do was venture outside the fence, which would take him beyond the border of the protective ward. "I mean, I'd at least feel better if you stayed inside the house."

He looked at her like she'd grown another head, but he nodded. "I can keep an eye on the perimeter with the monitors in the security office, if that's what you want."

"Yes, thank you." She started out of the room, but at the last moment, Declan grabbed her arm, halting her in her tracks.

"Suzanne?" His voice was soft, but his intelligent gaze was hard as steel, and she resisted the urge to shiver. "Is there...anything I should know?"

Startled by the question and the suspicion in his tone, she swallowed. Hard. "Like what?"

"I don't know." He released her, which should have made her feel better, but the truth was that she liked it when he touched her, no matter why he was doing it. "I just get the feeling there's something you're not telling me."

"Maybe," she said lightly, her attempt at trying to deflect, "I'm just a private person with an air of mystery."

He smiled, completely disarming her. "Okay, mystery lady. I'm going to shower and then make rounds." Stepping back, he ushered her the rest of the way out. "I'll see you later."

The door clicked shut behind her, and she blew out a breath of relief. He was mollified for now, but she had a feeling he didn't miss much, and it was going to be harder and harder to explain the weirdness that surrounded her life.

But for now, he was safe, and ultimately, that was all that mattered.

* * * *

Declan had no idea what was up with Suzanne, but he knew very well what was up with him.

Namely, his dick.

Damn, but the woman was hell on his libido. Or maybe it was the food. Spicy, sexy food. It was ridiculous, of course, but his errant cock didn't think so. Besides, those strawberries had been incredible. Sweet and peppery, with the slightest tang. Unexpected, just like Suzanne.

Who was hiding something. He'd bet his comic book collection on it. But what?

So yes, there was an air of mystery about her, but as for her other claim, that she was a private person? Bullshit. She was the type of woman who wore her emotions like her expensive-ass jewelry, on display for everyone to see.

His cell rang, and he cursed as he picked up the phone. "'Sup, Ian."

"Just checking to make sure everything's okay and that you haven't collapsed or some shit. You know, from *mild dehydration*."

Declan was never going to fucking live that down. "Yeah, I'm good. I was just getting ready to take a shower, so if I'm lucky, I'll just collapse and drown. That'll take care of the dehydration issue."

Tag snorted. "Just keep in touch. Let me know if you need anything. I can send over the Culligan man."

"Hilarious."

On the other end of the line, Tag laughed and hung up, leaving Declan to utter curses as he stripped and got into the luxurious shower.

The hot water fell like rain from the giant, ceiling mounted rain shower head above and the six body sprays on the walls. He'd like to say that the fixtures, including a panel that allowed him to program each of the sprays, as well as the water temperature and flow, were overkill, but really, he could hang out in this thing all day long.

The stall was also large enough for five people, but he'd be happy with just one more. His mind took him instantly to Suzanne, who would look perfectly at home bent over, clutching the teak bench as the body sprays misted water on her breasts and thighs. He pictured himself on his knees behind, licking water off her ass—*fuck you, Tag, I wouldn't be dehydrated anymore*—working his way in, until his tongue found the sweet spot between her legs that made her moan.

Closing his eyes, he gripped his erection and kept the fantasy going, only now it was Suzanne who was on her knees, her strawberry-red lips wrapped around his cock as she caressed his sac with those long, graceful fingers.

He groaned, letting his soapy hand slide slowly down his shaft, pretending Suzanne's mouth was doing the deed. She'd be good, and it would still feel amazing. She was so full of life and enthusiasm, and he had no doubt she tackled everything with the kind of energy she cooked with.

In his mind, she sucked him deep and then swirled her tongue around the head of his cock before swallowing him again. His legs trembled as the orgasm built, and he had to throw out his hand to brace himself against the wall as the tingle of imminent explosion spread from the base of his spine to his balls.

Squeezing the base of his shaft, he held it off, just long enough to imagine Suzanne coming to her feet and bending over again so he could spread her legs wide and bury himself deep in her dripping pussy. Fuck, that was it, game over, and he suppressed a shout as he came in a long, powerful climax that shocked him with its intensity.

Jesus, he thought, if sex was that good just thinking about Suzanne, what would it be like to actually be with her?

Not that it could happen. Sex with clients wasn't exactly forbidden, but unless it was part of the job, it wasn't encouraged, either. And Declan had long ago learned that getting too close to anyone, including teammates, could lead to mistakes and pain.

Out of the corner of his eye, through the steamy glass, he saw the blurry reflection of the tattoo on his back, reminding him of that pain. He fucking hated it, had tried to have it removed, but the freakish thing couldn't be altered or erased. It was as if The Man Upstairs wanted him to see the evidence of his arrogance and stupidity every day.

So, no, he wasn't going to get involved with Suzanne no matter how attracted to her he was.

His dick would just have to deal.

Chapter Seven

Suzanne was like a kid in a popcorn-scented candy store. Or, to be totally accurate, a kid in a popcorn-scented comic book store. She munched on a bag of complimentary popcorn as she walked up and down the aisles, stopping to admire superhero-themed artwork on the walls and action figures and memorabilia on shelves. When she saw the TARDIS replica from *Dr. Who* in the corner, she actually giggled with delight.

"This store is so cool. I can't believe I've never been inside one of these places." She glanced over at him. "You come here often?"

He shrugged. "Now and then."

"Hey, Dec!" The store owner, Stuart, waved as he emerged from the back room, his arms loaded with boxes. "I have the new *Hellboy* and *Black Panther* you asked for last week."

Suzanne gave him a "you're busted" look. "Now and then, huh?"

He felt his face heat. "Okay, yeah, I practically live here."

"Practically?" Stuart called out as he walked by. "I buy his favorite brand of popcorn for the popper, he has a designated spot on the fridge shelf in the back for soda, and one of the chairs in the sitting area has a permanent dent in it from his ass."

"Thanks, Stu. That doesn't make me sound pathetic at all." He plucked a couple back issues of *Demonica* from the backlist bins and handed them to Suzanne. "These'll get you started."

"Thanks." She bounced on her toes and grinned. "This'll be fun. Like I said, I grew up with *Mighty Mouse*, *Alley Oop*, and *Blondie* and *Dagwood*."

He shook his head in dismay, but what he really wanted to do was kiss her. He'd bet that kissing her would be just like her dessert, sweet but with a touch of spice and a little heat. And the way she was looking at him now could be described using those same terms.

Damn, he *really* wanted to kiss her. And then strip her the way he had in his shower fantasy last night. And again this morning when he'd woken with a raging hard-on.

She looked up at him, her eyes bright. He wondered if they'd be that bright if she knew what he was thinking. Would they be surprised? Appalled? Or smoky and heavy-lidded as she considered all the dirty possibilities? Maybe all of the above? Suzanne herself was a blend of contradictions, making it impossible to predict how she'd react to anything. She seemed both inexperienced and wise, an innocent seductress, a grounded dreamer.

"So how much time do you really spend here?" She held the comics to her chest as they walked toward the front of the store.

"Are you asking how much of a nerd I am?"

A pretty shade of pink bloomed in her cheeks. "Maybe. Have you been to any comic conventions?"

He grabbed a copy of the newest *Justice League* as he walked past a rack. "I'm a pretty big nerd. And yes, I've been to a convention, but it was only because I was working security." Still, it had been awesome. "I got to meet Kevin Smith and Robert Kirkman."

She put her comics on the sales desk. "Who?"

"You don't know?" Stuart gasped in mock horror as he rung up the sales. "Declan, you brought a heathen into my store!"

"Come on, Stu," Declan teased. "How else can we infect them with our obsession?"

"True." Stuart bagged the comics and glanced over at Suzanne. "You're welcome in my store whenever you want."

"Thank you." She paused with a delighted laugh as she dug around in her purse. "Hey, I just realized your name is Stuart and you run a comic book store. It's very *The Big Bang Theory*."

"Excellent taste in TV shows." Stuart sent a teasing wink Declan's way. "A woman after my own heart."

"Don't get too excited," she said with a good-natured wag of her finger. "I only catch it in passing when my assistant is watching TV." She pulled her wallet from her purse and gestured to the comics. "I'll pay for Declan's too."

Declan shook his head. "Stuart already put them on my tab."

"You have a tab?"

"His tab bought my new car," Stuart said with a wink, and Declan groaned. The guy was making him sound way nerdier than he really was. Mostly.

"Okay," Declan said to Suzanne, eager to change the subject, "I've shown you what I do for fun. How about you show me what you do?"

"I eat," she said brightly. "Every day I like to do something new. Breakfast in Toronto, lunch in Paris, dinner in Shanghai."

"Every day, huh?" he teased. "Do you have a personal transporter that beams you from place to place?"

"Oh, uh, no. I mean, I'd love to do that every day. I, ah, go out a lot here in Dallas. But I do love to travel as much as possible." She checked her watch. "And look at that. It's lunch time. Why don't we go to Top?"

"Good idea. I can't think of a safer place to eat, actually." Not when a considerable number of staff members or their spouses had military training.

Even better, in a public setting full of people he knew, he'd be too busy to fantasize about Suzanne in the shower.

Probably.

* * * *

Suzanne really loved the atmosphere at Top, but it was less about decor and more about the staff and the food. The moment she and Declan stepped inside the restaurant, the aroma of the savory beef lunch special made her smile, and the hearty greeting for both of them by several staff members filled her with warmth that reminded her of life with her human family.

She loved her angel brothers and sisters, but to say there was much in the way of warm fuzzies from them would be a gross overstatement.

They were seated immediately at one of the best tables, and they both ordered the lunch special. While they waited for their prime rib French dips, Declan told her funny stories about his experience at the comic book convention, but when she asked about his experiences in the military or growing up, he evaded the questions or gave vague, generic responses.

When the food came, he changed the subject, asking questions about her past and plans for the future, both topics making her extremely uncomfortable. Yes, she had most of her bases covered when it came to her backstory, but she tried to stay as close as she could to the truth, not only for the ease of remembering her story, but because she hated lying to Declan.

Her plans for the future were a bit more complicated, in part because she couldn't tell him the truth, and in part because her path forward, planned for her since the moment she was conceived, wasn't what she wanted anymore.

It was something she admitted to herself when she said it out loud to Declan.

"I used to have my life planned out," she sighed. "But a few things have happened recently to make me question my plans."

"Like what?"

Like you. "Someone I cared about died unexpectedly," she said, her voice catching in her throat as she thought about Meera. "There were so many things she wanted to do, and now she'll never get that chance."

He finished the last bite of his lunch and took a drink of tea. "So how does that change your future plans? You seem to have the time and money to do whatever you want."

God, she wanted to tell him everything. *No, I can't do whatever I want. I was born into the service of Heaven and I've been told I have no choice in the matter and that to stray from that path would be selfish. But dammit, I want to be selfish. I want to have a cooking show and I want to have love. What I don't want is to be a Heavenly warrior.*

She damned near fell out of her chair as the truth hit her like a blow.

She didn't want to be Memitim.

Fortunately, she was spared from having to think too hard on that revelation when Deena appeared at the table with a tray in her hands.

"I brought you a special treat." She placed a shot glass, filled to the brim with three layers of liquid in front of each of them. "Linc invented a new drink, and we're having a contest to name it, but the word 'top' has to be in it. Give it a try. So far, the frontrunners are Top Heavy and Woman on Top."

Shaking his head, Declan pushed his drink toward Suzanne. "I can't. I'm on duty and I'm driving Suzanne's Jag. But I'm sure Suzanne can come up with a name for both of us."

Alcohol was another one of those things that was originally forbidden to Memitim, but over time the rules had loosened, and it was now generally agreed that wine was okay, but not hard alcohol. But Suzanne was over being Memitim, over all the dumb rules, and if she was going to break one, she might as well break them all.

Or, at least, the fun ones.

She eyed Declan, her feminine senses locked onto all that raw, untamed masculinity, and knew, without a doubt, that sex with him would be one of those rules that would be fun to break.

For now though, she picked up one of the little glasses. "I would be honored to try your alcoholic creation, Deena."

She knocked it back, taking it all like a pro. At least, she felt like a pro for all of three seconds. And then the burn made her eyes water and her breath feel like dragon fire.

"Does the word 'top' really have to be in the name?" she wheezed. "Because I'm thinking it should be called a Burning Oil Slick."

Deena laughed. "You don't drink hard alcohol much, do you?"

She shook her head and eyed the remaining glass like it was full of demon piss. But hey, she was a demon slayer, of sorts, wasn't she? She could slay that drink like a champ.

"Let's try this again." Bracing herself, she drained the second glass. This time she barely wheezed.

I'm a big girl now!

She laughed at that thought and it occurred to her that she could already feel the alcohol bubbling in her veins. Hmm, maybe there was a reason Memitim were supposed to avoid liquor.

"Well," Deena said, "what do you think now?"

"I think I shouldn't have a third," Suzanne said, even though she kind of wanted one. "But thank you. And thank you for lunch. It was awesome as usual."

Deena picked up their empty dishes and stacked them neatly on her tray. "You know, I don't think I've ever shown you around. Would you like to see the kitchen?"

Suzanne nearly bounded out of her seat. "Would I? Yes, please!"

Deena signaled for Dec and Suzanne to follow. And as expected, the kitchen was amazing, with top-of-the-line appliances and cookware. The stainless steel prep tables gleamed and the floor was so clean she was afraid to step on it. Compared to the huge kitchens she worked from in Sheoul-gra, this one was small, but it was less industrial and far more personalized, from the group photographs of the staff through the years hanging on the walls, to the white board that contained not only the daily specials, but also comic artwork from the line chefs.

Suzanne inhaled the delicate saffron aroma coming from a steaming stockpot and admired the precision Macon was using to decorate a fruit tart. She could happily hang out here all day and just take notes.

Someone banged a door against her, which earned that someone a sharp word from Deena, but Suzanne barely noticed, too preoccupied by what she'd glimpsed on the other side of the door before it closed.

"Ooh, is that the famous supply closet I've heard about?" She started toward it, and each step was like walking in a crooked funhouse. Was the alcohol really affecting her so quickly? The pleasant tingles spreading over her skin said yes.

"It's not that exciting," Deena called out as she checked her phone. "Oh, hey, Declan, can you finish the tour for me? I've got something to take care of."

"Sure thing. If we don't see you before we leave, thanks for everything. See you later."

Suzanne waved and reached for the door knob. As the door swung open, she wasn't sure what she expected, but a boring closet entirely full of cleaning supplies and toilet paper wasn't it.

"You look disappointed," Declan said, his big body so close to hers that she felt the heat pouring off of him. "Were you expecting a sex swing or whips and fuzzy handcuffs hanging on the wall?"

Yes.

"No." She stepped into the little room and wondered how people managed to have sex in such a small space. "I'm just trying to work out the mechanics. Come inside with me."

"Suzanne—"

She grabbed his arm and tugged him inside, using her empty hand to close the door behind him. He bumped up against her, his hips meeting hers, his chest pressing into her breasts, and her skin got hot all over.

"You're freakishly strong," he muttered as he stepped back.

For a human, yes. For a Memitim...meh. She was average. Her best fighting skill was her speed. And her sharp-as-a-scythe wit.

She giggled, because she didn't normally think of herself as being particularly witty. The alcohol was kicking her angelic ass. And why was it so hot in here?

Declan gave her a funny look. "Are you okay?"

"Absolutely." She put her palm just above the neckline of her low-cut blouse and nearly moaned at the heightened sensitivity of her skin. "I feel tingly, like there are bubbles in my blood." Reaching over, she took his hand and replaced hers with his. "Can you feel it?"

Those incredible gray eyes became smooth, dark pools of molten metal, and around her, all the shelves laden with paper towels and cleaning supplies seemed to fall away, leaving her sole focus on the man standing mere inches from her. The muscles in his throat rippled as he swallowed, his gaze locked with hers, his hand burning her skin like a brand.

Her shoulders twitched, the wing anchors aching as if trying to release wings she didn't even have yet. But instinct was strong, compelling within her a need to extend her nonexistent wings and wrap them around Declan in the possessive embrace of angels. The ache intensified, her stupid body insisting on something she couldn't do. But at the same time another sweeter ache began to throb in her pelvis, spreading up to her breasts and deep into her core.

"Suzanne..." he trailed off as she stepped closer.

"Can you feel it?" she repeated, but now she wasn't talking about the bubbles in her blood. She was talking about what was going on between them. Right here in this closet.

"Yes," he rasped.

Time stood still for a moment, their gazes locked. His jaw clenched, the muscles twitching, the tendons in his neck straining as if he was reaching deep inside for control. Control she didn't want. She wanted him to unleash everything he had on her. Everything.

"Declan," she whispered.

As if his name was the key to breaking him, he abruptly hauled her against him and covered her mouth with his.

Oh, sweet Heaven, his lips were magic, and now she tingled for reasons other than alcohol. Well, it was still mostly alcohol, because *damn* it was hot and the room was spinning.

"Come on," he breathed against her lips. "I need to get you home."

"Why?" She hooked her leg around his thigh, holding him where he was, keeping the hard ridge of his erection pressed against her. "I like it here." She swore she heard him curse, which was super cute. "But it's hot. I need to take off some clothes."

"Ah...hey, I have an idea." He gently peeled her off of him, but mostly she was just messing with him. She might be drunk, but she did *not* want to get caught in an awkward situation at the restaurant she frequented so often she might as well move in. "Let's wait to do that at home, okay?"

"Promise?"

"I promise to let you take off all the clothes you want."

"I'm going to hold you to that." She was not messing with him about that at all.

He cursed again, and all she could do was smile.

Chapter Eight

Heart pounding and body buzzing with unquenched lust, Declan somehow got Suzanne into her car and buckled in without mauling her against the side of it. He'd practically had to drag her out of the restaurant, but she sat quietly as he settled into the driver's seat and started for her place. She stayed quiet for a few minutes, so silent and still he thought she'd fallen asleep, but then she turned to him, as perky as ever and showing no signs that she'd nearly gotten him to try out the sex closet.

"I had fun today. Thank you."

He glanced over at her, amused by the tipsy slur in her voice. "No need to thank me. I had fun too." His cock twitched as if to complain about the *lack* of fun. Stupid bastard. He gestured to the bag of comic books. "You'll have to let me know what you think."

She cocked her head, and even through the drunken glaze in her eyes, he saw a glimmer of focus. "What made you a fan of comic books?"

The traffic light ahead turned yellow, so he hit the gas and got them through the intersection without stopping. Totally missed the red...and a ticket from the cop hanging out in a nearby parking lot.

"I've been reading them since I was a kid," he said simply. "My mom wasn't around much, and even when she was, she was so busy working her way up in society that I never saw her, so *Batman* and *The Avengers* kept me company."

Wow, that had come off as crazy bitter, hadn't it? Which was why he never talked about this shit, but once again, Suzanne was getting under his skin and getting him to open up.

Jules had tried to warn him.

"I'm sorry." Suzanne reached over and rested her hand on his forearm, and he wanted to hate her pity, but strangely enough, he liked that she was trying to comfort him. When was the last time anyone had tried to make him feel better about anything?

When Gareth died.

His teammates had been there for him. They'd been there when he'd gotten self-destructive, taking stupid risks with his life. And they'd been there when he'd taken the early out offered to him by the Air Force.

A twinge in his spine spread through the shading in his tattoo and became a dull ache, as if the damned thing had a direct line to his heart, so he shoved that shit down hard and was grateful when Suzanne asked, "What about your dad?"

What a joke. "He's not my dad. He was a sperm donor."

"My dad too," she murmured, taking her hand back to tuck it tamely in her lap. "I mean, he's stepping up now, but I wasn't conceived out of love. It was all hate and duty."

"Hate and duty?" He entered the highway, easing between two semis. Her Jaguar ran like a freaking dream. He still wouldn't trade his Rover for it, though. "And, uh, aren't your parents dead?"

"Yes," she said quickly. "Of course. I was talking about my birth father. I was adopted."

Huh. That tidbit of information hadn't been in any of the research he'd done, but it wouldn't be that difficult for a family to keep an adoption private.

She held her hand in front of her face and waggled her fingers. "Now I know why I'm not supposed to have hard alcohol."

Not supposed to? "Who told you that?"

"I dunno." She looked up at the roof of the car, which made her breasts lift and strain at the low neckline of her blouse. "It's just known." She rocked her head back and forth as if testing its weight, and her breasts tested the neckline. They were going to get into an accident if she didn't stop that. "You'd think I'd be able to handle it better. My dad drinks like a bile-bone fire fish. Except they drink blood."

"A what?"

"Nothing," she sighed. "I guess I have some pent-up feelings about my family. I miss the ones who are gone and I don't understand the ones who are around."

"I get that," he muttered. He didn't have much family, but he had a lot of friends he missed. "I really get that."

It must have been something about the way he'd spoken, because once again, she reached over, but this time she took his hand, twining her fingers with his. He was so surprised that he just sat there in silence, unsure what to do. Which pissed him off, because he generally always knew how to handle any situation.

"Where does your family live?" Suzanne asked, her gaze fixed on something outside the passenger window.

"D.C.," he said, offering nothing else. But Suzanne being Suzanne, she didn't take the hint.

"Is that where you're from?"

"Yeah."

"Brothers and sisters?"

He exited the highway and merged onto the road that would take them to one of the wealthiest neighborhoods in the city. "I have four half brothers and sisters I've never met."

She let out a quiet laugh. "We have so much in common." Squeezing his hand, she looked over at him. "I'm guessing your parents are divorced?"

"They were never married," he said. "My father barely acknowledges my existence."

No, Declan was an inconvenient secret Senator Thaddeus Cantor III had wanted out of the way since the first time he'd pressured Declan's mother to have an abortion...even as he'd campaigned on an anti-abortion message. And while it was just a suspicion on Declan's part, he was pretty sure his father hadn't given up on trying to get rid of Declan, even to the point of asking favors to have Declan sent on high-risk missions in the military.

"That's really shitty," she said softly. "Are you close with your mother?"

He turned into Suzanne's driveway. "Not at all."

Declan had been a means to an end for his mother, blackmail material to get what she wanted from a powerful United States senator. Jeanne Burke hadn't been able to convince Thad to leave his wife and family, but in the years since Declan was born she'd gotten a lot of money, a high-powered job as a Pentagon spokesperson, and she lived the social life she'd always craved.

"*And I did it all in spite of you,*" she'd once told Declan.

Thank God she never expected him to go home for the holidays. Hell, he was lucky if she personally signed the Christmas card her assistant sent with his annual holiday fruit basket.

After punching in the gate code, he parked Suzanne's car, but before he even shut it off, she was out of the vehicle and heading toward the house.

"I gotta swim," she called out, even as she started peeling off clothes.

Shit. She was going to drown her drunk self. He hurried after her, picking up the clothes she tossed to the ground like breadcrumbs.

He had no idea how she'd gotten so far ahead of him, but by the time he got out to the pool, she was in it, naked.

And floating motionless, face down, on the surface.

"Suzanne?" He moved to the edge, his heart beating a little faster. "Suzanne?"

She didn't move. Son of a bitch! In seconds, he'd kicked off his shoes, peeled off his shirt, disarmed, emptied his pockets, and was diving into the water. As a PJ trained for water rescues he'd pulled a lot of people out of the sea. But this was the first time he'd gone into a pool after a naked woman.

Well, after an *unconscious* naked woman.

He reached her upon breaching the surface, but even as he pulled her into his arms, she roused, blinking her big, drowsy eyes at him.

"What the hell were you doing?" he practically shouted. "Holding your breath? You scared the shit out of me."

Her mouth quirked in amusement. "It's hard to drown us." She reached up, curling her arm around his neck as she dropped her legs so she was standing on his feet and her bare body was plastered against his. "I was hot. Were you hot? The water feels so much better."

Okay, sure, the water felt great. But her slippery, hard body felt even more incredible.

It's hard to drown us.

What did that even mean? God, could this assignment get any weirder? He was going to kick Ian's ass for this. Assuming Ian didn't kick Declan's first, for getting involved with a client.

Not that he was involved. Not really. Although he knew exactly what Ian would say if he walked up on them in this position right now.

"Not involved? Are you fucking kidding me? She's naked, you're practically naked, and you know damned well how this is going to end."

Imaginary Ian would then either rip Declan a new asshole or hand him a condom.

The guy was unpredictable as fuck.

Suzanne's hands caressed his shoulders and slid around to his back as she buried her face in his neck and nuzzled the sensitive skin between his jaw and his ear. Holy shit, her water-slick body felt good sliding over his. Her breasts rubbed against his chest as she undulated, and her delicate moans vibrated him all the way to his balls.

One of her hands dropped, and her fingers found the fly of his jeans. But before he could stop her, she stopped herself and pulled back with an impish grin.

"Let's go inside." Her voice was husky, dripping with wanton desire. "My room."

Okay, he could do that. He could get her to her room and put her to bed to sleep this off. Granted, right this minute there was nothing he wanted more than to fuck her into submission, but there was no way he'd do that while she was intoxicated. If he was going to risk his job, he was going to do it while they were both sober.

Taking her hand, he turned toward the steps, but she jerked him to a halt with her freakish strength. It made him wonder how she'd manage that strength in bed. Was she a gentle, playful lover, or did she like it rough and dirty?

"Wait." She reached for him, and he went taut as her palm came down on his shoulder blade. "That tattoo is amazing."

"Don't touch—"

Too late. He shivered as her deft fingers traced the outlines of the angel wings that spanned his skin from mid-back to his shoulders. The wings were sensitive, painfully so at times. But sometimes, like now, they became erogenous zones.

"The detail is exquisite. The tattoo almost feels...alive." Yeah, it felt that way to him too. "When did you get it?"

"Few years ago." His voice was clipped, spoken through clenched teeth. He really didn't want to talk about this.

"Why?"

Rage and pain hot-loaded like acid into his chest, burning like a mother. He hated the question so much, but he couldn't find the willpower to tell Suzanne to fuck off the way he did everyone else.

"Declan?" she prompted, her fingers stroking the inked feathers at the bottom of one of the wings. Erotic sensation shot straight to his cock, becoming the only reason he was still standing there when he wanted to bolt. "What's it mean?" Her voice became teasing. "Are you some kind of guardian angel?"

"I'm no angel, Suzanne." he growled. "The tattoo means nothing."

He started to pull away, to get out of this damned pool where he was trapped with a naked siren who tempted him to not only unload his cock inside her, but to unload his past as well. But then he froze as he felt a different sensation on his back. Something warm. Soft. Wet.

Her tongue.

A gasp escaped him as she dragged her tongue across his shoulder blade, where he knew exactly which feather she was tasting. Her lips pressed into his skin as she kissed him there, and he shuddered at the erotic tingles that spread from every point of contact.

"Suzanne," he groaned. "You have to stop."

"Why?" She kissed him again, this time at the very top of the right wing, her wet breasts pressing into his back.

Because I'm tempted. "You're drunk."

"Yes. But I knew what I wanted before I took a drink."

Shit. This wasn't going well. Gently, he reached behind himself and caught her wrists, but in a surprisingly powerful and quick move, she slipped his grip and spun him around so he was facing her, his chest against hers, his erection pressing into her belly through his soaked jeans.

Smiling, she leaned in, burying her face in his neck. Her soft lips nibbled at his throat as her hands roamed downward, sliding from his chest to his waist, the tips of her fingers sliding beneath his waistband.

A small plane flew overhead, and didn't it figure that it was an expensive-ass private jet, probably heading for the hoity-toity private airport nearby. He would have rolled his eyes if he hadn't been standing in a luxurious infinity pool with a rich heiress who was tempting him like no one ever had.

But what was her game?

As the plane's engine drone faded away, he pulled back so he could see her face. "What is it you want? Really."

"Huh?" She blinked, but her gaze was still unfocused. "I want to have sex with you. And I want you to tell me about the tattoo."

Closing his eyes, he let out a long, strained breath. He wanted sex too, but in all reality it couldn't happen. He already cared about her more than he should, and sex would only deepen his feelings for her, making him less effective in his job.

"Well?" Her palm found his fly again, and his eyes flew open. "How about you tell me about the tattoo and then we have sex?"

His fingers circled her wrist as he reluctantly pulled her hand away. "Suzanne, listen to me. We can't do this—"

Lightning fast, she took his other hand and settled it on her mound. "Right there," she said softly. "Oh, yes..." She pumped her hips so his fingers slid between her folds and he nearly came in his pants. "Touch me, *please.*"

There was a desperation in her voice unlike anything he'd ever heard. Oh, he'd made women beg before, had delighted in their pleas for release, but this was different. There was pain behind this request for pleasure.

"Suzanne..." His voice sounded tortured to his own ears. "I can't."

Her fingers dug painfully hard into his wrist. "But what if I die?"

"From not having an orgasm?" He tried guiding her toward the steps. "I don't think that's possible."

"No." She shook her head, her damp curls slapping against her cheeks. "What if I die and I *didn't* have one?" She was serious, her brown eyes swimming in unshed tears.

"What's this really about, Suzanne? Your stalker?" He lifted her face with one finger under her chin, making sure she saw the determination and promise in his expression. "I won't let him hurt you. I swear it. Nothing is getting past me."

The tears threatened to spill, and he couldn't stop himself from tugging her close. She came willingly, folding herself into his arms as she pressed her forehead against his chest. They stood like that for a long time, until her sobs settled down and she sagged into him.

"Suzanne?" He kissed the top of her head. "Hey. You okay?"

There was a soft snore.

Unbelievable. She'd passed out. Standing up. In a pool.

And he now had a new What's The Strangest Thing That Ever Happened To You On A Job story.

Damn, this job was bizarre.

Chapter Nine

"Come back to bed, Hawk."

Hawkyn finished buttoning his shirt and swung around to his mate, biting back a groan at the sight of Aurora lying tangled in the sheets, her blond hair spilling over the pillow, her breasts peeking out from beneath the comforter. They'd spent an hour this afternoon making love, and then they'd fallen asleep...until the incessant ringing of his phone woke him.

"I wish I could, but Sexy called. She's busy with one of her Primori and can't check in on Suzanne, so I'm going to pop in real quick."

Aurora propped herself up on one elbow, the comforter falling away to reveal those full, heavy breasts he'd kissed earlier, and the swell of her pregnant belly he liked to rest his hand on when he fell asleep every night.

"I'm sure Suzanne is fine," she said on a yawn. "She wouldn't have been assigned a Primori if you hadn't trained her properly. Maybe you should give her a little space."

He shoved his feet into his boots. "I'd love to, but she's...Suzanne."

"She's not a child."

No, she wasn't. But she was young. Innocent. Not cut out for this at all. "I'll just look in on her. I won't interfere."

"Pfft." She rolled her eyes. "You? Not interfere?"

Yeah, yeah, so he was a bit overprotective. "I'll be there two minutes, tops."

Aurora fell back into the pillows with a little growl of frustration. "What are you worried about? Seriously. That she can't protect her Primori by herself?"

"It's not just that. I worry that she has feelings for him."

She rolled onto her side and propped herself up again. "I know

Memitim/Primori relationships are forbidden, but come on, the Council made an exception for us."

"Our situation is different for a lot of reasons."

"Well, it's still stupid." Aurora thought a lot of the rules Memitim had to follow were as stupid as he did, but in this case, the rules were sound. "Okay, so worst-case scenario?"

"She doesn't Ascend to full angel and is relegated to human status."

Aurora frowned. "But she's Memitim. How can she just be changed into a different species?"

"She wouldn't technically be human. She'd have her powers stripped, which would leave her defenseless and mortal. I can't let that happen. Especially not over a human male."

"Aren't you a bit of an elitist?" she murmured, but she was teasing. Well, she was teasing, but she wasn't necessarily wrong.

"Well, it's a good thing you aren't human then, isn't it?" He patted her on her firm ass and bent to kiss her on the lips. "I've got Council business after this, so I'll see you in a couple of hours."

She slid her hand up his thigh and squeezed. "Don't be too long. I have the day off at the spa and I want to spend it with you. And with the way this baby drains my energy, I'll need to recharge soon."

Recharge, in this case, meant sex. As a Wytch, she fed on the energy of others to fuel her abilities, and her favorite method of drawing power from him was via orgasm.

He was okay with that.

"I love you," he murmured against her mouth.

Her whispered "I love you too" echoed in his ears as he extended his wings and flashed out of there.

For a heartbeat he thought about materializing outside the gate of the mansion and going in like a normal person, but really, he just needed to do a quick look to make sure Declan was doing his job and that Suzanne was...well, doing whatever Suzanne was supposed to be doing in her role as a spoiled heiress. So he activated the *shrowd*, allowing him to move in complete invisibility, and popped into her backyard.

She wasn't lounging by the pool like he'd expected. But her clothes were there. Including her bra and panties.

And next to her pile of clothes was Declan's pile, which included his boots, shirt, cell phone, keys, and a weapon.

Hawkyn's gut twisted.

She didn't. She *wouldn't*.

Holy shit.

He didn't think. Didn't hesitate at all. He flashed into Declan's bedroom, momentarily relieved to not find his sister tangled in the sheets with the guy. So he tried Suzanne's room, extra relieved to find her alone. The relief didn't last though, not when he saw her naked and sprawled on her bed. He averted his gaze and flung the covers over her.

"Suzanne." He shook her shoulder. "Suzanne! Wake up."

"Declan," she sighed, a secret smile curving her lips.

Hawk knew that smile. Knew it because he saw it every time he woke Aurora with intimate caresses.

Irrational anger spun up, heating his blood until he could practically feel steam coming out of his ears. Warning bells rang in his head, reminding him that this kind of fury came straight from his father, directly from the DNA of a fallen angel whose evil had blackened his soul for millennia.

Flames of heat licking his skin, Hawkyn ignored the warnings.

Primori or not, Declan was going to take a beating.

Chapter Ten

After he showered, and while Suzanne slept off her alcohol-induced whatever-it-was, Declan patrolled the grounds and reviewed security measures. At one point he'd even called Deena to ask what the hell was in the drink Suzanne had guzzled, but it hadn't contained anything out of the ordinary. He hadn't expected to hear that it had been spiked with anything strange, but he'd been hoping that maybe there'd been an exotic food ingredient that could explain her behavior.

Nope.

Now he was looking over security footage from the last two days. He hadn't expected to see anything other than maybe a raccoon or cat walking on top of the fence or on the grounds, but something strange caught his attention.

Last night, shit got real fucking weird.

At the 19:37 mark, just a couple of minutes after she'd gotten up from the dinner table to check on dessert, Suzanne entered the grounds from outside the security gate. What the hell? He hadn't seen her exit. Frowning, he reversed the feeds, but no, she hadn't gone outside. Not unless she knew of a way to get out of the house and outside the fence without the cameras catching her. There were a few blind spots, but they were limited, and he'd personally tested them to ensure that it was impossible for anything larger than a cocker spaniel running a complex pattern to get from the fence to the house and vice versa without at least one camera catching them.

Was there a glitch in the feed? He'd check the electronic gate logs to see if she'd been recorded going out as well as coming in, and maybe he could—

The hair on the back of his neck stood up and his fucking tattoo screamed out a warning, as if a lightning bolt had zapped him in the spine. Instinctively, he reached for the comfort of his sidearm, only to realize it was still sitting next to the pool. Idiot!

"What the fuck did you do to her?"

Declan surged to his feet and spun toward the office doorway, but he didn't even have time to square his stance before Suzanne's assistant, Hawkyn, had him by the throat and pinned to the wall. His feet weren't even touching the damned floor.

"I said," Hawkyn snarled, "what did you do to her?"

Declan swore flames danced in the guy's green eyes, but that was probably just the result of a lack of oxygen in his brain.

"Nothing," he rasped. Jesus, Hawkyn's grip was like a fucking steel clamp. "She had a couple of drinks. She's sleeping it off."

Hawkyn growled and slammed Dec against the wall again. Pain cracked in his spine and ribs, and damn, he was going to be feeling that for a couple of days. "You gave her alcohol?"

"The fuck?" The guy made it sound like Declan had given her meth or a venereal disease. "I didn't give her jack shit," he rasped. "And buddy, she's an adult. She drank it willingly. At a restaurant."

"Did you take advantage of her?" Baring his teeth, Hawkyn squeezed harder. "If you so much as touched her—"

"I didn't," he croaked, but even as he said that, he realized that kissing her was touching her. His hand between her legs was *definitely* touching her. And he'd have done a lot more than that to her if she'd been sober. Probably best not to say any of that to this lunatic. "I put her to bed. That's all."

Time stretched as Declan's vision grew blurry and blotches of alternating lights and shadows danced in front of him no matter how hard he struggled against Hawkyn's hold.

"Son of a bitch." Finally Hawkyn released Declan, and he gave silent thanks for the wall behind him. "Don't let her do that again. Some of us can't tolerate it."

Some of us? "What the hell are you talking about? Don't *let* her? I'm her bodyguard, not her nanny. If she wants to drink an entire fifth of Jack and have an orgy in the pool, that's her choice." Her choice, yes, but there was no way he'd stand by and let it happen no matter what he'd just told her overbearing assistant. The thought of her engaging in an orgy made him a little ragey. "And who are you anyway? Her dad?" He rubbed his throat and wondered if there'd be bruises in the shape of hands there later. "Jesus. Does she know you're a fucking psycho?"

Hawkyn laughed, apparently cool with being called crazy. "Just do your job and keep your paws off her."

The sound of a throat clearing shut them both up as they swung to face the doorway. And the very angry Suzanne, lips pursed, fists balled at her sides, standing in it.

"What the hell is going on?" she snapped. "I could hear you two from the other side of the house."

God, she looked adorable in the short silk robe, her hair mussed, her small feet hidden in fluffy slippers. When she looked at Declan, her cheeks turned rosy and he wondered how much she remembered of the pool incident.

Hawkyn grabbed her arm hard enough to make her gasp in outrage. "We need to talk." He started to drag her out of the office, but something inside Declan snapped. Hard.

With a growl, he clamped his hand down on Hawkyn's shoulder and spun him into the doorjamb. "I don't give a fuck who you are or how insane you might be. You do not handle her like that."

This time, the flames in the other guy's eyes were not in Dec's imagination. No way. Not with the way they were kicking out a blast of heat. And yet, it was impossible. He was losing his fucking mind.

Hawkyn hissed—fucking *hissed*—but before he launched into what Declan was sure would be a brutal, no-holds-barred battle, Suzanne was between them, one palm on each of their chests. Too bad, because at this point, Dec was spoiling for a fight, and clearly Hawkyn was too.

"Hey, boys. Let's all take a deep breath. Dec, I'll be back in a minute. Hawk, let's talk."

Declan stood down, content to let Suzanne handle this. But if he heard a single sound that made him think she was in trouble, that Hawkyn bastard was going to get the brawl he was looking for.

* * * *

Suzanne. Was. Furious.

And she had absolutely no doubt who was deserving of her fury.

The moment she and Hawkyn stepped into the massive, soundproof first floor library, she slammed the door shut and rounded on him, fists clenched at her sides, her breath burning like fire in her throat.

"Okay, bro, what the hell was that about?"

"I'm the one who gets to ask questions here." Hawkyn gestured out the window at the backyard. "I came to check on you and I found your clothes...and his...next to the pool, and then I found you in bed. Naked."

Her face grew so hot she felt as if she was standing in one of Hades's inferno prison cells. "You were in my bedroom?" She tugged her robe tighter, wondering exactly how much he'd seen. "Are you kidding me?"

He had the grace to look chagrined. "I thought you and Declan were—never mind. But you—"

"Hold on." She held up a hand to cut him off. "You thought Declan and I were having sex, didn't you? Well, I have news for you. Even if we were, it would have been none of your business. None. If I want to do a...a...reverse cowgirl in a restaurant supply closet or a...a wheelbarrow in the pool, you have no say in it at all. Got that?"

He gave her a droll look. "Do you even know what those positions are? Or maybe you think potentially drowning is erotic?"

"That's not funny." And no, she didn't know what those positions were. She'd heard of them, but whatever. That was a matter for Google.

"I'm not trying to be funny," he snapped. "This is serious, Suz."

She huffed, tired of being treated like a child. "Do you think I don't know that? Do you think that after fifty-plus years of you drilling me about all of our laws and customs and rules that I don't know what they are or what I'm doing? I'm protecting Declan, and I'll do it however I see fit."

"So that includes getting naked with him."

"He wasn't naked." She'd only *wished* he was naked.

"But you were."

Her face heated again. "Obviously."

"Shit." He scrubbed his hand over his face. "I'm assuming you didn't have intercourse..."

"Don't say that! I don't want to hear any of this from my brother." So gross. "And not that it's any of your business, but no."

"Then the guidelines are murky. If he touched you"—He paused and swallowed, as if he felt physically ill—"then you can get away with not declaring it when you Ascend."

"Ascend?" She threw her hands up in frustration. "Is that all you care about? I'm sick of hearing about it. Ascend, Ascend, Ascend. Screw that. I'm young, Hawk. It's not going to happen for centuries, so can we stop talking about it?"

She didn't even want to *think* about it. Unlike all her other brothers and sisters who constantly fantasized about earning their wings and joining the "real" angels in Heaven, Suzanne liked it here on Earth, and she wanted to experience its history as it happened. She wanted to live it, not watch it unfold from the impersonal distance of the Other Side.

"No, we can't," he said. "Because it's the single most important event that can happen to a Memitim, and if you don't live your life with that goal in mind, you can stray. I won't let that happen, Suzanne."

"Yeah?" She crossed her arms over her chest, digging in. "Well, it's my life, and how I live it is my choice. Mine. And right now I choose to be alone, so kindly get out."

"Dammit, sis. I'm trying to protect you."

She flung her hand at the door. "Get out! And don't you dare threaten Declan again."

"You need to fire him and come back to Sheoul-gra."

"No."

"It's not a suggestion," he said, his glittery wings erupting from his back. "It's an order."

She sucked in a startled breath. He'd never pulled rank on her. He'd certainly never flared his wings in a show of superiority. How had things gotten so bad between them? How could he not see that she had to do this? Declan would die without her constant protection.

She'd die if she was stuck in Sheoul-gra.

"I said no. Declan needs twenty-four seven protection."

"Our brothers and sisters will help watch over him," he argued, making perfect sense.

She knew she could count on her Memitim siblings to help, but what if the person who was keeping watch got called to their own Primori? Declan would be vulnerable, even if it was only for a few minutes until she could get there.

"You're too close," he continued. "And if I have to go to the Council to have him transferred to another Memitim, I will."

Anger swallowed her whole. "How could you? You...you...asshole!" Squaring her shoulders, she stomped over to the door and flung it open. "You need to leave."

He spat out a nasty curse, but he didn't argue. He put away his wings and stormed from the library, his heavy boots cracking on the tile and echoing through the house until he slammed out of the front door.

Crap. She hadn't wanted that to happen. She loved her brother and hated fighting with him, but she also hated being treated like a newbie Memitim who hadn't even fought her first demon. Yes, she'd made mistakes, and no, she didn't have centuries of experience under her belt like most of her brothers and sisters, but she wasn't completely clueless.

She uttered obscenities under her breath as she made her way back to the security office, where Declan was standing in front of one of the monitors, the muscles in his broad back rippling with every tiny movement. Her stomach churned with anxiety as she stood in the doorway, wondering what to say. He was probably pissed at Hawkyn and confused by her behavior in the pool.

So embarrassing. She wished she didn't remember, but it was all way too clear. She could blame her actions on the alcohol, but deep down, she knew that everything she'd done and said originated with real desires and feelings.

But what about Declan? His mixed signals constantly left her off balance. He'd kissed her, and she'd felt the evidence of his desire pressing into her belly in the restaurant closet and the pool. But he kept turning her down. Granted, it had been the gentlemanly thing to do given her inebriation.

Maybe it was time to find out where they stood. She just hoped they were standing in the same place. It wasn't as if she was looking for marriage, after all. She wanted just one night in bed to break a rule and a hymen.

A figurative hymen, anyway. Memitim didn't have them.

She took a deep, bracing breath and stepped inside the security room, where Declan was hovering over a camera monitor, his gaze focused on the screen. He was dressed in black military-style pants with boots and a black tee, and no one who saw him would doubt he was a force to be reckoned with.

"Declan. Hey. Look, about earlier..."

He didn't look up, but his grip on the table turned white-knuckled. "Your assistant is a nutcase and you should fire him."

"Hawk is a little overprotective," she hedged. "But he means well."

He spun around, his expression carved from granite, his eyes as cold and gray as winter in England. "Then what would he say about this?"

He gestured to one of the camera monitors, where a screenshot of her outside the fence, night before last, was on full display.

"Oh, that." Shit. She'd forgotten about all the security crap. Maybe Hawkyn was right to worry about her. She sucked at Memitiming. "Yes, um, while I was checking on dessert, I looked out the window and thought I saw a cat and I went to check."

"A cat. Really." Skepticism dripped from his voice. "And how, exactly, did you get outside the wall without triggering any of the motion sensors or showing up on camera?"

"Obviously some piece of equipment is glitchy. Why don't you take a look into that?"

"I considered that," he said. "But then I found something else that didn't make sense." He pointed to a screenshot of the gate logs. "Maybe you can explain why there's a record of you entering through the gate but no record of you leaving the property, and while you're at it, explain how Hawkyn got inside the house without the gate logging him in?"

Shit, again. She shrugged. "Like I said, glitches."

"In two different, independent systems?" Declan took a step closer and she fought the urge to step back. "Why are you lying to me?"

"What? Lying?" She tried to sound both innocent and offended. The combination made her sound guilty instead. "I'm not."

"Bullshit. You're flushing. Your pupils are dilated. And unless you two can teleport, there's another way into this house that you didn't tell me about. Where is it?"

Oh, crap. How the hell was she going to explain this? She couldn't. She'd have to deflect.

"Look, I'm sure there's a logical explanation that doesn't involve secret tunnels or superpowers or something." Palms sweating and her heart fluttering around in her chest like a trapped bird, she started toward the doorway. "I've got to plan my next cooking show episode, so I'll just get to work—"

He blocked her path, his big body a virtual wall between her and the exit. "I take security failures personally," he said, "and I really, really don't like being lied to." His gaze locked on hers, holding her as captive as if he'd fitted her with power-neutralizing Bracken Cuffs. "There's no glitch."

Caught in a lie, she panicked and took another tack. "Well," she said briskly, summoning her father's aura of command, "I'm your boss, and if I say there's a glitch in the security system, then you should check it out. Now get to work or I'll find someone who will."

Disappointment darkened his expression, but it was gone in an instant, replaced by something harder. And colder. "Go ahead. I didn't want this job anyway. Consider this my three-day notice."

Stung and even more panicked because she couldn't lose him as a "bodyguard," she lashed out. "If you quit, I'll go straight to your supervisor at McKay-Taggart. I'll make sure you're fired."

She didn't mean it. In fact, she regretted saying it before she even finished talking. But now it was out there, and Declan's head snapped back as if she'd hit him.

"I thought you were different," he said roughly. "I really did."

"Different? Different than what?"

The contempt in his gaze chilled her to the bone. "Than other rich people."

"Well," she said softly. "Sorry to disappoint you."

He barked out a bitter laugh and brushed past her on the way to the desk. "Being disappointed is nothing new." He gestured to the screens. "I'll just get back to work since you'll tank my job at McKay-Taggart if I don't."

"I didn't mean it, Declan. I don't want you to quit. Please stay."

Turning away from her, he tapped on one of the keyboards. "Close the door behind you. Ma'am."

She hated the distance between them. Hated the frosty tone of his voice. Hated herself for putting it there.

So she told herself that this was for the best. His hatred would keep them both out of trouble. He'd be more alert and ready for danger, and she'd be in no danger of not Ascending.

It was a win-win.

So why did she feel like she'd just lost everything?

Chapter Eleven

Suzanne spent the next three days avoiding Declan and preparing to tape her next episode of *Angel in the Kitchen*. She still cooked meals, but Dec would take his plate into the security room and eat there.

If he'd found a secret entrance to the mansion, he hadn't shared that information.

Guilt pinched at her heart. She'd panicked and treated him like shit. He'd have been right to walk out on her right then and there, but for some reason, he'd stayed. And just yesterday he'd told her he'd accepted her apology and would continue on the job.

But things were still chilly, and she still felt guilty for being a jerk and for lying. She hadn't lied about the existence or non-existence of a secret entrance, but she'd definitely lied about the security equipment being glitchy. She wanted to tell him the truth, all of it, but revealing her identity to a human was another one of those forbidden things. Unlike other laws that governed forbidden actions, this one made sense. The knowledge would change his life and, perhaps, his destiny. The truth, in this case, would not set him free.

Her phone buzzed on the counter next to the stack of recipe note cards she'd been preparing for future *Angel in the Kitchen* episodes, and Cipher's name popped onto the screen.

"Hey, Cipher. You're on speaker," she said as warning to be careful with whatever he was going to say in case Declan was nearby.

"Gotcha, doll. Hey, I got some exciting news."

"Yeah?"

"Yeah. And thanks for letting me know you listed me as your contact person for *Angel in the Kitchen*, by the way."

"You're welcome," she chirped, amused by his sarcasm. "So is this related to my show?"

"You could say that. This is huge, lady." He paused, probably for effect. He was a drama queen sometimes, but it worked. She was practically bouncing on her toes while she waited for him to continue. "That big science fiction network wants to venture into food programming for nerds or something, and they want you to fly out to New York so they can discuss signing you for a cooking series."

Too stunned to speak, she stood there. And kept standing there, even as Cipher called out her name.

"Suzanne? Yo. You there? Suzanne?"

She stared down at the phone, her thoughts scattered all over the place. This was what she'd always wanted. A dream come true. Cipher better not be screwing with her.

"Yeah," she finally croaked. "Yeah. I'm here. Are you serious?"

"As Azagoth's condemnations."

"Holy shit," she breathed. "Holy shit!"

"They're up against a deadline and they want you there tomorrow. They're willing to buy you a plane ticket, but I figured I'd get you a D'Angelo private jet."

"You can do that?" The fallen angel had somehow maintained his ability to navigate the angelic network even after he'd lost his wings, and his reach constantly surprised her. So did his willingness to help. Assisting Memitim in their duty to protect Primori must be part of his plan for earning his way back into Heaven.

"Consider it done," he said. "I'll text you the deets and the network's schedule for you."

The network's schedule. This was real! "I can't believe it. This is crazy. Have you told Hawkyn?"

"*Hell* fucking no. I'll let you do that. You know what he's going to say, right?"

She picked up the cell, clicked it off speakerphone, and lowered her voice. "He's going to say I can't do it because we're forbidden to have too much human interaction or to draw attention to ourselves by getting famous or some crap."

"Bingo."

"Well, let's just keep this to ourselves for now, okay?"

"I'm not going to lie to him."

"I'm not asking you to," she assured him. "But do you expect him to ask if you've been contacted by a TV network about me?"

Cipher hesitated. "Well, no..."

"Then you won't have to lie." She heard footsteps in the hallway. "I gotta go. Send me the details when you can. Bye!"

Declan walked into the kitchen and went straight for the coffeemaker. Damn, he looked good in his jeans, a navy T-shirt that hugged every rigidly-defined muscle, and his sidearm at his waist. His leather flip-flops slapped softly on the tile as he shifted to grab a mug from the cupboard next to the fridge.

"Good morning," she said brightly, knowing by now that he wasn't a morning person.

His gruff "Morning, ma'am" amused her even though she hated that he still called her that. She wanted to be Suzanne again. Her name sounded so sexy when he said it.

"I have some news." She couldn't contain a grin, despite the fact that things between them were a bit tense.

Okay, a lot tense.

He poured steaming coffee into his mug. "Yeah?"

"We're flying to New York tomorrow."

"Great." He took a sip of his coffee as he swung around to face her. "Why?"

She couldn't wipe the smile off her face. He must think she was a loon. "Because a cable network wants to talk to me about *Angel in the Kitchen.*"

For a long moment, Declan said nothing, his expression unreadable. "Congratulations," he said, finally breaking his silence. "How long of a trip should I pack for?"

His response, or lack of it, stung. She'd felt as if they'd connected, and she was sure he'd told her things he didn't normally tell people. Especially not people he barely knew. Now he was back to the gruff, serious soldier he'd been when he'd first arrived, and it was all her fault. She had to fix this.

"A couple of days, at least," she said, going full-out cheery in case it was contagious. "I'll need to go shopping later this afternoon though, so make time in your schedule for that."

"Aye-aye, boss." He started to leave, but she hurried around the island and blocked him.

"Look, can we talk?" At his twitch of one shoulder that she took as a shrug of assent, she launched into her apology tour. "I'm sorry about the other day. I shouldn't have said the things I did. I shouldn't have threatened your job. It was a shitty thing for me to do."

"Yeah, it was." This time he gave a real shrug. "But like I said, I'm used to it."

"You should never be used to it," she said, suddenly angry. "Being treated like you're lesser than someone is bullshit."

"I'm used to it," he said. "But that doesn't mean I believe it. I know who I am."

"Well, I'm still sorry."

He moved a little closer, his gait slow and predatory, and her heart beat a little faster. She felt like a gazelle being stalked by a lion. "You sorry enough to tell me why you lied to me about how you got outside the perimeter fence?"

"Declan." She looked up at him, wishing for the first time that she had Maddox's gift to Compel. Compelling Declan to believe her would come in real handy right about now. "There is no secret tunnel from this house to outside." On that, at least, she didn't have to lie. "I promise."

"I've gone over every piece of equipment, every frame in every video, hundreds of times. I even sent the digital files to McKay-Taggart for expert analysis. Nothing has been tampered with, and there's no missing data. So how can you explain Hawkyn getting in and you getting out without being recorded on any of the cameras or setting off any motion alerts?"

"I can't." She really couldn't. Forbidden, and all that. "I wish I could prove to you that I'm telling the truth about there being no secret entrances to the house."

He eyed her speculatively, and then one corner of his mouth curved in a grim smile her father would envy. "There's a way to prove it."

She wasn't sure she wanted to know, and she hesitated before finally asking, "How?"

He gestured toward the grand staircase with his coffee mug. At first, she didn't understand. But as he started toward the stairs, she realized that he had no intention of going up to the second floor.

He was heading for the torture chamber *beneath* the stairs.

* * * *

Declan was at the end of his rope. In three days he hadn't found a reason for the lack of video showing Suzanne leaving the house and Hawkyn coming inside the house, and even more baffling, the doors and windows, which registered every instance of opening and closing, hadn't recorded activity during those times, either.

Why Suzanne would lie, he didn't know. And truth be told, he didn't think she was lying. But unless someone tampered with the evidence, there was no other explanation. But why would someone tamper with the evidence? Besides, McKay-Taggart's best techies, including Steve, confirmed that no tampering had taken place.

Something wasn't right about this entire situation, and he was about to get to the bottom of all of Suzanne's secrets, one way or another.

He stopped at the door beneath the stairs and tested the knob. It was as locked as it had been every time he'd tried, which was at least twice a day. And yet, Suzanne was able to turn the knob with no trouble.

Had to be some sort of advanced touch-sensor technology in the hardware. But when he asked, she just shrugged and claimed to know nothing about it.

Yeah, something definitely wasn't right.

"What are we doing in here?" she asked, her fists planted firmly on her hips. Hips he could picture himself gripping as he pounded into her no matter how hard he tried not to imagine it.

Sure, she'd crossed a line when she'd threatened his job, but he believed she was sorry, and he knew she'd been panicked and desperate when she'd done it. She was truly afraid of something—he could only guess that something was her stalker. The fear in her eyes had dimmed his anger and reminded him that he'd promised no one would get past him, and he'd meant it.

"Are we looking for anything specific?" Suzanne twirled in a circle as she took in the room. "Like a secret door behind the... What is that thing?"

"It's a bondage horse." An exquisite one, in fact. The four legs and punishment stocks on one end were wooden, but the rest was padded and covered in leather.

"Okay..." She stood there, looking confused and delectable in her blue and yellow sundress.

"Come here, Suzanne."

"What?"

"I said come here."

She swallowed, the delicate muscles in her throat rippling, and he had a sudden urge to nibble his way along each one. He wanted to nip a little too, a pleasurable punishment, but not for treating him like a serf, which he'd forgiven her for. No, she was still keeping something from him and despite that he wanted to fuck her in the worst way.

Angry sex was still sex.

But that wasn't what this about. Not entirely, anyway.

"Why?" she asked.

"In the pool you said you wanted sex. You begged me to touch you. Do you remember that?"

She swallowed again, her face going bright red. "Yes," she whispered.

"Do you still feel that way?" At her wide-eyed nod, his cock twitched, all stupidly happy. *Down, buddy.* This might not end that way. This really wasn't as much about sex as it was about opening up, breaking down barriers, and building a connection. Sure, it was unprofessional as hell, but, as he was discovering on a daily basis, this wasn't a conventional job. And he wouldn't do anything she didn't want. "Do you trust me?"

She didn't hesitate. "Yes."

"Do you really?" He gestured to the bondage horse and stocks. "So if I cuff you to this, you would trust me not to hurt you?"

Her chin came up, and her eyes sparked with determination. "Absolutely. But why do you want to do that?"

"Because *I* don't trust you, and that's a problem."

She folded defiant arms across her chest, pushing her breasts together and deepening the cleavage. God, she was killing him. "You really think you can torture me into telling you what you want to hear?"

"Yes...and no." He snagged two sets of handcuffs from where they hung on the wall. "This is going to be an exercise in trust, Suzanne. For everything you tell me, I'll tell you something. That's how it works."

For a moment she stared at the handcuffs, and then she squared her shoulders and marched over to the bondage horse.

"Go ahead. You'll see that I'm not hiding anything." Smirking, she held out her wrists to him, almost taunting him.

She was going to learn a lesson about teasing.

Without warning, he moved on her, slipping the cuffs on her wrists even as he maneuvered her body, angling her over the bench so she was lying on her belly, arms outstretched, her legs spread and her feet barely touching the floor. The fabric of her dress was stretched tight around her knees, so after he secured the cuffs to the stocks, he hiked the dress up to her hips.

He wasn't counting on the sight of her creamy, toned thighs and the bunched-up pink silk panties that barely covered her tight round ass to grab him right by the cock. An instant erection strained at his fly, the impatient bastard.

"Declan!" she gasped. "W—what are you doing?" She tried to look back at him, but her position didn't allow much movement.

"Your safe word is...halo." He wasn't sure why that word popped into his head, but it seemed to fit Suzanne, and it definitely matched up with his damned angel wings tattoo. "If you want me to stop at any time, say it."

"Stop...what, exactly?"

He slapped her ass, just a light one, and the sound echoed off the walls. "Shh. I ask the questions."

"But—"

He slapped her again, a little harder, and a rosy blush began to bloom on her right cheek.

"I ask the questions," he repeated. "I told you that's how this works. You have a safe word, and you can use it if anything I do makes you uncomfortable." He pitched his voice low, quiet with an edge of command. "Understood?"

Irritation put color in her cheeks and a hot flare in her eyes, but she nodded and looked forward again.

"Good girl." In reward, he cupped her bottom, feeling the heat from the spanks in his palm, and used his thumb to stroke her inner thigh. She trembled when his thumb brushed the fabric of her panties, and when he added pressure, she squirmed.

Nice.

"Now, tell me if there's a secret entrance to this house." He slipped his finger beneath the fabric and used the tip to caress, ever so lightly, the smooth, plump flesh between her legs.

"There's not," she blurted. "I told you."

He deepened his touch, adding more pressure and easing his finger inward, so he was stroking the seam of her labia. She went utterly still, but her breaths came in small bursts that shook the bench.

"Are you sure?"

"Well...there could be." She broke off on a moan and when she spoke again, her throaty voice had gone even lower. "But if there is, I don't know about it. Like this room."

Despite evidence to the contrary, he believed her and moved to reward her. Gently, he dipped his finger between her folds and nearly groaned at the silky moisture he found. She did groan, a hearty, needy sound that made his balls clench.

"Okay." He kept his voice to a low, soothing murmur. "Do you have the building plans to the house?"

"No."

He believed that, too. "Now it's my turn to tell you something."

"Your tattoo," she blurted breathlessly. "I want to know about that."

Reflexively, he jerked his hand away. He didn't want to talk about his fucking tattoo.

"First of all," he said, as he pinched the tender area he'd spanked, "you don't get to ask the questions." He brought his hand down on the spot he'd just pinched, and she hissed even as her lovely ass, framed by all that flowing fabric from her dress, rose as much as she could manage to meet his palm. Hmm, she liked this. It opened up a lot of fun possibilities. For later. Right now this was business. Mostly. "Second, my tattoo is off the table."

He swore she growled. "Then this isn't about trust, is it?" she asked. "If so, you need to give me something you don't want to give up."

As right as she was, he didn't want to hear it. This time, he pinched her between the legs. Not enough to hurt, but enough to startle her into making a squeal of both surprise and outrage. But when he began to pet her there, easing the throb he knew she was feeling, she moaned.

"Tell you what," he said softly. "You tell me who you really are, and I'll tell you what you want to know."

She went still. Even her breathing stopped. "What do you mean?"

Her wetness soaked through her underwear, proof that she wanted everything he was doing to her, and he had to hold back an appreciative moan of his own.

"I mean, take away your money, and who are you?" He slipped two fingers under her panties and pushed them between her labia, loving her shocked gasp. "Tell me, Suzanne."

"I—I don't know."

He withdrew his touch and brought his palm down on her hot ass. "I don't believe you." He slapped her again. "Who are you?"

"I don't know!"

Another, and she cried out with a sob. "Tell me."

"I. Don't. Know!"

"Bullshit." He drove his hand between her legs again, cupping her intimately but not giving her any stimulation. Just the hint of it. "Some people are defined by their money. You're not. You act like you are, but I don't believe it. You're hiding something, Suzanne. What is it?"

"Please, Declan..."

"Please what? Do you want me to stop? Do you want me to uncuff you?"

She shuddered, and her voice trembled. "No."

"Then what?"

"I want you," she whispered. "Since the first time I saw you, I've wanted you."

God help him, he wanted her too. But not yet.

"What else?" When she said nothing, he started rubbing circles on the pillowy pad of her pussy, still over her underwear, taking care to put extra emphasis over her clit. "Come on, Suzanne. Tell me what else you want."

Several moments of silence ticked by, and then, as if a dam had broken inside her, she blurted, "I want to be free. I want to cook. That's what I am." She let out a sob. "I'm a cook, and I'm social, and I want to choose my own path and be free of all the damned rules!"

Rules? There were rules for being rich? But actually, when he thought about it, maybe for people like her, there were. Maybe she felt constrained by her family name or the expectations that came with belonging to the D'Angelo empire. All that money, and she still felt trapped.

For a moment, he wanted to tell her to snap out of it. There were worse problems than having money. But obviously, her feelings were real, and she was sobbing as if this was the first time she'd admitted it.

For all of that, she deserved as much from him.

He tunneled his fingers beneath her panties again, and this time, he eased one finger just inside her. They both groaned as he tested her slick, tight channel.

He wanted to do more. He wanted to drop to his knees and lick her until she screamed, but unfortunately, he had other plans for his mouth.

He had to give her something he didn't want to give up.

He had to tell her about the tattoo.

This was going to cut deep.

"Back when I was in the military," he began roughly, "I had a friend named Gareth. We were part of a joint special forces team made up of members from the Air Force, Navy, Army, and Marines. He was a Ranger." The team had gone on dozens of missions together, and Declan had patched them all up at one point or another. "I earned a reputation of being a good luck charm, and Gareth got everyone calling me their guardian angel. It was a fucking stupid nickname, but it stuck because whenever I was with a unit or team, no one ever died. Hell, we were freakishly lucky all the time. Enemy RPGs would fly off course and hit empty buildings, IEDs would fizzle out before they detonated... Once, a mountain landslide took out thirty enemy combatants before they could ambush us. So anyway, once when we were on leave, Gareth got me drunk and made me get this tattoo. I don't even remember getting it." Which was probably a good thing, because his life went to shit afterward. He drew his finger up her slit, spreading her satin cream over her swollen flesh. "Back to you now." He made some slow circles around her clit, and she began to pant. "You say you want to be free. Why can't you be?"

"I—I think I can. I think...this is a start."

"This?"

She wiggled, rattling her cuffs. "I've never done anything like what we're doing. It's terrifying. But I have to take risks if I want to be happy, right?"

If she thought he'd be surprised by the fact that she'd never toyed around with BDSM, she was as crazy as her assistant. But he got what she was saying. Sometimes your comfort zone doubled as a prison.

"Keep doing that," she whispered, straining to push into his touch. "And tell me why the tattoo bothers you so much. I don't think it's just because your friend got you inked while you were drunk."

No, it wasn't. "I wasn't even mad. I was cocky. I was a fucking good luck charm, a guardian angel." And after a childhood of being invisible at best and a means to an end at worst, being needed, being important, was something he'd craved. "But then we got back to work. And one week later, Gareth died when the Humvee he was in ran over an IED. I was in the vehicle behind his. Saw the whole thing. And I couldn't save him."

"I'm so sorry, Declan." Her soft voice held a slight tremor, a testament to her ability to feel empathy for others. "You know it wasn't your fault, right?"

His heart jerked painfully against his ribs. It *was* his fault. Because everyone, including him, believed he had some kind of good luck mojo going on, and they'd gotten careless. Gareth had paid the price, and that emotional laceration was never going to heal no matter how many times someone used the words "It wasn't your fault" like a bandage.

"Whatever." He moved between her legs and let his fingers play on the satin skin of her inner thighs and ass. Touching Suzanne was far more pleasant than reliving the past. "Now you know something no one else does. Please don't make me regret telling you."

"Never," she swore, the tremor still in her voice. "But Declan?"

"Yeah?"

"Halo."

Chapter Twelve

Halo.

Suzanne couldn't believe she'd used a safe word. Someone had once told her that safe words were for people who wanted the freedom to say no during sex play without stopping the action. There were other reasons too, she supposed, but she'd simply never seen herself having the kind of encounter that would require a safe word.

But now she understood what the safe word meant to Declan. Like he'd said at the beginning, it was about trust. It was a contract, a guarantee that she was safe with him. She hadn't needed it—she knew in her soul that he wouldn't hurt her. And if her soul was wrong, well, he was no match for her power and abilities.

On the other hand, she was no match for his skilled hands and cool, commanding voice, and she'd been on the verge of letting him take her virginity on a bondage horse while in cuffs.

She was *not* wearing cuffs for her first time.

But more than that, she was in a state of overload. She'd admitted things to him that she hadn't even admitted to herself. He'd told her things he held private. And he was touching her like no male had ever touched her.

She'd never felt like this, like she was going to explode from her skin, and she just needed a minute to gain control of the situation before she let Declan take command of her desire and her body. She definitely trusted him with those.

As the safe word faded in the air, Declan froze, his fingers digging into her hips. Then, slowly, deliberately, he released her, unlocked her cuffs, and freed her from the stocks.

"I'm sorry if I upset you." He offered his hand to help her up off the bench.

"You didn't upset me." She pushed up on her elbows and resisted the urge to pull down her dress to cover herself as she lay on her belly, her legs still draped on either side of the bondage horse. She felt so exposed, but at the same time, she felt a sense of power every time Declan's hungry gaze drifted to her legs and backside. "I want to tell you anything you want to know, and I want to learn more about you, but not right now. I need... I want...more."

He stood there, his body as tense as a steel rod, a massive erection straining at the fly of his jeans. "More of what?" His voice was raw, as if every word hurt. She got that. She ached all over...but she was certain she knew the cure.

Summoning the erotic advice of every women's magazine article she'd ever read, she reached down and pulled her dress up, defying the instinct to shove it down. *If you want it, ask*, they said. *You're responsible for your own pleasure.*

She was also responsible for her own wings, which she most likely wouldn't get if she did this. If someone found out she did this. Yes, she could keep her mouth shut and no one would know, but during the Ascension ritual, when it came time for Confessions to the Council, she knew she'd tell the truth.

I had sex and didn't regret it.

That, she knew, would be the truth.

The hard, cold, steel gray of Declan's eyes became molten as he took her in, her dress now hiked up around her waist as she bent over the bondage horse, her panties damp and begging to be torn off.

"Tell me exactly what you want, Suzanne," he said softly. Was he kidding? Her ass was hanging out all over the place, and if that wasn't an invitation to sex, she didn't know what was. But she wasn't entirely sure how to do this. There was a little more to it than she'd expected, which was a happy surprise.

She could start with something basic and obvious. "Your fly. Open it."

His fingers found the top button of his jeans, but there they rested, waiting for her command.

"Yes," she whispered, her gaze glued to his hand.

She squirmed as he popped the button. Then the next one, giving her a glimpse of dusky skin. Was her mouth supposed to water? Because it was.

He stepped closer, popping two more buttons, and his erection, a magnificent column of smooth skin and bulging veins, sprung free.

Oh, my.

She'd never been this close before. Not like this. Something in her belly fluttered wildly as she reached for him, her fingers skimming the underside of his shaft. The hitch in his breath when she touched him made her own breath catch. She loved his reactions, loved the heady hit of feminine power she got when she caused them.

"It's so...velvety," she murmured.

"I'm not even sure what to say." Holding her gaze with his, he covered her small hand with his big one, tightening her grip around him. "Like that."

Shifting her weight on the horse so she wasn't squashing her breasts, she squeezed his hard flesh, taking it from the thick base to the plump head.

"Faster." His voice was a lash of command, and she didn't even consider disobeying. Licking her lips, she pumped her hand and watched him rock into her fist, listening to his breath as it became ragged. "That's right, Suzanne. Just. Like. That."

A shudder shook her body at the praise, and all she could think about was how his cock was going to feel inside her. She'd pleasured herself, one of those Memitim rules they weren't supposed to break, although Hawkyn had recently gotten that particular mandate revoked. But sex with another person, especially sex with one's own Primori, was bad.

Whatever. Right now she felt like being bad. Very, *very* bad.

As if Declan could read her mind, he pulled out of her grip and moved behind her, his fingers trailing over her butt as he maneuvered himself around the bondage horse. His warm hands felt like fire against the place where he'd spanked her, and she moaned as the most decadent sensation filled her. She'd been shocked at first by the bursts of pain followed by moments of a soaring bliss that she wanted to hold onto forever.

"Talk about velvet," he murmured as he stroked her hot, spanked skin, and then she squeaked in surprise when she felt his lips on that same spot. Oh, how she wanted to feel more of his lips, but then he straightened, gripped her panties, and pulled them down her legs.

She couldn't have prepared herself for the sudden vulnerability of being naked in front of him, bent over and spread-eagled. Instinct made her try to close her legs, but he cupped her intimately, pressing gently in a soothing, tender massage that chilled her out like he'd hit a switch.

"This is going to be amazing, Suzanne." Declan stepped back and suddenly, shockingly, he replaced his hand with his mouth.

"Dec—" She broke off with a cry as his tongue probed her slit, the tip teasing her entrance.

This was incredible. Decadent. So sinful she almost expected to be struck by lightning right through the roof of the house. With a moan, he spread her with his thumbs and delved into her slick heat, his tongue-lashing becoming a merciless torture as he licked and nibbled at her intimate flesh. And when he latched onto her clit and sucked, she sobbed with the need to come.

He seemed to know when she was right there at the edge, and then he'd cruelly change the rhythm or focus on a less sensitive spot. He teased and tormented her until she was a writhing, panting ball of need. And then, just as she gathered enough breath to beg him for release, he stopped.

Momentarily confused, she tried to crank her body around to see what he was doing, but right then he moved against her, pushing the blunt head of his condom-covered cock into her entrance.

The condom wasn't needed since un-Ascended Memitim weren't fertile, but she wasn't surprised that he'd been prepared to protect her.

"Damn," he breathed. "Oh, damn. I'm going to embarrass myself."

That wasn't going to happen, but she didn't have the words to say it. Not when he was pushing inside her, stretching her to the very edge of pain. A good pain. She'd never known such a thing existed, but it did, and she wanted more.

As he pushed deep, her core clamped around him as if trying to hold him there. Her body hummed with lust, and the slow, easy thrusts weren't enough.

"Faster," she rasped. "I think I need...faster."

As if he'd been waiting for permission, he hammered into her, his hard flesh stroking her slick channel. Every pump of his hips brought a new sensation and wrung a different sound from her. She especially loved how every time he came close to pulling out, the crown of his cock hit something near her entrance that made her wild. She nearly bucked herself right off the sex furniture until he gripped her hips harder, holding her for every punishing thrust of his hips.

Yes, oh...yes...*there*!

Every cell in her body quivered with ecstasy, making her shake and sob and see stars. Nothing she'd ever done by herself could compare to this. Nothing but Declan could make her blood steam through her veins with the hottest pleasure she'd ever known, and she knew it. She was spoiled now.

She'd need this again.

He shouted in his own release, his hips pumping violently, ramming her forward on the bondage horse. From this position she couldn't see him, but she felt his fingers digging into her hips, felt every spasm that made his body jerk with ecstasy.

Finally, with a deep, tortured groan, he collapsed on top of her, his breath fanning across her neck as he panted in exhaustion.

"Declan?" Her voice sounded like she'd swallowed a mouthful of sand.

He grunted, but before he could say anything, the video monitor on the wall beeped, revealing a vehicle at the gate.

"Fuck." He gently pulled free of her body, and she nearly wept at the loss. "That's Steve. He's here to help me figure out what's going on with the security system."

Bullshit. Oh, Steve was probably here for the reason Declan said, but she had no doubt he was also going to help Dec scour the place for a secret entrance. She hoped they didn't find one. She didn't know much about this house, and for all her denials, it wouldn't surprise her if they discovered a portal to another dimension or some crap.

It was already proving difficult to lie to him, and she didn't want to have to do it again.

There was, however, one thing she did want to do again, and that definitely wasn't going to happen if Declan believed she was lying.

Chapter Thirteen

Azagoth hadn't seen his mate in four months.

Everyone expected him to go full Grim Reaper over it. And, as he stood in his office, black clouds churning overhead and lightning striking all around him, he couldn't blame them. He was known for his temper.

But for all these months he'd managed, more or less, to control his inner demon. When he needed to release it, he went to the Inner Sanctum and tortured a few evil souls. And not just tortured them, but scared them. He became their worst nightmares. He'd spent a full day on a new resident of the 3rd level, a serial killer from the human realm who'd gone by Jason Drayger. Hawkyn would be happy to know about it.

So, yes, he sometimes got to release the monster within, but on this side of Sheoul-gra, he'd kept his displays of fury limited to shit like this.

Except this shit was just for show.

Mostly.

Jim Bob, one of his Heavenly spies, had just revealed the identity of the person who had helped Lilliana get out of Sheoul-gra, and after four months without her, he really wasn't in the mood for this.

"I know you're a big fan of killing the messenger," Jim Bob said, his face nearly obscured by the hood of his cloak. "But if you fry me, you'll miss me."

Azagoth snorted, but the angel was right. Jim Bob was, by far, his best source of Heavenly intel, and it would be a shame to electrocute him. It might even take a little more effort than usual, given that the force of the guy's angelic ability was tangible even here in Sheoul-gra, where Azagoth limited all power except his own.

"Then maybe," Azagoth said, shutting down the storm, "you should bring me better news."

Jim Bob shrugged. "I would think that learning Reaver helped your mate escape would have been good news. You know he'll keep an eye on her."

"Lilliana didn't *escape*," he snapped. "She'll be back. And fuck Reaver." Reaver, the most powerful angel in the universe, had been a thorn in Azagoth's side for years, so it was no surprise that the haloed bastard had answered Lilliana's call for help in getting out of Sheoul-gra.

He'd have to get Cipher to find out how she'd contacted Reaver. That was assuming he could get the Unfallen away from the flaxen-haired female he'd been doing every chance he got. Flail, a True Fallen, had been living here for a couple of months now, paying her rent in the form of intel gained from high-level demons and from cleaning toilets.

According to Hades' mate, Cat, cleaning toilets was a great way to knock arrogant fallen angels down a peg.

There was a rap at the door, and Zhubaal stuck his head in. "Hawkyn wants to talk to you. Says it's important."

"It's time for me to go, anyway." Jim Bob moved toward the doorway, his black cloak flapping around his boots. "Be well, Azagoth."

He ducked out, and Azagoth gave Z a nod. A moment later, Hawkyn entered.

"Father," he said, bowing his head in greeting. "Thank you for seeing me on such short notice." His formality said he was here for Memitim concerns, but the worried thread in his voice said it was personal.

Which meant Azagoth was probably going to make it personal as well. "What is it?"

"It's Suzanne. She's gotten in too deep with her Primori, and she won't listen to me. I was hoping you'd talk to her."

If Hawkyn was asking Azagoth to talk to his favorite sister, the situation must be bad. "What do you want me to say? I'm going to need more to go on here."

Hawkyn hesitated, and Azagoth resisted the instinctive urge to snap. But Lilliana had left for a reason. She'd left so he'd learn to deal with his children and his emotions without using her as a crutch.

It pissed him off.

But he wasn't going to get her back until he figured this shit out, so instead of giving in to his impatience, he was going to wait for Hawk to speak.

He waited two more heartbeats. Fuck it. "Fucking spit it out, son. I have a backlog of souls to inspect and Lilliana is going to Skype me in"— He glanced at his watch—"five minutes."

She Skyped every day, and seeing her face was the only thing that kept him sane. Yes, she was gone, but he had to admit that their chats had been...fun. Almost as if they were dating over the Internet. They'd skipped the whole dating routine, what with Lilliana being forced to mate him. Things had been rough at first, but they'd found love quickly. Maybe too quickly.

As much as he hated to admit it, he liked the way things were going between them. Lilliana was always flirty and full of laughter, and they sometimes talked for hours, learning things about each other that they hadn't known before.

And the Skype sex was incredible.

But it was time for her to come home, and he was going to tell her that today.

"Suzanne is living with her Primori."

Azagoth blinked at Hawkyn's blunt statement. "She's what?"

With a frustrated growl, Hawk jammed his fingers through his hair, which was already a mess, probably from doing just that. "A Siecher demon is after her Primori, and its psychic attacks don't trigger her *heraldi*. So she thought it would be a good idea to hire her Primori as a bodyguard to keep him close. And I think she's falling for him."

Azagoth cursed, but he wasn't surprised. Suzanne had never been cut out to be Memitim. She was too soft-hearted. Too...human. Of all his children, she was the only one who made a special effort to see him every day, even if it was just to say hi or ask how his day went. She'd once told him that it was "a thing" she'd done with her human father. She'd either seen him or called him every single day from the time she was six until the day she was plucked out of the human world and deposited into the Memitim one. Only she hadn't called the human her father. She'd called him Daddy.

And he just now realized that he hadn't seen her in days. Shame at not having noticed clawed at him, and his inner demon stirred. He tamped it down with the promise of blood later and addressed Hawkyn. "Why is the Siecher after her Primori?"

"We weren't sure, but I just got back from going through some of the records filed by his prior guardian. Looks like during the near-apocalypse Declan killed the head of the demon's family. He slaughtered a lot of demons. He was a surprisingly lethal and prolific demon slayer for a human."

"This...Declan. He's aware of our world?"

"No." Hawkyn glanced over at the massive fireplace, where flames as tall as Azagoth licked at the inner walls. Since Lilliana had gone, the flames had been cold. "His memory was altered afterward."

"Huh."

Hawkyn stared. "*Huh?*"

Azagoth glanced at his watch. Lilliana was going to call at any second. "I'll talk to her," he assured Hawkyn.

But he didn't need to. Unless Suzanne was in physical danger, he probably wasn't going to. As someone who could read souls, he'd come to sense when one was in flux. Suzanne was at a crossroads, and she needed to be in charge of her own destiny. Whatever mistakes or successes she made, she had to own.

"Now," Azagoth said, as his laptop beeped, "I need some privacy. Oh, and Hawkyn?"

"Yes, sir?"

"Keep an eye on your sister. I would be...inconsolable...if anything were to happen to her."

"Of course." Hawkyn bowed his head. "Thank you."

Azagoth barely heard Hawkyn leave. His entire focus was on Lilliana now, and somehow, he had to convince her to come home.

* * * *

Lilliana missed Azagoth so much it hurt, and as she looked down at him on her cell phone's screen, she absently stroked her finger over his cheek.

"You're at the beach today, I see." She missed his smoky, deep voice, too.

"Ares's island is lovely." Waves lapped at her feet as she sat in the warm sand, a salty breeze teasing her chestnut hair.

Azagoth frowned, his eyes narrowing. "Is that a hellhound behind you?"

She looked over her shoulder at the pitch-black creature watching her from behind a dune and sighed. "That's Maleficent. She's been following me around for weeks."

"I don't like that," Azagoth growled.

"It's fine. I feel sorry for her. She's really small for a hellhound, and the rest of the hounds torment her."

Ares's mate, Cara, was some sort of hellhound whisperer, and their island was crawling with the things. Maleficent had latched onto Lilliana from almost the minute Reaver had brought her to stay with the Horseman and his mate. Lilliana had yet to be able to pet the young hound, but she hadn't pushed it, content to let Maleficent come to her when she was comfortable.

Azagoth cocked a dark eyebrow. "How small is small?"

She shrugged. "I don't know. About half the size of a normal one?" Considering the damned things were the size of a bull moose, Mal was still big at half of that.

"You shouldn't be there," he said, the change of subject giving her whiplash.

Feigning ignorance, she rolled her eyes. "The beach is perfectly safe."

"I'm not talking about the beach and you know it. Come home."

She twirled her hair around her finger and flipped the subject around again. "How are the children you brought from the human realm settling in?"

His expression said they'd come back to his choice of topic but that for now, he'd humor her. "Some of them are handling their situation well."

"And the others?"

He frowned, his frustration putting deep creases between his dark brows. "They're troubled. And strange. Their slang is obnoxious."

She bit back a laugh. He'd had the oldest children brought in first, which meant he was dealing with teenagers. She'd actually like to see that.

"Well, remember, they're usually taken for fifty years of training at Memitim centers before you ever meet them." She smiled. "They're civilized by then."

"I don't have the patience for it. What if this was a mistake?"

What he was really asking was, "What if *I* make a mistake?"

Azagoth was so wracked with guilt for allowing his children to be abandoned at birth in the human realm and raised in the worst conditions imaginable. Once upon a time, he didn't care. He had been an evil, unfeeling monster until Lilliana had come along. Since then he'd opened his realm—and his heart—to his children, and for the most part, it had gone well. But emotion was a new drug to Azagoth, and it was taking time to figure out the right dosage.

"It's not a mistake," she said gently. "These are the older ones, and they're going to need more time to adjust. You'll feel differently when the little ones start arriving."

"I don't think so. Children don't belong here, Lilliana."

"And you think they belong in the human world, in the worst possible homes they could have?"

"So it's a choice between Hell and hell." He shook his head. "What if I lose my temper and whip out my demon or decapitate someone in front of them?"

She'd tell him to stop being dramatic, but there was actually a decent chance of either of those things happening.

"You'll just have to work on controlling your temper," she said. "And it isn't like they don't know what you are. I think you're going to find that they'll be pretty accepting. After all, you're a legend, and they're going to be powerful angels. All in all, I'd say this is an amazing thing for them."

Azagoth blew out a long breath. "There's another bright side. Hades did point out that I get to be the one to fuck 'em up instead of some other asshole."

"That's the spirit," she said, trying to keep things light. Azagoth's mood seemed a little grim, and she didn't want to fight. "Hades is wise." The Jailor of the Underworld was a jackass, but he wasn't stupid. "Oh, and I have news. Cara is pregnant. She told Ares this morning."

A shadow passed over his face, his expression going as dark as his mood, and her gut clenched. "How'd he take it? Was he upset?"

"Was he upset?" she repeated, incredulous. She hadn't expected him to jump for joy, but this? "Are you serious? He was thrilled. Why would you think anything different?"

"Ares has lost children before," Azagoth said. Just dropped that bomb in the space between them.

And now she got it. She understood his reluctance to completely let his children in. On top of his guilt, Azagoth had been dealing with the grief of losing his children. Meera might have been the most recent to lose her life in the service of Heaven, but there had been hundreds before that.

She wanted to go home right this instant and hug him, but she couldn't. Not yet.

"Poor Ares. I didn't know," she said softly.

"It was a long time ago. Before he became War."

A bird called out as it soared along the beach toward Ares's Greek mansion, where a Ramreel demon was playing tug o' war with a hellhound pup on the lawn in the very spot where Ares had learned he'd be a father.

"Well, you'll be happy to know that he was so excited by the news that he whisked Cara away to go tell their family."

"So you're on the island alone?"

"Azagoth, I'm fine. Ares's island is hidden from all eyes, and only a few approved people can pass through the wards. Plus, the place is crawling with Ramreel guards and hellhounds."

"Oh," he said, his voice dripping with sarcasm, "if you'd only told me the island is infested with demons at the beginning, I'd have felt much better."

"Hon, you're being a bit of a jerk, so I'm going to go. I love you."

He opened his mouth to argue, but she didn't give him the chance. She disconnected the call and took a deep, calming breath. She wanted to go home, but she had to be sure that he'd gotten control of his emotions first. She couldn't be blamed for his pain again.

A warm nose nudged at her hand, and she nearly screamed. Then she froze as Maleficent nudged her again before moving a few feet away and plopping down in the sand to look out at the waves.

That was the first time the canine had gotten this close, let alone touched her. Cara said the things were sensitive to the emotions of those they bonded with. But surely it hadn't bonded with her. Not that Lilliana knew what was involved with the bonding process.

"Well, Mal," she murmured. "What do you think Azagoth would say if I took you back to Sheoul-gra with me?" The hound turned to her, tongue lolling. "Yeah, he'd freak."

But that would be nothing compared to what he was going to do when he found out that telling him about Cara's pregnancy had been a test of the waters.

Because Lilliana... Well, there was another reason she'd left Azagoth while he dealt with his inner demon.

She was pregnant too.

Chapter Fourteen

Declan wasn't used to being nervous. No, not nervous. Jangly. Was jangly a word? Because that was how his insides had felt all day. He'd only seen Suzanne once since he'd kissed her good-bye and left her in the understairs dungeon, and that had been when she'd brought him and Steve lunch. She'd showered and changed into a pair of khaki shorts with a matching, flowing pink and khaki top, and if Steve hadn't been there, he'd have had that sexy little outfit on the floor.

She'd given him a flirty smile, probably thinking she'd been covert about it, but the moment the office door had closed behind her, Steve went playground.

"Ooh, damn." Steve whistled. "What was that about? You nail her?"

"No, I didn't *nail* her." He reached for what Suzanne had called a French grilled cheese. Declan wasn't normally one for bucking the grilled cheese tradition of plain white bread and American cheese slices, but this croissant sandwich with pepper jelly, sliced granny smith apples, brie, and turkey was fucking awesome. He paused before taking a bite. "And shut up."

Steve snorted. "You nailed her." At Declan's glare, he'd grinned and held up his hands in defense. "Shutting up."

That lasted for approximately three seconds.

"But aren't you always the one preaching about how it's harder to protect someone you care about than someone you don't give a shit about?" Steve grabbed a homemade French fry and dragged it through the garlic aioli Suzanne had made. "That's bullshit, you know. Just ask Liam and Avery or Case and Mia. If anything, I'd argue that you'll be even better at keeping someone you care about safe."

"Yeah, well, you're an IT guy. If your computer dies, you can get another one."

"That's harsh, man," Steve said with mock seriousness. "My computers are my babies."

"That's because you can't get a woman."

Steve considered that as he popped another fry and chewed. "Did you know there's sex doll porn? Like, dudes fucking sex dolls. On video."

"What does that have to do with you not being able to get a woman?" Declan grimaced. "And why do you know that?"

"Not important." Steve ate another fry and wiped his fingers on a napkin. "My point is that I'm not that hard up."

"Not that hard up to do what? Get a sex doll?"

"To watch some dude bang one. I mean, how fucking lonely do you have to be to watch someone have sex with a *doll*?"

Declan really hadn't wanted to think too hard on that.

He and Steve had finished lunch and then got back to searching the house, but Dec hadn't been able to get Steve's words about Suzanne out of his mind. *You'll be even better at keeping someone you care about safe.*

Maybe. But the cost of failure was also much, much higher.

Now, hours later, Steve had gone and Declan shook himself out of thoughts that weren't doing anything but making him crazy as he pulled Suzanne's Jag up to the front door. He was not a fan. Sure, the car was nice. Luxurious, plush, drove like a dream. But he felt like a douche driving it. Like he should be wearing a two-thousand-dollar suit and paying three hundred bucks for the same haircut an average person could get for twenty at the local barber.

He'd take his Rover over her kitty any day.

His breath caught when she came outside, still in her shorts and blouse, but she'd added a light sweater and strappy sandals, and a lot of blingy jewelry. She was practically glowing, her hair in a high ponytail that bounced as she walked down the sidewalk. If he had to choose just one word to describe her, it would be vibrant. She was a bundle of positive energy that engulfed everything around her, and as he got out to hold the passenger door open for her, he reveled in the way she made him feel.

"Thank you," she said, giving him a shy smile that was as bright as the diamond around her throat.

He wanted to kiss her. Maybe ravage her a little.

Shit. This was why getting involved with a client was dangerous. He was thinking about getting her into bed when he should be alert to threats.

Mentally re-ordering his priorities, he shut her door and got back into the car. He put the Jag in gear, waited for the gate to fully open, and then he eased the vehicle down the driveway. Next to him, Suzanne put on her sunglasses, completing her effortless, angelic look. There was even a golden halo surrounding the crown of her head, a trick of a sunbeam striking her glossy hair.

She was too good for him, and that was something he would never have thought he'd say just a few days ago.

"Well," she said, giving a sassy toss of her head as she turned to him, "did Steve find the secret entrance? Or did you guys just work on security issues?"

Busted.

"No," he said sheepishly. "But did you know there's a storage room full of some really old and bizarre artifacts and religious stuff?"

"Really?" Her eyebrows climbed up over the rims of the sunglasses. "Huh. I'd like to see it."

She seemed genuinely surprised, and he didn't doubt it. The room's entrance had been hidden behind a door disguised as a bookcase, and if Steve hadn't been specifically looking for a secret door, he never would have found the storage room.

Declan flipped on the Jag's blinker and pulled out onto the street.

Suddenly, a man was there, standing in the middle of the road, his finger pointed at the windshield.

"Oh, shit!" Suzanne lunged at Declan, slamming her palms into his knee and pushing down, forcing his foot on the gas pedal. "Hit him!"

"*What?*" He cranked the steering wheel, and he swore he saw the guy smile as the car swerved wildly.

A flash of light, so bright it made the noon sun seem dim, blasted his corneas, blinding him with searing pain. Suzanne shouted as he mashed down hard on the brakes. The car skidded sideways to a halt, the squeal of tires fading into the sound of the passenger side door opening.

Somehow, his vision returned, partially, at least. He saw well enough to watch as Suzanne bailed out of the car and ran toward the man in the road.

Except it wasn't a man anymore. He stared, blinking madly, as if doing so would eventually change the image in front of him. Holy fuck, it was a monster. A horned creature straight out of his nightmares. And Suzanne was running right for it.

"Suzanne!" His hands shook as he simultaneously drew his weapon and opened the car door. As his foot hit the hot pavement, the beast swung a massive ax at Suzanne, and his heart shot into his throat. "*Suzanne!*"

She disappeared. Right before Declan's eyes, she disappeared, and the ax cut through empty air. A split second later, she reappeared behind the creature, scythes whirling like blender blades in her hands. Where had those come from? What the everliving fuck was happening?

The monster-thing leaped into the air. One of Suzanne's blades caught it in the mouth as it spun into her, knocking her thirty feet away into a telephone pole. She slid to the ground in a heap, but before Dec could take a single step toward her, she threw her hand out, and a fireball—an actual fireball—shot from her fingertips.

The beast easily stepped aside, and the ball of fire shrieked through the air before plummeting into a nearby mansion. Time seemed to stand still as the roof caved in and then blew out in an explosion that shook the entire block. Debris rained down and smoke choked the air.

Before that moment, Declan had actually thought that maybe, just maybe, he was being punked. Or that they'd inadvertently driven onto the set of a Hollywood movie.

But no, this was all too real. Unbelievable as it was, it was real, and he knew it.

The monster snapped its arm in an arc and launched some sort of round weapon at Suzanne. Blinded by a veil of black smoke, she didn't see the sphere, and Declan didn't have time to warn her before it struck her in the head, knocking her to the ground. The monster charged at her, jaws snapping, its massive, serrated teeth clacking together like demonic thunder.

A sense of déjà vu washed over him. As if he were divorced from his mind, a feeling of calm took over, and he leaped into action. Taking a knee, he used the Jag as cover and fired at the horned creature. It roared and rounded on Declan, its gaping maw dripping saliva and blood.

He fired again, and the thing charged, the bullets bouncing off its hide as if they were nothing more than BBs hitting the hull of a tank.

Hawkyn materialized on the monster's left flank and attacked it with bolts of lightning, slowing it. And then Sexy was there, and three other people he'd never seen.

Suddenly, skull-shattering pain knocked him to the ground, and his body convulsed so hard that he heard the crack of bone. Hellish agony ripped him apart for what seemed like hours, until finally everything went dark.

Chapter Fifteen

Declan woke to the sound of Suzanne's hushed voice. Opening his eyes, he found himself on her couch. She was standing a few feet away, speaking quietly with some big dark-haired, leather-clad dude he'd never seen.

Why? And why had he been sleeping?

Suzanne turned to him, her face smeared with blood and soot, and it all came back. He jackknifed up so fast his head spun.

"Hey," she said, rushing over to him. "Be careful. Sexy loaded you up with some healing waves, but she's not very skilled at that, and you probably still have a concussion."

Did she say *healing waves*?

"And maybe some fractured bones," the guy added. "We really should have called Darien."

Suzanne rolled her eyes. "I wouldn't trust Darien to heal a paper cut. Look what he did to Hawkyn."

Leather dude tugged at the plug in one of his ears. "All he did was make him fertile."

"By accident," she said. "Which is even worse."

"Excuse me," Declan said, his voice rough, like he hadn't used it in years. "But what the fuck is going on?"

Before Suzanne could say anything, the guy put a hand on her shoulder. The silver skull ring on his middle finger glinted in a ray of sunlight streaming through the window, and Declan swore one of the ruby eyes winked at him. "You sure you want to do this?"

"There's no other choice, Journey. Declan's seen too much. He needs to know the truth. Besides, he's the only person we know who can tell us

128/*Larissa Ione*

how to defeat Morroc."

"Aaaand I say again, what the hell is going on? I'm losing my patience here. Morroc? The truth? Yeah, that would be good. Because what the hell was that thing that attacked us?" Declan glared at Journey. "Also, get your fucking hand off her."

Suzanne and Journey exchanged glances. The guy shook his head, clearly not wanting her to say anything, but she shrugged and turned back to Declan.

Journey removed his hand and casually picked up the overhead fan remote as if that had been his plan all along.

"It was a demon," she said, sounding dead serious. "A nasty one."

"Are there non-nasty ones?" Journey toyed with the remote, turning it off and on. "Seriously?"

"You know there are." She snatched the remote away. "Now, will you please go tell Idess what's going on? We need help."

Journey scowled. "I thought Ciph was handling Idess."

"Cipher is handling damage control at the house I blew up. Humans have to think it was a gas leak." She glanced over at Declan. "No one was hurt, and it doesn't look like there were any witnesses."

Humans have to think it was a gas leak. Why was Suzanne talking like she wasn't one of them? Declan was fucking lost.

He tried to corral his thoughts as Journey grumbled under his breath and walked out of the room, but once they were alone, all he could do was blurt, "A demon? Are you fucking kidding me?"

Suzanne walked over to a table where someone had placed a pitcher of ice water. "I'm serious." She poured water into one of the glasses on the tray, all cool and calm. Like a house didn't blow up, lighting hadn't come out of Hawkyn's hands, and a man hadn't turned into a twelve-foot horned beast right in front of the mansion. "Do you have a better explanation?"

"The military is always experimenting with crazy shit..."

"You really think the military created that thing?"

No, he didn't. Hell, he was starting to question his sanity. "Maybe we're under the influence of some kind of drug."

"Yeah, whatever." She put the glass of water on the coffee table in front of him. "Or it was a Siecher demon."

"Right, right..." He reached for the water, forcing himself to stay calm. "And you know this, how, Suzanne D'Angelo, rich heiress with a cooking show? Do you put on a superhero suit and slay demons by night?"

"Something like that." She inhaled deeply. "You're gonna want to sit down."

"I am sitting down."

"Well...lean back." When he glared, she held up her hands. "All right, geez. Okay, so, maybe you've guessed by now that I'm not who I say I am."

"I'm starting to figure that out. So I'll bite. Who are you?"

"I'm an angel."

"I see." Jesus. He always got the loony ones. Then again, he was having a hard time explaining the things he'd seen, like how she'd disappeared and then materialized someplace else. Or how she'd thrown a fireball that took out an entire house. "I don't suppose you can show me your wings?"

She averted her gaze. "I don't have them yet."

Of course not. "Then how are you going to prove your story?"

"I'm going to tell you the truth, and hopefully you'll remember all of it."

He wasn't sure what to even say as she moved over to the window and pulled the curtain back. Out on the street, fire engines and police cars had gathered to attend to the burning house nearby.

"A few years ago," she said as she turned back to him, "we nearly lost the human realm to an apocalypse. Demons emerged from Hell, and humans fought them alongside angels, three of the Four Horsemen, and even other demons. Evil was defeated, and for a few months, humans tried to rebuild and cope. But you humans are fearful and power hungry, and when religious wars threatened to break out and politicians seized on the idea of using the threat of demons to control their populations, angels decided to step in and once again to repair a lot of the damage and make humanity forget."

Once *again* make humanity forget? She was crazy. Certifiable. A virus was responsible for the violence and destruction that had spread across the planet a few years back.

"You want me to believe that demons not only exist, but they attacked humans, we fought back, and then had our memories erased by angels?"

"Erased and replaced with an explanation your primitive human minds could understand," she said. "Well, most of you. Angels kept some humans in the loop because the existence of an otherworld can't be kept secret much longer. Human technology is exposing more and more every day, and restlessness in all the realms is causing instability and frequent incursions by demons. Angels are hoping that a more gradual introduction to the Otherworld will keep humans from freaking the hell out."

"Uh-huh." He took a drink of his water and wished it was vodka. "So you're saying that the viral outbreak that caused mayhem didn't happen. It was demons. My *primitive* mind just doesn't remember that."

"Yes. And can I just say that you're taking this really well?"

That was because it was always best to stay calm when dealing with a crazy person. But Jesus... How was he supposed to handle this?

"Look," he said softly. "Maybe you could explain why that thing attacked you." He paused, remembering her fighting skills. Assuming all of this was real—and that was still up in the air—she could take care of herself. "And also, why the fuck did you hire me to be your bodyguard if you can fight like that?"

"I hired you and moved into this angel-owned house to keep you near." She came closer, her expression uncharacteristically grim. "Because that demon wasn't after me, Declan. It was after you."

Whoa. He put down his glass with a shaking hand. "Me? What the fuck did I do?"

"You don't remember, but you killed a lot of demons. I didn't even know until Hawkyn told me after the battle. Apparently you were a fucking badass. And you killed the patriarch of a powerful demon family. That family now wants you dead."

Angry at this incomprehensible freak show, he slammed his fist into the table. "Stop it! Stop with this psycho-ass bullshit!"

"Whoa." Hawkyn's voice, booming from behind Declan, made him jump to his feet like a twitchy cat. "Suzanne, you told him?"

"I had to. He knows already, Hawk. He saw everything, and deep down, he knows."

Naturally, her lunatic assistant was in on this insanity. Maybe they'd broken out of the same asylum.

"Just...prove it to him," she said. "Show him your wings."

"I thought you don't have wings," Declan snarked.

"I don't. But Hawkyn does."

"Uh-huh." He came to his feet to face Hawkyn. "So let's see these wings of—"

Glowing, glittery wings erupted from Hawkyn's shoulders, filling the space and brushing the ceiling. Declan sucked air, rocking back a step before catching his balance. It was a trick. There was no way the dude was an angel.

Suzanne sighed. "I don't have wings, but..." She held out her hand, and in the time it took him to blink, she was holding a scythe, its graceful, curved blade glinting in the light. Then it was gone, and she was holding a sword. In moves almost too fast for him to track, she performed a series of battle stances and sword strikes that would have killed a dozen people before they even saw her move. Then she made the weapon disappear in a ball of light.

Very slowly, Declan sank onto the couch. It was real. Everything she'd told him was real.

And somehow, he'd known all along.

* * * *

Suzanne watched as Declan attempted to process everything he'd just learned. She couldn't even imagine what he was going through. Well, she could imagine—her life had been turned upside down when she was torn from her happy college life and plopped down in a new world with a new reality. But she hadn't felt any shock. The moment she met her first sibling, reality had washed over her and she'd felt as if she'd always known the truth. Unlike most of her siblings, she hadn't necessarily been ecstatic. She'd had a good life and was happy.

Being forced to leave that life had been a little traumatic.

While Declan drained his glass of water as if it were whisky, Hawkyn put away his wings. "I'm going to make sure Journey caught up with Idess. We're definitely going to need her demon in-law for this."

"Demon in-law?" Declan croaked. "God, this is going to take a minute to sink in."

"Don't worry," she said. "We're going to help you out with that. We think we can restore your memory." She tapped Hawkyn on the shoulder. "Isn't that right?"

"Right," he said. "I'm outta here." With no reason to hide anything from Declan anymore, he flashed out.

"Holy shit." Declan stared at the empty space where Hawkyn had just been standing. "This is crazy." He scrubbed his hand over his face. "Why me? How did I get mixed up in all of this?"

She took a seat on the opposite end of the couch, not wanting to crowd him. "You are what we call Primori. Primori are people whose lives are important to the future of the earthly realm. I belong to a class of angel called Memitim. We are the official guardians of all Primori. Keeping you safe is how we earn our wings and entry into Heaven. Like Hawkyn. He's special, though, because usually once we Ascend we no longer have contact with other un-Ascended Memitim."

Hawkyn also didn't have *complete* access to Heaven, but his was a complicated situation that she could explain to Declan after he'd absorbed the more urgent information.

He blinked at her from where he sat, his legs spread, forearms resting on his knees, his gorgeous eyes a little glazed. "You're saying you've been my guardian? For what, my entire life?"

"I've only been your guardian for a year," she explained. "Before that, you were assigned to one of my brothers."

"Where did he go? Did he...God, I can't believe I'm saying this...did he earn his wings?"

"He was killed while protecting another Primori."

"I'm sorry," he said, sounding a little numb. Or shell-shocked.

"It's okay." It really was. It was always sad when a sibling died, but she'd never even met the brother who had watched over Declan for three years before she'd inherited him. "I didn't know him. I don't know most of my brothers and sisters."

"How many do you have?" He straightened, perking up as if a subject as normal as siblings was a welcome break from the bizarre reality that had just been thrust upon him.

"Thousands. Most of them have already Ascended, so I won't meet them until I earn my own wings."

"Thousands?" Declan sounded a bit strangled.

"Well, most of them are half-siblings. We all have the same dad. I've only met four others with the same mom, too. Hawkyn is one of them."

"Hawkyn is your brother?" He groaned. "Now shit makes sense. Crazy motherfucker."

"He can be a little overbearing," she admitted.

"Yeah. A little." He rubbed his throat absently. "So he's your full brother, right? Who's your mom?"

"An angel named Ulnara. I've never met her, but Hawkyn has." At his quizzical look, she explained. "Our parents don't raise us like most angels. We grow up with human families."

"And I'm assuming your dad is...God?"

She laughed. "Sorry. It's just funny because angels have always treated us like lessers, and for thousands of years they told us that they were created by the hand of God, while we were sinned into existence."

"Sinned?"

"You know. Sex. My parents had sex. But so did theirs. Bunch of liars."

"Damn." Declan flopped back on the couch and looked up at the ceiling fan as it spun like a helicopter rotor thanks to Journey's fascination with the remote. The thing could fly off its base and decapitate them all, and it still wouldn't be the weirdest thing that happened today. "You know what's crazy? I spent my entire childhood reading about fictional worlds and the supernatural, and I always thought I'd be cool if I ever found out any of it was real."

"I think you're being pretty cool about it."

He barked out a laugh. "I'm so freaked out right now." And then, shocking the crap out of her, he held out his hand. "Come here."

It didn't occur to her to say no, even though the last time he'd commanded her to come to him, he'd cuffed her to sex furniture.

She'd totally let him do that again.

Pulse fluttering madly, she took his hand and let him pull her down on his lap. "I can't believe you're an angel. I'm not sure my mind has processed all of this yet, but I'm glad you're here." He frowned. "Wait. You're an angel. Holy shit. Are there rules about us? Humans and angels?"

Damn it. She hadn't wanted to address this. Not yet. There was so much going on all around them that they didn't need any more complications.

Which didn't mean that she was going to let the subject of their relationship go. No, she was in it for as long as he was. That, she now realized, had been decided from the moment she'd first laid eyes on him.

"There are definitely rules." Reluctantly, she pushed away from him. "We can't let anyone see us. We definitely can't let anyone know we had sex."

"Oh, Jesus." The blood drained from his face. "I had sex with an angel."

Now was probably not the time to tell him she'd been a virgin. No, definitely not.

The doorbell rang, and a heartbeat later, her sister Idess was in the doorway to the living room, looking gorgeous as usual in low-slung jeans and a jade tank top, her thick brown braid draped over one shoulder. A blond guy stood next to her, a sleeve of tats extending from the tips of his fingers to where they disappeared beneath his green Heineken T-shirt, only to reappear on his neck, entangled with a double ring around his throat.

"More siblings?" Declan asked.

"One of them is. Declan, this is my sister Idess. We also have the same mother, but she's a few thousand years older than I am. And she's not an angel anymore." She gestured to the male next to her. "And this, I'm assuming, is one of her demon in-laws."

Declan surged to his feet. "Demon?"

"It's okay," the demon said. "I'm one of the good guys." He stuck out his hand.

For a long moment, Declan did nothing. And then, with a muttered "What the hell," and a shake of the head, he clasped hands with the demon. "I'm Declan."

"Nice to meet ya, human. I'm Wraith." The demon grinned, flashing vicious-looking fangs. "And I'll be your guide to the nightmares that live in your brain."

Chapter Sixteen

Declan couldn't believe this was happening. A demon was standing right in front of him. A real, honest-to-god demon. The statuesque woman with him, Suzanne's sister Idess, walked into the living room with a smile and a light step, which seemed surreal. She'd been an angel once, and now she was buddy-buddy with a fucking demon?

He eyed Wraith. The guy didn't look anything like the demon that had attacked them. Muscular, tall, and with a shiny, shoulder-length mane of blond hair Thor himself would envy, Wraith could easily grace the cover of any magazine, and if he walked into any Hollywood studio, he'd be on the big screen the next day.

They might have to disguise those fangs, though.

"So...you're going to restore my memory?"

"I'm going to try." Wraith shrugged. "But angels are dicks, so who knows what they did to you? Might have whipped your brain into scrambled eggs."

Idess sighed. "You can't be normal for two seconds, can you?"

"What's normal?" Wraith asked. "Because, hello, you're asking me to reconstitute memories erased by angels after a demon apocalypse. So, you know, define normal."

"He's got a point," Suzanne said.

Idess groaned. "Don't ever say Wraith has a point. Or that he's right about anything."

Wraith nodded. "Totally. I'll use it against you for eternity."

What the hell was happening? This was so not what Declan had expected of demons. Or angels, for that matter.

I had sex with an angel.

"Declan?" Suzanne prompted. "You okay? You look a little pale again."

"Yeah." He cleared his throat. "Yeah, I'm fine. But I'm not sure I'm comfortable with this..."

Suzanne took his hand in hers and squeezed. Her thumb stroked his skin in long, soothing passes, an intimate gesture he might not have been ready for just days ago. Intimacy with women had always been limited to the sexual kind. This emotional stuff was brand new, and he was ready for it. Hell, he needed it. Given all that had happened, who wouldn't?

"You don't have to go through with this if you don't want to," Suzanne said. "But if you do, I'll be right here."

"Do you know this...demon?"

"No, but if Idess trusts him, I do too."

"Plus," Wraith chimed in, "I saved the world once or twice. I'm totally trustworthy."

"It's true." Idess rolled her eyes. "I hate to stroke his already enormous ego, but it's true. He's on our side."

How? How could a demon be on their side? He frowned. "Wraith...sounds familiar." He racked his brain and finally, something clicked. "There's a character named Wraith in the Demonica comics. Looks like you, actually."

Wraith grinned. "That's because it *is* me. I'm a rock star."

"But the comics... They're fiction."

"No," Idess said softly, "they're not. I don't know who is responsible for them, but they're pretty true to real life. Wraith did help save the world, just like in the comics..." She gave the demon another eye roll. "...and we hear about it on a regular basis. My theory is that the comics are sanctioned by someone high up in Heaven in order to get humans used to the idea of demons and angels, and to tell the story of what happened before human memories were erased."

"An angel is definitely the author," Wraith said. "You can tell because the comics are totally biased against demons. The author makes me look like an idiot."

"That's because you *are* an idiot." Idess turned from Wraith to Declan. "Wraith aside, I think the purpose of the comics is to prepare people like you for the truth. They're way behind in the timeline—the near apocalypse hasn't happened yet, and they haven't introduced the Four Horsemen of the Apocalypse."

"The...what?" He vaguely remembered Suzanne saying something about humans fighting alongside three of the Four Horsemen, but at the time it hadn't registered that she'd been talking about *those* Horsemen.

Suzanne waved her hand. "I'll fill you in later. Right now we have to get your memories turned on."

Sure, sure. Mining important information from his head was a priority over the Four Horsemen of the damned Apocalypse.

Jesus.

On the other hand, how often had he read a comic book or seen a movie and wondered how he'd react if he were one of the characters who learned that superhero powers, or aliens, or vampires existed? He'd always thought he'd adapt quickly.

And he'd always thought it would be awesome.

In reality, it was just fucking weird and at times downright terrifying.

"So," Wraith said, "you cool with this?"

Nope. "I have to be."

"It could be painful," Wraith warned. "Try not to resist."

Declan nodded, and before he'd even finished, Wraith was behind him, one arm slung around Declan's chest, and a searing, piercing pain sliced into his neck. Faintly, he heard a chorus of, "Wraith! You don't have to bite him," and "What the hell are you doing?" But just as he started to struggle, the pain turned to pleasure, and Declan felt himself sag against the big demon.

Then the mind-fuck started.

Agony ripped through his head, as if a clawed hand was inside his skull, tearing at the vault that held his memories. At first, he resisted the unnatural invasion, but it wasn't long before bits and pieces of visions, like second-long film clips, began to flash before his eyes. There were monsters there. And friends from McKay-Taggart who fought the monsters. Declan engaged in a life-or-death brawl with some creepy, pale, eyeless thing.

Good...god. As if the door containing his memories had been thrown open, they flooded his brain. So many demons. So many battles. Declan saw himself in Africa, fighting alongside people he'd been sent to capture. But in a time of desperation, all humans became the good guys when you were up against the spawn of Hell.

The memories flipped through his brain in rapid succession, barely giving him time to absorb them. But he suspected he didn't need to.

They'd been unlocked, and once Wraith disconnected himself, Declan had a feeling he would be able to pick through each snapshot for more details as needed.

Finally, Wraith pulled away and eased him onto the couch. Declan hated feeling helpless and weak, but if not for the couch, he'd have been nothing but a puddle on the floor. He felt a warm hand on his knee and knew without looking it belonged to Suzanne.

"Hey," she said softly. "How are you doing?"

"Good," he wheezed. "A little thirsty."

Wraith licked his lips. "That's the blood loss."

"Did you really need to do that?" Idess asked, and yeah, Declan was wondering the same thing.

"I was hungry. I skipped lunch. Sue me." Wraith glanced over at Declan. "You have a lot of shit in that noggin of yours. And dude, your dad is a douche."

Declan was torn between feeling violated and feeling vindicated. After all, if a damned *demon* thought your dad was a douche...

"I'll get you some juice or something." Idess headed toward the kitchen.

"So," Suzanne asked hesitantly. "What did you remember?"

Hell. He remembered utter hell. "Demons," he croaked. "And most of them didn't look like Wraith."

"That's because the ones that look like Wraith have been living among humans for centuries without causing much trouble. When Pestilence's Seal broke, it released a lot of really bad demons from Hell."

Pestilence? One of the Horsemen? A memory flashed through his brain in slow motion, a horde of umber-skinned monsters with claws like knife blades and teeth longer than his hand squeezing through some kind of rip in the ground. They came at him and the team of hotel security guards at the place he'd been staying in South Africa while on a job. The battle had been vicious and gruesome, but the memory cut out before he found out how he'd gotten away alive. Another memory came on its heels, of flying into Houston and getting off the plane just as some sort of horned monster rampaged through the terminal.

"Declan?" Suzanne squeezed his hand. "You're getting pale again. You okay?"

"Yeah." He scrubbed his hand over his face, hoping she couldn't tell he was lying. He was tired of being asked if he was okay. Because this wasn't okay. None of this was okay. Well, except Suzanne. She was literally his guardian angel, and right now, she was his entire world. "I'm just a little overwhelmed."

Idess returned with a glass of orange juice. "Here. Try to relax. You don't want to be flooded with too many memories at once."

Too late. But even as the thought cleared his mind, another memory invaded the space. This one was close to home. Literally outside the McKay-Taggart offices, three demons, like the one that had attacked today, had ambushed him, his friend Steve, Remy, and Tag. They'd all been armed, but bullets hadn't so much as scratched the bastards...again, just like today. Then, out of nowhere, people he'd assumed were human, dressed in black BDUs and combat gear, had rushed in and joined the battle with swords, strange S-shaped blades, and squirt guns filled with a liquid that made the demons screech.

One of the demons had gone down after being hamstrung by a sword strike, and Declan had leaped on it and jammed a dagger deep into the creature's eye. The sound it had made...a screech that right now pierced his ears, had frightened off the other demons, who disappeared as suddenly as they'd arrived.

But the one he'd stabbed... It had shriveled up and disintegrated. The newcomers, people who called themselves The Aegis—just like in the comics—had explained that the demon was dead, and then they'd gone and he'd never seen them again.

"I remember something," he said, optimism sparking for the first time since this happened. "I remember demons like the one that attacked us. I remember killing one."

Suzanne sat up straight. "How?"

"I stabbed it in the eye."

Suzanne practically deflated. "I put a spear through that demon's eye today, and it barely even noticed."

"So if these demons don't have an obvious vulnerable spot," Wraith said, "look to the person who killed it." He gestured to Declan. "When I was in his feeble human head I saw him getting a tattoo. You guys know it's not a normal tat, right?"

Declan started. From the beginning he'd sensed that something wasn't quite right about his tattoo. Hell, he'd known it was messed up. But he'd told himself that the ink was defective. Or that the needle had damaged his nerve endings, causing the strange sensations he felt emanating from it now and then. He'd rationalized. Maybe the demon was right and his mind *was* feeble.

"Not normal?" he asked. "What do you mean?"

The demon shrugged. "I got a look at the artist. I'd bet both my nuts that he's not human."

Didn't that just figure.

"Sounds like it's time for a road trip," Suzanne said, sounding way too perky. "Where are we going?"

"San Francisco," Declan said as he dug in his pocket for his phone, which was buzzing so fiercely it nearly vibrated itself out of his pants. When he looked at the screen, his stomach dropped to his feet.

No. Oh, God, *no*.

"Declan?" Suzanne asked. "What is it?"

Pain twisted and clawed at his insides, like a monster was trying to get out. "It's my friend. It's Steve." The phone slid from his numb fingers into his lap. "He's dead. Someone...or something...tore him apart in his own home."

Suzanne clapped her hand over her mouth. "Oh, Declan, I'm so sorry."

"Torn apart?" Wraith cursed. "That's what Siecher demons do to send a message. Fuckers."

"Steve was there that day," he rasped as he struggled to keep it together. "He fought beside me."

"Morroc couldn't get to you, so he went after your friend." Suzanne came over and sat beside him, the scent of her tropical perfume a welcome comfort. "No one you know or love is safe, Declan. We have to stop this thing."

His fingers trembled as he retrieved his phone and Googled the tattoo shop. Closed today. But tomorrow? He was going to be there with bells on. And he was going to get some answers. Steve hadn't deserved to die, but fuck if he was going to die in vain.

Chapter Seventeen

"The kitchen smells amazing."

Suzanne looked up at Hawkyn and gave him a tired smile. With everything that had happened, they hadn't had a chance to talk about their blowout yesterday, but maybe they didn't need to. Hawkyn had chilled out, and she was happy to just let it go. She'd never liked conflict anyway.

"Thanks. I'm making chicken biscuit pot pie and cherry hand pies."

"You make pie foods when you want to comfort someone." His accusatory tone made her bristle. Obviously, Hawkyn hadn't chilled as much as she thought.

"Declan just found out his memories have been altered, that I'm not who I said I was, and that his friend is dead, most likely killed by the demon that attacked us today. I think he can use a little comfort, and you're not going to shame me for it."

"Whoa." He held up his hands in defense. "I'm concerned about you, but I learned my lesson."

No, he hadn't, but she wasn't going to argue. "Well, thank you for checking to see what Declan did to earn being hunted by a Siecher. Hopefully we can figure out how he was able to kill one. And thank you for getting help to fight the bastard."

He eyed her as if trying to decide if her change of subject was intentional to get away from talking about how much she wanted to comfort Declan, and if he wanted to let it go.

"You're welcome," he said. "You're just lucky I dropped by to tell you about the demons Declan took out and saw your car and Morroc in the middle of the road. I flashed back to Sheoul-gra and caught Journey, Maddox, and Ilsa on their way out for pizza." He shook his head. "I can't believe how much things have changed since Azagoth opened up his realm to us."

Apparently, Memitim hadn't always been team players, but the structure in Sheoul-gra lent itself to a family atmosphere and team building, and now, more often than not, Memitim had help when they needed it simply by asking.

"I wouldn't know." She grabbed a bottle of water from the fridge. "I came straight from training to Sheoul-gra, and as you like to point out, I'm a baby angel."

That got a smile from him, seeing how she hated being called that. "Let me know how it goes at the tattoo place."

"I will." A soft hiss escaped her bottle of sparkling water as she removed the cap. "Oh, and Hawk? When you got into Declan's records at the Memitim Embassy, did you find out why he's Primori?"

He shook his head. "Any information even slightly related to what their future actions are is available only at the highest levels. I mean Archangel levels. Not even the Memitim Council has that kind of intel."

That was disappointing.

"And, sis?"

"Yeah?"

"Be careful." He wasn't talking about the tattoo parlor. He was talking about Declan.

"You keep saying that," she reminded him. "I think I'll be fine."

Hawkyn's skeptical expression remained with her as he shook his head and flashed away. Damn him. She knew what she was doing. She was going to keep Declan alive, and she was going to get an awesome job on a TV cable network—

Oh, no.

She was supposed to fly out to New York in the morning. Quickly, she dialed Cipher.

"'Sup, Suzie Bear?"

Always with the nicknames. She'd have to come up with something for Cipher. "Hey. Can we reschedule the meeting with the network people? I can't get away right now."

"I'll see what I can do, but don't get your hopes up. They indicated that they were under a deadline. I'll hit you back in a few." He hung up just as the timer on the oven indicated that dinner was ready.

A few minutes later, she had a tray loaded with pot pie, sautéed veggies, and little cherry pies, as well as a couple of sparkling waters, and was standing outside Declan's door. She tapped lightly with the edge of the tray.

"If you're an angel," he called out, "come in. If you're a demon, give me a minute to arm myself."

She elbowed the door handle and walked into his room, where he was sprawled on the couch, surrounded by *Demonica* comics. As soon as he saw her, he leaped to his feet and took the tray.

"You didn't have to bring this," he said as he set the tray on the coffee table. "I would have come to the kitchen."

She shrugged. "I just figured you might want to be alone. You've been through a lot, and my family can be...overwhelming." Reaching out, she touched his shoulder. "And I'm sorry about your friend."

"Thank you." He looked down at the tray, where her phone was buzzing. "You have a call."

It was Cipher. "Excuse me for a second." She hit the answer button. "Give me good news, buddy."

The heartbeat of silence on the other end made her heart sink. "Sorry, Suz. The network can't wait. They canceled your meeting."

Shit. Closing her eyes, she gave herself a moment to get past the disappointment. Her dream had just been pulled out from under her, and it hurt more than she would have thought. She should have known it wasn't in the cards. Her fate had been cemented in place since conception. Maybe she needed to accept that and move on.

But the thought of moving on made her want to cry.

"Suzanne?" Cipher's voice called out gently over the airwaves. "You there?"

"Yeah." She turned away from Declan so he wouldn't see the tears stinging her eyes. "Are you sure they can't hold off the meeting? Just for a couple of days?"

Obviously, accepting and moving on wasn't going to happen right away.

"They said it's tomorrow or nothing. Can you leave Declan with Hawk or something and just flash there?"

As tempting as that was, she couldn't do it. She wanted the cooking show more than anything. Anything except making sure Declan lived. She trusted Hawkyn with his life, but she had a duty. She might not like that she'd been forced into this life, but Declan was more important than her dreams.

"It's fine, Cipher. Thank you. I'll talk to you later." She hung up before he could reply, and then she just stood there, looking at the floor.

"Hey." Declan's hand came down on her shoulder. "Is something wrong?"

"No," she said, but even to her own ears it sounded like a lie.

"Bullshit." He turned her around, the gray in his eyes tempering from hard, cold steel to a soft mist. "What's wrong, angel?" His words, spoken in a hushed whisper, broke her.

Tears blurred her vision as the first sob shook her body. "I lost the TV deal."

"That was real? It wasn't part of the cover story?"

When she shook her head, Declan pulled her into his arms. "I'm sorry."

She felt like an ass for needing him when he'd just lost his friend and *she* should be the one comforting *him*.

"It's okay. I'm fine." She tried to push away, but his arms tightened around her.

"You're not fine, and this isn't about the TV gig, is it?" He pulled back just enough to look down at her. "I know pretty much nothing about angels, but I know when people are lying and when they're telling the truth. All those lies you told me about who you were? A rich heiress? It didn't fit you."

"Didn't fit me?"

He wiped away a tear with his thumb, his touch so tender she nearly sighed. "You seemed as comfortable in this house as a cowboy in pantyhose. But when you talk about food and cooking, you light up, and you get the slightest hint of a Southern drawl. That's the real you."

"I'm an angel," she said, the weight of that fact sitting heavily on her shoulders. "That can't be the real me."

"See? That's why I said this isn't about the TV gig. It's about who you are."

She peered up at him, amazed by his ability to parse through the background noise and focus on what was important. "How do you know that?"

"Because I don't know who the fuck I am, either." His voice started out gruff, but when he dipped his head and pressed a kiss into her hair, his tone gentled. "Especially now."

And again, she felt like a piece of crap for whining about her own situation when his entire world had been turned upside down. Her dreams had died, but her world was still the same.

"I know who I am. And I know who I want to be. I just can't be that person." She dashed away the tears and stepped back. "It doesn't matter. What's important is that you're safe."

"Fuck that." He guided her over to the table of food. "I want to be safe, but I also want to know more about you. Things are a bit lopsided between us, seeing how you've been spying on me for a year and I just found out that you're an angel instead of a rich heiress. So tell me who you are. I mean, I know precisely nothing about angels."

She sank down in a chair. "There's not much to tell. I'm a Memitim who lives in Sheoul-gra with over a hundred of my un-Ascended brothers and sisters. They're all really great warriors, but I've never felt like I fit in."

Declan took a seat on the couch kitty-corner from her. "Why not?"

No matter how many times she explained her feelings to her siblings, they didn't understand. Maybe Declan, as a human, would.

"I grew up with a wonderful family in Georgia, and I was happy." She smiled with fondness at the pot pie. Cooked in a cast iron skillet, it had been one of her mother's favorites. "I thought I was human, and then I was plucked out of college and dropped into this world. I know it sounds selfish, but I didn't want this for myself. I want to cook, and have a family, and just be normal, you know? Instead, I have this awesome responsibility and no freedom. But at least I got you as my first Primori." She held out her right arm to show him the *heraldi* he'd asked about a few days ago. "What I told you about this was a lie. It's actually an alarm system tuned to you. When it burns, that's how I know you're in danger. Well, it's supposed to alert me to danger, but it's kind of glitchy."

"Seriously?" Reaching out, he took her wrist and gently rubbed his thumb over the raised, flesh-colored lines. "That's cool. But Sheoul-gra? The Demonica comics say it's where demons and evil people go when they die."

"It is. My dad and Hades run it."

"And your dad is...?"

"The Grim Reaper."

She expected him to freak out, but he just nodded. "Of course your dad is the Grim Reaper."

"You're taking this well."

He laughed, a deep, rich sound that warmed her all over. "In the last few hours I've been attacked by a demon, I've had a demon drink my blood while he unscrambled my brain, I learned that I killed a bunch of demons, that my girlfriend is an angel, and that her psycho assistant is really her super-powerful psycho brother. I think I've hit my shocked-out limit for today."

My girlfriend is an angel. Suzanne hadn't heard anything after those words. He'd called her his girlfriend! She felt like she was back in high school, giddy and smitten by this amazing man.

"Yeah, well, don't count on it." She scooped some of the chicken pot pie into a bowl, making sure to get a lot of biscuit. "I'll bet you're still shockable."

"Try me."

She shouldn't. She really shouldn't. But that cocky set to his jaw practically begged her to win this challenge.

"Well," she said as she pierced a big chunk of chicken with her fork, "since we Memitim are forbidden to have sex, and I didn't sleep with anyone during the years I thought I was human..."

It took a couple of seconds for her words to sink in. And then he rocked back in his seat. "Oh my God. You were a virgin. Holy shit, I...I..."

"You deflowered an angel."

Yep, she was right. He was definitely still shockable.

* * * *

Declan wasn't struck silent often, but man, it felt like his voice had taken a permanent leave of absence. Or maybe it was his brain that was on the fritz. Either way, it took him forever to finally manage a highly articulate "Huh?"

"It's no big deal—"

He exploded to his feet, nearly knocking over the coffee table and the tray of food. "No big deal? Come on. You said there are rules about humans and angels. 'We can't let anyone see us. We definitely can't let anyone know we had sex.' You said that. What happens now? I mean, taking an angel's virginity? Holy shit. Your nut job brother is going to kill me."

"He can't kill you." She made it sound like the guy hadn't already tried. "You're Primori."

"What the fuck is Primori? You never really explained that. And why am I one of them? Because I killed some demons?"

She took a bite of her pie, and his stomach growled even though the thought of eating didn't sit well with him right now.

"We don't know why anyone is ever Primori." She washed her food down with a swig of sparkling water. "We're assigned a human or demon and we protect them—"

"Demons? You protect demons too?"

"Sometimes. I told you that Primori are people—human or demon—who will play an important role in the fate of humanity. They aren't always good people. The worst people in history were Primori because their actions shaped the world we live in today."

He sank down on the couch again. "So you're saying I'm important to humanity in some way?"

"Exactly." She gestured to the *Demonica* comics. "Maybe someday someone will write one about you."

That would be the coolest thing ever. Hopefully he wouldn't be a villain. Or the clueless jackass who deflowered an angel and got struck down by lightning.

Oh, Jesus... She'd been a virgin. What if she wasn't of legal angel age? Whatever that was.

"I hope this isn't a rude question, but...how old are you?"

"I'm in my mid-seventies," she said with a defensive sniff, as if this was a touchy subject for her. "I'm *not* a baby angel no matter what everyone says."

Whoa. She looked pretty damned good for being the age his grandfather had died. "You said you grew up in Georgia? With a human family?"

She nodded. "All Memitim grow up with humans. Well, that's changing now that my father isn't breeding anymore."

Breeding? He was going to let that go for now. "Did your human parents know the truth about you?"

She shook her head. "My mother replaced their human baby with me. It's what happens to all Memitim babies. The practice is the basis of Changeling folklore."

Made sense, seeing how Changelings were supposedly the offspring of fairies who had been swapped out with human infants. And hey, look at that, Declan's nerdy knowledge was coming in handy now.

Take that, everyone who ever made fun of me. Tag. Remy. Shane. Steve. Gareth. Every person who had ever met him outside the comic book store.

Thinking of Gareth and Steve threatened to drag him down when he needed to be alert, now more than ever, so he went back to concentrating on learning as much as he could about this new world that had just been revealed to him.

"So what happens to the biological children of these humans?"

Suzanne waved her fork as if gesturing to the Heavens. "They're adopted through angelic channels."

"That's kind of fucked up."

"It's better than it used to be before adoption agencies. There was a time when the infants were left at churches or in town squares." She suddenly looked sad. "Trust me, the human babies usually get the better end of the bargain."

"So why do they go through all this trouble?" He finally reached out to dish up some pot pie, but at the last second went for the cherry pies. This felt like a dessert-first kind of day, when life came at you hard and fast and you didn't know if you were going to live to have another meal. He and his special military team had been firm believers in eating dessert first before a mission, and if ever a situation called for having pie before dinner, having a demon trying to kill you was it. "Why are you raised by humans instead of your mother?"

"It's so we'll learn the ways of the humans we'll be protecting," she explained. "And they make sure we have awful childhoods so we'll be tough."

"Didn't you say you had a great childhood?"

She nodded. "I was lucky. My human mom was supposed to marry the abusive dirtbag who got her pregnant, so I guess the angels thought I'd have a crappy home. But at the last minute, she called off the wedding, went back to the family that disowned her, and she met a brilliant, handsome doctor and lived happily ever after."

"Did they have kids?"

She smiled fondly, and maybe it was selfish and stupid, but he felt a twinge of jealousy that she'd had the kind of childhood he'd craved. "I grew up with two brothers and a sister. My brothers died within a year of each other about ten years ago, and my sister died more recently. I visited her every day in the nursing home."

"So if they didn't know the truth about you, how did you hide the truth from them? You obviously don't age beyond, what, twenty-five?"

She beamed. "I'll take it."

"Seriously," he said as he licked sweet glaze from the pie off his finger. "Do you age?"

"We naturally stop aging in our twenties. But once we earn our wings, we can choose to appear any age we want. It's the same with humans in Heaven. Everyone looks like they're in their twenties unless they change their appearances to greet a relative crossing over from death in the human realm."

Stomach rebelling again, he set his hand pie down without tasting it. He'd give anything for a shot of whisky right now. This was way too much information to process. "So how did you find out the truth? What happened with your family?"

"A Memitim sister came to me when I was twenty. I was in college and having the time of my life. I was just starting to date, and I was going to be a chef someday... I had it all. Then Marisol showed up, and I had to go with her."

Declan would have been thrilled to learn that the people he'd thought were his parents weren't. But Suzanne didn't sound like she'd been happy about the news. "You believed her right away?"

"She didn't have to say a word," Suzanne said after taking a drink of her sparkling water. "The instant I saw her, the truth of my existence filled me."

"Was it hard to leave your life and everyone you loved?"

"It was awful." Sadness cast a shadow across her face. "I had to fake my disappearance and let my family believe I was dead. For years I watched them hope and pray and grieve. My mother went to her grave believing I'd someday come home." She inhaled a ragged breath and squared her shoulders. "So it was hard, but ultimately, I understood I was bred for this purpose. I had been tasked by Heaven to protect mankind," she finished, a little defensively. "It also helped that I got to join a new family."

That was how he'd felt about the military. It had been tough love, for sure, but after no love at all, it had meant everything to him.

Until Gareth died and he'd gone on a self-destructive binge that had led to his separation from the Air Force.

He swore under his breath, and Suzanne held out a bite of her chicken pot pie. "Here. Eat this. It'll help you relax."

"Why?" He eyed the fork with suspicion. "Is the gravy full of sedatives?"

"Nope. It's full of good, old-fashioned 'angel emo,' as Cipher calls it." She made an impatient gesture with her fork, so he took the bite. "When I cook, my emotions fuse with the food. And when I cook on my cooking show and people prepare the dishes while they're watching it, their food gets infused, too. It's why my show has a cult following."

He remembered her saying something about how, when her viewers prepared her dishes while they watched the show, they'd feel the effect from the food that she intended. He'd figured the whole thing was a gimmick. It was pretty incredible that it was real.

"It probably helps that your cooking is amazing," he said. And she was right. He'd only just swallowed the pie and already a sense of ease was spreading through him like warm sunshine. "Earlier today...the lunch you put together for me and Steve...what were you feeling when you made it?"

Her long lashes flew up. "We'd just made love. I was happy. You couldn't tell?"

Made love. Her words made him suck in a startled breath. He wouldn't call what they'd done "making love." They'd had sex. They'd fucked. In a room he could only assume was used by angels to torture demons.

She'd deserved better.

"Yeah, I could tell," he said gruffly. "And it put Steve in a great mood. Best I'd seen him in for a while." Closing his eyes, he gave himself a minute to breathe. Steve was a good guy, a good friend, and he was going to miss him. "Thank you for giving him that before he died."

"I wish I could do more. For him and for you." She put her food down and moved from the chair to the couch cushion next to him, sitting so close he could feel her heat on his skin. "What can I do?"

Looking into those sweet eyes, all he could think about was how they'd been drowsy, glazed, and sated after he'd made her come. He wanted to do that again. But mostly, selfishly, he wanted to take comfort from her. This new world was bizarre, and she was part of it, but she was tangible and real, and he wanted to ground himself in her. And against her.

Shifting to face her, he slanted his mouth over hers. Instantly, she melted against him, bringing her entire body into contact with his. She was so warm, her flesh firm except in all the places it should be soft.

"I want to be naked," she whispered against his lips. "And I want you to be naked too. On the bed. I want to be tangled in the sheets with you. And I want you to wake me up in a couple of hours so we can have sex again."

He smiled. "You're very demanding."

Her cheeks turned bright red. "I've seen stuff like that in movies. I've always wanted to know what it's like."

"You know," he said, as he stroked her bottom lip with his thumb, "you seem very different from your brothers and sisters. Are you typical for an angel? Or are they?"

Her gaze dropped as if she was ashamed. "They are. They like battling demons and sparring with each other and hunting down evil. They love what they do." She looked back up at him, her brown eyes swimming in what he could only call disappointment. "I hate it. I want to serve in some other way, but we're born for a purpose, and I just have to suck it up." All of a sudden, a wicked smile curved her glossy lips. "Speaking of sucking..."

Her fingers found the fly of his jeans, and before he could stop her—not that he would—she'd ripped it open. Then, just as she started to slip off the couch to drop to her knees, he gripped her arms and stood them both up.

"What are you doing?"

She made a sad little noise. "Am I doing it wrong already? I've read books..."

Jesus. She was so...innocent.

What did you expect? She's a damned angel.

It felt so wrong to want to see her doing dirty things.

You fucked her on a bondage horse.

And he wanted to do it again. But maybe not until they'd done it right. She needed a better "first time."

"You did nothing wrong." His voice sounded raw and needy, maybe because his balls were tight with anticipation. "I just want to do this in a bed. Tangled in the sheets, like you said." He drew her in and kissed her before sweeping her up into his arms. "You deserve to be worshipped."

"Because I'm an angel?"

"No," he murmured. "Because you're Suzanne."

This time the noise she made wasn't born of worry that she'd done something wrong. This time, it was because she'd done everything right, and as he carried her toward the bedroom, she wrapped her arms around him and settled against his chest, holding him tight.

Something inside him loosened at that moment. All the resistance that had hardened his heart when it came to relationships started to break apart like hard-packed snow on a mountain. An avalanche of affection crashed over him, and he knew that, after today, nothing would be the same.

Chapter Eighteen

Suzanne rested her head on Declan's shoulder as he carried her to the bedroom. It felt good to hold her like this. If he correctly understood what she'd told him, she'd been a warrior for over fifty years, and she deserved a few hours of being a *person*.

"Hey, I have a question." Declan pressed a kiss into her hair. "You guys do sleep, right?"

She covered up a delicate yawn that must have been invoked by the use of the s-word. "We don't need it the same way humans do. We won't go insane or die or anything, but sleep does help us regenerate. Personally, I love to sleep."

He tucked her against him, and she wiggled up as close as she could get. "Good, because I think we might be needing the rest."

"Are you worried about going back to the tattoo place?"

He stopped to draw the curtain on the south window. "It's a little disconcerting that my tat was done by a non-human," he admitted. "I want to know why. And what it's done to me."

"For what it's worth," she murmured, "I don't get an evil vibe from it. But it'll be interesting to get the story behind it."

Interesting wasn't the word he'd choose. Disturbing, maybe. But whatever. There was no sense stressing out about it. Yet.

He had tomorrow to do that.

Tonight he was going to take comfort in Suzanne. Thing was, he didn't need sex. He wanted it, sure. But he'd be happy to just lie with her. To wake up with her and do the intimate things lovers did, from talk about movies to sharing fantasies.

This was all new for him. Not the sex, nor the fact that Suzanne was an angel. Although the angel thing was new, he supposed. It was the rest of it, the simply wanting to be with someone, that was unfamiliar.

He set her on the bed, but before he climbed in, he excused himself to brush his teeth. When he got back to the bedroom, he nearly swallowed his tongue.

Suzanne was reclining on top of the comforter in a skimpy, sheer blue baby doll nightie that left very little to the imagination.

"While you were in the bathroom I flashed to my room and brushed my teeth and changed." She toyed with the lacy neckline, her fingers stroking the creamy skin above the swell of her breasts.

Breasts he was going to be tasting in about two seconds.

"Oh, and you might be interested to know that Memitim aren't fertile until they Ascend." A naughty smile ruffled the corners of her mouth. "So we don't need condoms."

Oh, hell, yeah.

He undressed in record time, his male ego soaking up how Suzanne watched him, hunger swirling in her mocha eyes.

As he climbed onto the bed, she welcomed him with a shy smile and open arms, the perfect picture of an angel and a temptress.

"Are you sure about this?" He paused as he hovered over her legs, not wanting to go any further if she needed more time.

"I'm three quarters of a century old, Declan. I think I know what I want by now."

He slid one hand up her thigh, drawing a ragged breath from her. "Do you really?"

This time when she spoke it was with less confidence and more breathlessness. "Of course."

"Then tell me. I'll do anything you want."

One skeptical eyebrow arched. "Anything?"

"If you can imagine it, Suzanne, I'll do it." He was counting on her not having too extreme of an imagination when it came to sex, in part because he planned to help her fill her sex chest of imagination, and in part because there were some lines he wouldn't cross.

But there were a lot of lines he'd slide right up to.

Her eyes shot wide and a pink blush spread over her cheeks. Exactly as he'd thought. But he wasn't ready to let her off the hook. If she was going to learn about sex, she was going to learn how to express her desires. She was a kitten now, but male instinct told him she'd be a tiger once she found her voice.

He wanted that tiger, and he heard himself growl with possessiveness as he eased his hand further up her thigh, until the tips of his fingers were brushing her panties.

"Well?" he prompted. "You want me to maybe tease your nipples?"

Shifting, he cupped one of her breasts through the fabric and circled her nipple with his thumb. The slightest catch in her breath through slightly parted lips spurred him on. She liked the dirty talk and the teasing. Good, because he liked it too.

"Do you want me to suck on it?"

"Yes," she croaked.

"Say it."

She shocked him by leaning forward and saying boldly, "I want you to put your mouth on my breast." Then her vixen persona faded with a soft "Please?"

Yeah, they needed to work on the tiger thing.

Later.

Eagerly he lowered his mouth to her breast and took the nipple between his teeth, pinching just a little, enough to make her squirm, and then he laved it, dampening the material stretched across the areola. He wanted to chew right through the baby doll and suck her deep, but he could do that another time.

There was so much to show her.

"Oh, Declan," she sighed as she arched into him, her hands coming up to caress his shoulders and stroke his back. Her fingers found the lines of the tattoo, and instant streaks of pleasure shot straight to his groin. Damn the erotic effect of that. He might actually be able to come from her touch.

"That feels so good," he whispered against her skin.

"Mmm. So does that."

Gently, he blew air across the wet fabric, loving how the cool contrast made her nipple pucker. He watched her expression as he rolled it between his fingers, the wonder in her eyes driving him crazy. It was clear she didn't know her body that well, didn't know how it reacted to someone else's touch, and he wanted to be the one to show her.

Every inch of her body was going to know his, and only his, caress.

"What next, angel? Want me to kiss you all over? Kiss my way down your belly?"

She nodded. "Yes, please."

He nearly laughed. So polite when what he was going to do to her would be anything *but* polite.

Shoving the baby doll up to expose her perfect, flat belly, he kissed a path from her breasts to her navel. She quivered as he rimmed it with his tongue, and his balls quivered with her. They felt heavy, achy, and if he didn't get inside her soon, things were gonna start hurting.

He moved lower, spreading her legs as he went.

Suddenly, she jacked upright. "Wait."

"What's wrong?"

"Nothing. I just... I want to do that to you."

His cock got all fucking excited as she gripped his shoulders and tugged him back up her body so he was straddling her, his knees in her armpits, his erection so close to her mouth he could feel her warm breath.

He expected her to be shy. But nope, his angel swallowed him whole without hesitation.

"Holy shit," he shouted as she sucked him hard. Her mouth was hot and wet and perfect, the scrape of her teeth just rough enough to keep him from spilling down her throat.

Perfection.

Her tongue swirled around the crown of his cock before she licked her way down the shaft, and when she brought one hand up to fondle his sac, his entire body jerked reflexively. So she fondled harder.

That was when he decided she was no angel. Suzanne was a cruel succubus who was going to end this before it began.

"Okay," he said as he pulled from the hot depths of her mouth. "Your turn." He backed his way down her body again, kissing her swollen lips on his way. "Don't you want my mouth between your legs? My tongue pushing deep inside you as I taste every drop of your arousal?" He spread her with his fingers and inserted one into her core. "Or do you want this?" He pumped his finger in and out, spreading her cream through her sex. She was so ready for him. Shifting, he withdrew his finger and replaced it with the head of his cock. "Or this?"

"All of it," she breathed, and he chuckled.

"You're a greedy, naughty angel, aren't you?"

She arched her back and pushed herself onto his cock. "Not naughty enough. Fuck me, Declan."

Even as she said it, her voice cracked and her cheeks lit up with embarrassment. Being crude was not in her DNA, but she was trying, bless her heart, and he was already on edge, so he'd give her what she wanted.

But next time? Next time he was going to spend half an hour between her legs and make her come half a dozen times before he sank inside her gorgeous body.

Groaning at that thought, he plunged deep into her satin core. Her cry of satisfaction fueled his own passion. He planted his palms on either side of her head and hovered over her so he could watch every nuance in her expression. He wanted to see her teeth sink into her bottom lip the way she was doing now. And he definitely wanted to see the way her lips would part and her eyes would close when she reached climax. He'd missed all of that the first time, when she'd been facing away from him.

He wouldn't miss that now.

Her legs came up to hook around his waist, drawing him closer as he pumped into her, hard and fast. She gripped him with her powerful thighs, forcing his rhythm into the one she wanted. He'd always been in control during sex, always guiding his partners in the direction he wanted. It wasn't that he was selfish, unless being selfish meant making sure his partner climaxed first. There was nothing sexier than a woman deep in her passion, her soft cries urging him toward his own orgasm.

But Suzanne understood pleasure. Maybe not sexual pleasure, but being as tied to food as she was, she knew the power of satisfaction and she was taking the route she wanted. Forging her own path and making her own recipe.

As long as she tested those recipes on him, he could definitely deal. She was his now. His own personal chef, in and out of bed.

"D-Declan," she gasped. "Declan!" Her shout rattled the walls, and oh, yeah, that expression on her face was what he'd been waiting for. Ecstasy was etched into her expression, her mouth falling open, the tendons in her neck straining as she arched, her fingernails digging deep into his back.

He pumped his hips even faster as his climax built like a storm in his shaft. It hit him with the force of a tempest, the energy spreading through his pelvis and up his spine, making him lose control like never before. He roared in ecstasy, calling out Suzanne's name over and over.

Consciousness became fluid; he swore he was in and out a dozen times before the orgasm finally waned and he collapsed on top of her.

Groaning, he buried his face in the crook of her shoulder and tried to catch his breath.

"That," he said when he could finally speak, "was unbelievable."

"Is that good?"

He'd have laughed if he'd had enough air in his lungs. "Yeah. Oh, yeah."

He heard her yawn. "Declan?"

"Uh-huh?"

"Is it true that human males can only orgasm once?"

He lifted his head and caught her curious gaze. "Mostly. Why?"

"I was just wondering if we could do it again."

Instant erection. Smiling, he punched his hips against her so she could feel what she'd just done to him.

"What do you think?"

Her slow, sleepy smile made him even harder. "I think I could do this all night."

Growling with impatience, he gripped her hips and began to move, the wet sound of his cock sliding into her channel joining the soft creak of the mattress beneath them.

"So you're an angel in the kitchen and a demon in bed," he murmured against her lips. "You're every man's fantasy."

"I only want to be one man's fantasy," she whispered.

Oh, yeah. She was the fantasy. *His* fantasy.

And the crazy thing was, she was also his reality.

Chapter Nineteen

The tattoo parlor looked like every other tattoo parlor Suzanne had ever seen. Which was precisely zero. Still, nothing stood out about it. Nothing screamed This Place Is Run By A Demon.

There was also nobody around, despite the open sign that hung from the window as they'd come through the door.

Inhaling the unmistakable scent of smudged sage, she looked around the shop, one wall covered in pictures of tattoos she assumed had been done here, another wall plastered with tattoo templates.

"You're sure this was the place?" The fact that whoever worked here had used sage to cleanse and purify the space of negative or evil energy most likely meant that the artist wasn't a demon. But Wraith had said he wasn't human, either.

That still left a lot of possibilities, including shapeshifters, elves, werebeasts, faeries, vampires… The list was endless.

"Yup." Declan moved around the shop like a predator, his right hand poised to shove aside the hem of his blue button-down and draw his weapon even though he knew—from the comics—that bullets were ineffective against a large percentage of supernatural beings. "I was drunk as fuck, but I kept the business card the guy gave me because he wrote something weird on the back."

She frowned. "What did he write?"

A deep voice boomed from behind them. "I wrote that if he should ever have any questions about the tattoo he should come back."

An immense wave of power filled the building, stronger than anything she'd ever experienced outside her father's realm. Instinctively she summoned her own power, holding it in her fingertips as she and Declan spun around to confront the newcomer.

Her jaw hit the floor and she couldn't stop staring at the male who had emerged from a back room, his long, dark hair flowing over his T-shirt clad shoulders, his jeans and boots so different from the hooded robes she'd always seen him in. Hell, the only reason she recognized him was because of the intense vibe he gave off, one that was as unique as a signature.

"Jim Bob," she whispered. "Holy shit."

Declan looked between her and Jim Bob, his hand still hovering over his sidearm, which would be utterly useless against the male in front of them. "You know him?"

Jim Bob was a regular visitor of her father's, and she was pretty sure he was some sort of spy. But where did his loyalties lie? With Heaven? With Sheoul-gra? With another party?

"Go ahead." Jim Bob gestured to Declan. "Tell him."

She didn't take her eyes off Jim Bob as she spoke. "He's an angel."

Declan's gaze raked the angel from head to toe. "And his name's Jim Bob?"

"Not...really." She had no idea what his angelic name was. Her father had a habit of giving his spies ridiculous code names. Jim Bob. Ricky Bobby. A new one called Cletus. "It's a long story. I'll tell you later. But he's definitely an angel."

"Like you?"

Jim Bob's deep laughter echoed through the small space. "No Memitim is like me."

Annoyed, she translated Jim Bob's insult. "He was born a Heavenly angel," she explained. "He probably belongs to one of the Orders at the top of the hierarchy. They think they're better than us."

Jim Bob didn't even try to deny it. "Given that you're both here and that Declan is clearly aware of our existence, I'm guessing you have some questions about the tattoo."

"Yeah." Declan stepped forward to take a brochure off the counter, but when he turned back to speak to Jim Bob she realized he'd intentionally put himself between her and the big angel. He had to know that Jim Bob could crush him with his pinky finger, yet Declan didn't seem fazed. It was so cute. And halo-meltingly *hot*. "What, exactly, does the tattoo do, and why did you give it to me?"

Jim Bob didn't move, but the door behind them locked and the OPEN sign in the window flipped to CLOSED. Suzanne watched with envy; she'd never been able to manipulate objects like that, but some of her siblings could. He gestured to a small table with three chairs in the corner. Declan relaxed a little, but Suzanne noticed he still chose a seat that allowed him to keep an eye on the door.

"A man named Gareth brought you in," Jim Bob said once they were all seated. "You worked with him."

"He was a member of my team, yes." Declan's voice went hoarse. "He was killed not long after we were here."

Jim Bob snorted. "He wasn't killed."

"I fucking watched him die." Declan gripped the table top so hard his knuckles turned white. "I was there. I couldn't save him."

"You couldn't save him because he wasn't human," Jim Bob said calmly. "He's an angel. Alive and well and inserting himself into human business in…I want to say…Norway? Maybe Finland?" He shrugged. "In any case, it's a good thing he likes fish."

"What?" Declan rocked back in his seat. "I can't believe this," he said, his voice a mix of surprise and relief. "He let me think he was dead. And human. That asshole."

"He's a Nephunter," Jim Bob said. "He's an angel assigned to find humans with angelic DNA."

Interesting. Suzanne hadn't known that there were angels specifically assigned to find humans who had angel blood in their family trees. But then, there was a lot she didn't know about the goings-on in Heaven. And frankly, she didn't care. Let people like Hawkyn deal with the inner workings of angelic business.

"But why?" Declan asked, apparently still so shocked by the fact that his buddy was not only alive but an angel that he hadn't realized that Gareth must have zeroed in on Declan.

"They might prove to be valuable in the inevitable war between good and evil," Jim Bob explained. "That's why he was on your team. He was watching you. Sizing you up." He shrugged. "And stealing your blood when you weren't looking."

Declan got it this time, and his eyes shot wide. "Me? I have angel in my DNA?" At Jim Bob's nod, Declan closed his eyes and swore softly. "Man, these last two days have been surreal." He opened his eyes again. "So why did Gareth bring me here?"

"Because once we find someone like you, I mark them."

"Mark?" Declan's eyes narrowed. "Or track?"

Jim Bob didn't have to answer. The sly curve to his mouth said it all.

The tats were for tracking purposes.

"The tattoos are unique to everyone," he said. "They tap into a human's inner angel and give them little...tweaks."

"Tweaks?"

Jim Bob shrugged. "It depends on how far back in your family tree the angel DNA came from, and it depends on the angel itself. You, for example? You are, by nature, a guardian. It's why I gave you wings. Since getting them, you've probably noticed you have slightly faster reflexes and more heightened senses than people around you."

Suzanne grinned. "You're a superhero."

"I thought I was losing my mind." Declan raked his hand through his hair, coming to grips with all of this while shoving to his feet to pace in a circle. "I hear things long before other people do. I can see shit other people need a scope to see." He grimaced. "I don't want to discuss my enhanced sense of smell."

Jim Bob's cell phone buzzed on the counter, but he ignored it. "What is it that brought you here, anyway?"

"Declan has a Siecher demon after him." Suzanne cast a glance over at Declan, who seemed lost in thought as he paced. "He's killed one before, and we suspect that the tattoo might have been how."

Jim Bob shook his head. "The tattoo enhances abilities, but it wouldn't provide the key to killing a Siecher demon."

That was disappointing news. "What do you know about them?"

"Very little." Jim Bob drummed his fingers on the table as he spoke. "I've never encountered one, and the only angel I know who killed one used an ability you don't possess."

"How do you know?" Suzanne asked, feeling a little insulted. She might be a Memitim, but to assume she didn't have powerful gifts was a bit elitist.

Jim Bob gave her an even more insulting are-you-kidding-me stare. "Can you pull apart a body at a cellular level so that it rains down like microscopic glitter?"

Oh. Suzanne was at a loss for words, but Declan was right there to help out.

"Can you do that?" Declan asked her. "Because that would be cool. Terrifying, but cool."

He had some strange ideas about what was cool. "Ah, no."

Curiosity gleamed in Declan's eyes as he addressed Jim Bob. "Can you put them back together?"

"Hmm." Jim Bob considered that. "I don't think anyone has ever tried. I don't know why you'd want to. I mean, you exploded them for a reason. But I don't see why you couldn't put them back together as long as you did it quickly." His expression said he wanted to test that theory.

Suzanne shuddered. She'd grown up going to church on Sundays and believing in a wrathful God and compassionate angels, but she'd since learned that reality was the exact opposite. Angels were warriors capable of ruthless cruelty, winged believers in the ends justifying the means...as long as the ends were part of the Heavenly agenda.

Even Memitim, considered by most to be the "nice guys" of the angel world, were badasses. Well, she doubted any of her brothers and sisters considered her a badass, but she was certainly the exception

"Well," Suzanne said, feeling a little deflated, "that wasn't the news I wanted to hear."

"Sorry I couldn't help more." Standing, Jim Bob mentally unlocked the door and turned on the OPEN sign, their cue to leave. Suzanne and Declan got up to go, but as they reached the door he called out, "Oh, and Suzanne?"

"Yes?"

"You know not to tell anyone about this, right?" Jim Bob's deep voice was steeped in warning.

"Tell them what? That one of my father's most prominent Heavenly spies doles out enchanted tattoos from a seedy shop in San Francisco?"

"That's precisely what you can't tell anyone about. Anyone. Not your closest friend, not your favorite sibling, not even your father. Got it?"

"Got it."

Declan reached back and massaged his neck as if it was stiff, and given the last twenty-four hours, she'd be surprised if every muscle in his body wasn't strained to its limit. "What about me? I'm assuming I can't talk, either?"

"You're human," Jim Bob said, managing to not sound like the word "human" was an insult. "Few will believe you. But those few who do will either want to kill you or use you, so yeah, keep it to yourself."

"No problem." Declan gazed out the window, looking suddenly sad, and she wondered if he was thinking about Steve. "I just wish you'd had the answer we needed."

Jim Bob's eyes glowed as he looked at Declan. "You never said how you killed the demon. Most human weapons wouldn't even scratch their hides."

"No shit. Bullets didn't even make the thing flinch. It was like we were throwing pebbles at The Hulk." His fingers fluttered over the bump under his shirt where he kept his holster, as if reassuring himself that he had a weapon, even if it was useless against this particular threat. "I put a dagger through his eye socket."

"Really?" Jim Bob cocked his head in curiosity. "What kind of blade?"

"It was mine. A standard—" Declan broke off, his gaze turning inward. "No...it wasn't mine. My KA-BAR was knocked out of my hand during the fight. When I saw the demon go down, I looked around for a weapon." He shook his head. "I can't believe I didn't think of this sooner. I lifted the dagger from the demon's belt. I killed him with his own weapon."

"There you go," Jim Bob said. "You need that blade. Do you know where it is?"

"It's in my boss's wall safe."

For the first time since Declan was attacked outside his employer's building, Suzanne had hope that this would soon be over. And so would her status as a Memitim once it got out that she'd slept with her Primori.

But that little hiccup was something to deal with later. Right now they had a demon to smite. "Let's go see your boss."

Declan looked at her like she was mad. "I can't just walk up to Tag and tell him I need it without telling him why. If his memories were altered like mine, he probably doesn't even know he has it. He's going to want to know the truth."

Shit. Declan was right. She was already in it up to her chin with all the rules she'd broken with Declan, and angels were working overtime to repair some of the damage, namely the destroyed house across the street from the angel mansion. She was going to be in even more trouble if she revealed their world to yet another human.

Unfortunately, she didn't see another option. "We have to tell him everything."

"I don't need to tell you that's forbidden," Jim Bob said, his voice a low, ominous growl. Then he grinned, and his smile was just as ominous. "But there are ways to bend the rules."

Huh. She was starting to like this secretive angel. "Then let's do this."

Chapter Twenty

As Suzanne and Declan traversed the McKay-Taggart office hallways, he couldn't believe how surreal everything felt. The last time he was here, just days ago, he hadn't known demons existed. He hadn't known Suzanne was an angel.

He hadn't had sex with an angel.

And people were walking around, clueless. Like everything was okay. Like a Biblical apocalypse hadn't almost destroyed mankind.

It was maddening.

When they got to Tag's office, his assistant, a temp from an agency filling in for Sadie, balked at their lack of an appointment, but Declan insisted that this was important, and after consulting with Tag, she let them inside.

Tag was sitting at his desk, his bloodshot eyes glued to the computer screen. He looked up when they entered, his brows climbing inquisitively when he saw Suzanne.

"Declan. Ms. D'Angelo. This is unexpected." He let out a long, drawn-out breath. He looked tired, sad, and more than a little pissed. "You got the message about Steve?"

"Yeah." Declan shuddered. God, he was going to miss Steve, but Declan swore he'd take revenge. A dagger through the eye sort of revenge. "I can't believe it."

Tag growled. "I've got everyone I can spare working to find out what happened and who's responsible. We'll find the psycho cocksucker who killed him. I swear it."

"Yeah...about that." Declan and Suzanne sank into the chairs across from Tag. "I know who did it."

Taggart went as stiff and straight as the barrel of a rifle, his gaze locking onto Declan like a laser-guided missile. "Who?"

Here we go. "Okay, first, I need you to listen to us, and I need you to not think we're crazy."

"Or on drugs," Suzanne added.

"I can't promise anything, but I'll try. Probably not as hard as you'd like." Taggart jerked his head in the barest of nods. "Don't keep me in suspense. What's going on?"

Declan's gut churned. Tag was going to freak. "Yesterday something attacked us. I didn't know what it was, but Suzanne did." He shot a glance at Suzanne, who squeezed his hand reassuringly, a move Tag noticed. The guy didn't miss anything.

"Well?" Tag prompted sharply. "Spit it out."

Declan spit it all out. The whole damned story. In one jumbled rush. And he made sure to tell his boss that his sidewalk face plant hadn't been a life-altering medical issue. Just a life-altering demonic one.

Tag didn't say a word during the entire thing. He shifted uncomfortably at times, stared out the window more than once, and twice the vein in his temple throbbed with his rapid pulse. Finally, a full sixty seconds after Declan and Suzanne stopped talking, he sat back in his chair.

"Huh."

Declan blinked. "Sir?"

"I've been having these fucked-up dreams. I haven't told anyone because they'll think I'm insane. It's bizarre shit. Monsters coming out of the sewers. Angels blasting them with lightning. A big, armored dude on horseback popping out of thin air. The dreams feel real."

"Because they are," Suzanne said. "They're memories, not dreams."

"Okay, let's say all this psycho demon crap is true, and I admit I'm pretty skeptical. I might even be planning an intervention for you as we speak." He braced his forearms on the desk and leaned forward, his eyes hooded and unreadable. "So why are you telling me this?"

Man, Tag was handling this a lot better than Declan had. Probably the difference between the truth being revealed calmly in an office and being revealed in the midst of a demon attack.

"Because all of this started when I killed this demon's buddy a couple of years ago," Declan said. "And you were there. So was Steve. And Remy. You're both in danger now, but we might be able to stop this demon if we can get the dagger you stored in your office safe."

Tag scowled. "There's no dagger in my safe. You know I barely use that safe. It came with the building. I haven't put anything in it in years."

"You should check," Suzanne said softly.

Looking at her like he was just doing it to humor her while they waited for the guys with straightjackets to show up, Tag pushed out of his chair and went over to the panel in the wall that concealed the safe. Seconds later, he cursed under his breath and removed a dagger, its bone handle still stained with blood.

"Jesus," he breathed as he turned back to them. "It's been in there all this time, but I never saw it until now."

Suzanne shifted in her seat to face him. "That's because when angels altered your memories, they tapped into the part of the human brain that either invents outlandish explanations for what it can't understand, or it simply doesn't consciously 'see' objects that don't make sense. That dagger was part of a world you didn't remember, so your brain didn't register it. Demons have been using that human failing for centuries. They build structures and drive demon ambulances right in front of your noses, and humans don't even notice."

"This is some crazy shit." Tag handed the dagger to Declan. "I'm still not sure I believe it, but on the off chance that all of this is true, you're going to use this to kill the demon that murdered Steve, right?"

"Absolutely," Declan said.

A low growl rumbled in Tag's chest. "I want to be in on it."

"Absolutely not." Suzanne came to her feet, which were clad in strappy high-heeled gold sandals that seemed like a poor choice of battle footwear. But then, angels probably didn't need combat boots. "And no one else can know about this. It's bad enough that we told you."

Tag did not look happy about that. "Why can't anyone know?"

"It's not time. But I have a feeling it'll be soon. People who can handle the truth, the ones who adapted and fought well when demons breached the human realm, are being brought in first."

"So you're planning on just leaving me with this knowledge that I can't share with anyone?" Tag's fists clenched at his sides, anger rolling off him in a palpable wave. "That's fucked up."

"No." She tapped her phone's screen. "Your memory is going to be erased again."

"The hell it is," Tag barked, and Declan couldn't blame the guy for his reaction. He wouldn't want to go back to ignorance, either, and if angels tried to wipe him, he'd put up a hell of a fight. He and Suzanne definitely needed to have a talk later. "Demons exist and you want me to let my friends and family be at risk?"

"Yes, demons are real," Suzanne said, "but truthfully, right now your friends and family are in far more danger from other humans."

Tag looked like he was going to explode, so Declan stepped in real quick. "Isn't there another way?"

"I'm sorry," Suzanne said, genuine sympathy in her eyes. "But it has to be this way. I'm in enough trouble as it is for telling you the truth. If I let this go, I could earn a thousand years of punishment. Or worse."

Declan didn't know what could be worse than a thousand years of punishment, but he didn't want Suzanne to be subjected to any punishment at all, let alone centuries upon centuries of it.

Tag was just going to have to go back to being blissfully ignorant of the supernatural world for a while. It was probably better for his sanity, anyway.

A flash of light suddenly filled the room, and a heartbeat later, the tattoo angel guy, Jim Bob, was standing in the office, his massive white wings extended, the tips brushing the walls on either side of the office.

"Holy mother of…son of a bitch!" Tag leaped backward, slamming into a bookshelf, his eyes glued to the angel. "Who the fuck are you and what is up with the wings?"

Weird how Declan had already grown used to this insanity, because he hadn't even blinked in surprise when the angel popped in. Had Declan looked like Tag, all bug-eyed and slack-jawed when he'd seen his first set of wings?

Yeah, probably.

Okay, definitely.

Suzanne's voice went low and soothing as she tried to keep Tag from freaking out. "This is Jim Bob. He's an angel, and he'll be making sure you don't remember this conversation."

"Don't worry," Declan said. "I'll bring you some literature to keep you up on the truth."

Tag looked over at him, still all kinds of freaked out. "Literature?"

"You know how you make fun of me for my comic books?"

Tag's eyes were wild, rapidly shifting from Jim Bob to Declan. "Yeah…"

Declan grinned. "Mr. Jim Bob? Do you think that while you're in Tag's head you can give him an appreciation for the *Demonica* comics?"

When Jim Bob nodded, Tag cursed at Declan. "You nerdy motherfucker."

Yup. And proud of it.

* * * *

After leaving the McKay-Taggart offices with Declan, Suzanne flashed them back to the mansion, where Hawkyn, Cipher, Journey, Sexy, and Maddox were already waiting. She'd texted them while Jim Bob rearranged the mental files in Tag's head, and now they needed to brainstorm a plan.

"That's really cool," Declan said, after they'd materialized in the living room. "I always said that if I could pick a superpower, teleportation would be it."

"It's handy," she admitted. She glanced around at the waiting crowd. "Anyone hungry? I can whip up a quick snack to nosh on while we make plans."

Journey, who never turned down food, raised his hand. "I could eat."

"Dude." Maddox reached up from his chair and punched Journey in the thigh. "You just ate two large pizzas. Sit your ass down."

No one else wanted anything, so she dove into their situation. Well, she started to, but Declan interrupted.

"Before we start plotting, can I get some assurances that after this is over, I won't be flashy-thinged?"

Everyone stared, including Suzanne.

"What?" That was from Hawkyn and spoken with a good dose of annoyance.

"Flashy-thinged," Declan repeated. "From *Men in Black*. You know, Will Smith? Tommy Lee Jones? They wipe memories with a little flashy thing."

"I totally got your reference, man," Cipher chimed in, his fingers ripping on the keyboard. "Didn't need to explain it to me. The other losers in the room, however…"

"Okay, okay." Suzanne took a step forward into the center of the room. "I think we get the gist." She swung around to Declan, knowing he must be worried. Until it came up at Ian Taggart's office, she hadn't even considered what would happen to Declan's memory after all of this was over. Yes, they'd been busy, but this was only more evidence that she wasn't cut out for being a Memitim. "Declan, we'll petition the Memitim Council to make an exception for you. You're clearly an asset. It won't be a problem." She was totally talking out of her ass, as Maddox liked to say, but she'd always been an optimist. Besides, she had a brother with influence on her side. "Isn't that right, Hawkyn?"

She gave him a back-me-up glare, and he rolled his eyes. "Yeah, that's right. It won't be a problem at all."

"See?" she said brightly. "All good." Before Declan could ask for more detail, she launched into their coming plan of action. "We have the weapon Declan used to kill the Siecher that started this whole mess. We just have to make sure we meet Morroc in a controlled environment where we'll have the upper hand." She glanced around the room. "I don't suppose any of you can take apart a body at the cellular level?"

"Huh?" Maddox froze while unwrapping a stick of gum. "Can we do what?"

"Atomize them. Turn them into red mist," Declan said. "No chunks. Like spaghetti sauce."

"Not like *my* spaghetti sauce," she muttered. "Also, eew."

No one claimed to be able to make spaghetti mist out of people, but she'd expected as much. "Okay, so how do we draw it out?"

Cipher tapped a few keys. "Flail said the Siecher will be drawn to Declan's pain."

Flail. The fallen angel had been worming her way into Azagoth's service for the last few months, and Suzanne didn't like her at all. Not that Cipher cared about Suzanne's opinion. All he saw when he looked at the evil beauty was big boobs and long legs.

Which reminded Suzanne to ask about Lilliana and when she was going to go back home to Sheoul-gra. The slinky, flirty Flail didn't need to be sniffing around Azagoth.

Declan's brow popped up. "My pain? I need to hurt myself?"

"Or someone else can do it," Cipher said, his gaze still glued to the computer screen. "But yeah, you need to be in agony."

"Mental or physical?"

"Both is probably best."

Hawkyn stepped forward. "I'll volunteer to deliver the physical pain." At Suzanne's glare, he blinked innocently. "What? It's for a noble cause.

I'm noble."

"You're an asshole," Declan said under his breath, and both Maddox and Journey nodded in agreement. "But it's probably best that you do it." He took a deep breath and looked over at Suzanne. "And if it's mental agony you want, I think I have the perfect setting. It's in the middle of nowhere, good for a battle, and I swore if I ever saw it again I'd burn it down. So yeah. Agony."

It broke her heart in half to hear that he associated a place with pain. So if he wanted to kill one demon and exorcise others, he was going to get what he wanted.

Chapter Twenty-One

Declan fucking hated this place. He liked the woods, and he had nothing against million-dollar cabins in them. But this property, hidden deep near the Catskills in New York, belonged to his father, and the only memories he had of it were shit.

Suzanne released his hand after they'd all materialized on the grassy lawn between the cabin and the lake. "This is perfect. Wide open space but plenty of cover. Why do you hate it so much?"

He really didn't want to talk about it, but he wasn't going to keep anything from Suzanne. Didn't seem right after all they'd been through, and after all she'd done to protect him. Besides, angels seemed to be pretty uninhibited when it came to romping around in people's memories, and he didn't need some asshole like Hawkyn deciding they wanted to find out the truth.

"My mom brought me up here when I was a kid." He glared at the log porch. "I think she and my old man used this place as a getaway. They could meet on long weekends without his family knowing he was with his mistress."

"And she brought you with her?"

"She was always trying to get him to acknowledge me. When I was little, I didn't know what was going on, but looking back on it? Yeah, she was hoping he'd love us both and leave his family." He looked out at the pristine lake where he'd spent hours swimming and playing in the canoe. Unattended, of course. "But the bastard loathed me. He ignored me in front of her, but when she wasn't around..." He shook his head. "He tried to kill me."

Suzanne had been scanning the nearby forest, but now her head whipped around to him. "Are you serious?"

"I wish I wasn't." He hadn't understood the attempts for what they were until he'd learned, just last year, that his father had pulled strings to get him sent on the most dangerous missions while Declan had been in the military. That was when he'd put together the time his father had taken him on a hike and "lost" him in the woods, and that other time he'd "accidentally" knocked Declan off a cliff during another hike.

He looked around at the majestic mountain view, listened to the chirping birds and the soft breeze filtering though the trees, inhaled the fresh scent of earth and pine.

God, he fucking hated this place.

"We might as well get started. What's Hawkyn going to do to me?"

Hawkyn's voice boomed behind him. "Nothing that'll cause permanent injury. I know you can't afford more damage to the brain."

"Hawk, knock it off." Suzanne turned to the others. "Cipher, since you can't fight, I want you to hang back and call for help from our brothers and sisters if we need it. Hawkyn, you're in charge of the dagger, but anyone who gets a chance to use it on Morroc should. Sexy, Journey, and Maddox, find a place a few miles away to conceal yourselves. I don't want Morroc to sense your presence or he might not show up. Cipher can text you when Morroc arrives. I'll stay here with Declan and Hawk."

Cipher didn't look especially pleased to be relegated to hanging back in a support position, but Suzanne had explained that, as an Unfallen angel, he didn't have any abilities that would help him out in a battle with an underworld creature. He was stronger and faster than any human, but on the supernatural scale, he was at the bottom. Plus, just being outside of Sheoul-gra or a protected space like the angel mansion was dangerous for him since he was subject to being kidnapped by fallen angels. Or something like that. Declan had been inundated with so much information that he couldn't keep everything straight.

"Just FYI," Cipher said. "Siechers don't travel via Harrowgate or teleportation. They move through the earth, so Morroc will probably be emerging far enough away that we won't feel the tremors."

Suzanne nodded. "Okay, everyone. Stay sharp."

As the angels dispersed, she turned to him and in a blatant move, took his hand. Declan swore he saw smoke coming out of Hawkyn's ears.

"We're going to end this today," she promised.

"And then what?" He wasn't even sure why he'd asked that, given that he could very well die in a few minutes. And truth be told, he'd never been a future-planner. He'd always lived in the moment.

But suddenly he wanted to plan tomorrow. And next week. Next month. Next year. And he wanted to plan those things with Suzanne.

"And then you can go back to your life and Suzanne can go back to hers," Hawkyn said, his tone super assholish.

"Hawkyn," Suzanne said, "I was going to ask you to give us a minute of privacy, but you know what? I want you to hear this." She turned to Declan. "I don't know what's going to happen after we're done here. But I do know that my primary concern will always be for you, whether I'm a Memitim or not."

"What do you mean, whether you're a Memitim or not?"

"I mean that I've more than likely ruined my chances for Ascension—"

"Suzanne," Hawkyn snapped. "Don't say that. I will do everything I can to make sure you Ascend."

Silence dragged out for a moment. Finally, Suzanne said quietly, "I don't even care anymore. It's not what I want."

Horror flooded Hawkyn's face. "You don't mean that. You're young. You've let your feelings for this human cloud your judgment—"

"That's very insulting," she interrupted. "You think I can't choose for myself what I want? You think love has made me stupid? I've been feeling this way for a long time. I'm not meant for this. Fifty years later, I miss the life I left behind when I thought I was human. I was happy all the time back then. Now I'm only happy when I'm cooking." She cast a sideways glance at Declan. "Or when I'm with him."

Hawkyn cursed up a storm, but his voice was barely a buzz in Declan's ears. All that he could hear, over and over in his head, was what Suzanne had just said.

She inhaled deeply and turned back to Declan. "You probably feel differently—"

He didn't even think about it. He tugged her against him and kissed her, mentally giving Hawkyn a big "fuck you."

Which was aided by a flip of his middle finger. Hawkyn's eyes nearly popped out of his head, and the fury in their emerald depths promised pain.

Pulling back, Declan looked down at Suzanne, wishing he'd approached her long ago, back when he'd thought she was human. "You're the best thing that's ever happened to me. You...and this world you've opened up for me. I always felt like I wasn't going anywhere, like I was meant for more. I don't want to go back to the life I had. I want a life with you, and I want a life in your world."

"Hey!" Cipher called out from where he was lurking in some nearby bushes. "I have shit to do. Can we get on with it?" His hand popped out from some branches and he waved. "Sorry, dude. I know you're going to get tortured and shit, and possibly die, but I have a hot date."

"Yeah," Hawkyn shouted back, "with your laptop."

"It's with a real female," Cipher yelled. "Alice is later."

"Who's Alice?" Declan asked.

Hawkyn made an I-give-up gesture. "His laptop."

Despite the dire situation his was in, Declan laughed. Steve would have loved Cipher. The reminder that they were here to slaughter the demon that had killed Steve sobered Dec up quickly. Cipher was right. They had to get on with it.

Making the mental switch into battle mode, Declan backed away from Suzanne. "I'm ready."

"Declan, you don't have to—"

"Yes, I do, and you know it. My pain is the only way to draw Morroc out."

"Then let me do it."

"Never," he growled. "It would hurt you more than it would hurt me, and I doubt that's the case with your brother."

"Not even close," Hawkyn offered. "I promise that everything I do will hurt you a lot more than it hurts me."

Suzanne glared at her brother, and Declan almost expected a death ray to shoot from her pupils. Could angels do that?

"All right, all right," Hawkyn said. "I'll be gentle."

She shot him one last glare before walking away, but a few feet from the gazebo where she planned to wait, she paused and looked back over her shoulder at Declan, the soft waves in her hair catching the golden sunlight and making her look every inch the angel she was.

Tears shimmered in her eyes. "I'm so sorry."

Declan didn't have a chance to respond. Pain swallowed him whole, as if he was being chewed up by a giant shark. What the fuck was Hawkyn doing to him? Panting, his arm wrapped around his cramping belly, he looked over at the dickhead angel, who wasn't even looking at Declan. He was watching his sister, his expression etched with misery as Suzanne buried her face in her hands and slumped against the gazebo.

Hawkyn didn't care about Declan's pain, but his love for his sister was fierce.

"More," Declan gritted out. "I can take more."

"I don't know..." Hawk said, but dammit, Dec was tired of this bullshit. The longer he suffered, the longer Suzanne would suffer. He wanted the demon dead, and if he had to break every bone in his body to draw the thing out, that's what he'd do.

"More!"

"No," Hawkyn snapped.

"Why?"

"Because you want it."

Okay, Declan was done with this shit. It was time to get serious. Time to make Hawkyn really mad.

"Asshole," he spat. "You've been wanting to destroy me from the moment you saw me, all to protect your innocent little sister. Well, you failed."

Hawkyn went taut, and his lips peeled back from his teeth and those giant fangs. "What did you say?"

"Declan, don't!" Suzanne shouted, but too late. Declan had made his decision, and if Hawkyn killed him, well, at least Morroc would no longer be after him and Ian and Remy would be safe.

"I fucked her," Declan said, locking gazes with Hawk. "Twice. And damn, she was good—"

He broke off as agony ripped him apart. Dear God, maybe Hawkyn could do the red mist thing, because it felt as if he was coming apart at a molecular level. Dropping to his knees, he screamed, and somewhere in the background he heard Suzanne scream as well. He hated that this was hurting her too, and although he'd never prayed for anything in his life, he prayed that when he was gone she'd find peace.

Abruptly, as quickly as it began, the pain ended, and something struck him like a truck, knocking him into a tree. Shouts and roars erupted around him.

Morroc.

And not just Morroc. The demon had brought friends.

"Fuck!" Maddox shouted as the Siecher demons swarmed the clearing.

Lightning bolts and fireballs flew from the hands of the angels, who had materialized from out of nowhere. Declan groaned as he pushed awkwardly to his feet. His ribs and spine screamed in pain as he ducked around a tree trunk to avoid what would have been a lethal blow to the head. As it was, Morroc's fist punched a hole through the wood, stopping short of slamming into Dec's shoulder when it erupted from the opposite side.

Then Suzanne was there, a scythe in both hands. "Take cover!"

It felt wrong to hide while everyone else was fighting, but he was the target, and he knew from experience that it was hard to fight an enemy when you had to worry about someone else's safety.

Cursing his human shortcomings, he made a dash for the gazebo. Hawkyn rushed past him, dagger concealed at his side, but before he could reach Morroc, another Siecher tackled him, and they went tumbling into the lake. The dagger flew into the air, coming down in the grass a few feet from where Suzanne and Morroc were locked in mortal combat.

"No!" he screamed as Morroc pinned Suzanne, his razor claws punching through her torso and into the ground beneath her. Blood sprayed in a geyser, splashing the demon's face in a shower of gore. Suzanne's mouth opened, her silent scream gurgling through blood.

As Morroc raised his other fist in preparation to slam it down with the other one, Declan lost it. His agony, his terror, his instinct to protect the woman he loved, condensed in a ball of desperation and power that vibrated his entire body.

Heat built with searing intensity that concentrated along the lines of the tattoo on his back.

Morroc punched down, ripping once more into Suzanne's chest. He was going to tear her in half. The terror in her eyes as she stared into his face made it clear that she understood what was about to happen to her.

Rage launched Declan into the air, completely off the ground. He didn't consider how he was flying or why; the only thing that mattered was Suzanne.

He dipped low, scooped up the dagger where it was lying in a pool of her blood, and hit Morroc from behind so hard that it knocked the breath from Declan's lungs.

The demon tumbled forward, taking Suzanne's impaled body with him. Hawkyn, his leg twisted and one eye swollen shut, threw some sort of round weapon that looked like a sharp Frisbee made of ice. The disc sliced through the demon's flesh, severing one of his arms at the elbow.

Suzanne rolled free, but when her body came to a stop in a crumpled heap, she wasn't moving.

Roaring with the force of years of built-up rage, Declan slammed into the demon, coming down on its chest like Iron Man hitting the pavement. Morroc's ribs cracked beneath Declan's knee, and for the first time, fear flickered in the demon's black eyes.

"This," Declan snarled, "is for Steve."

With a shout of pure, rabid pleasure, he plunged the dagger into Morroc's right eye. The demon shrieked, his body bucking and quaking so hard Declan was thrown off with the force of a rodeo bull throwing its rider. He hit the ground and rolled instantly to his feet. All around, the other Siechers howled as their leader took his last breaths.

The angels, battered and bloody, moved in on the demons, but with their leader dead, the battle was over and, if Suzanne was correct, so was the vendetta against Declan. Tremors shook the ground as it opened beneath each of the monsters and swallowed them up.

"Hawkyn!" Cipher's terrified scream echoed off the mountains.

Declan spun around, his jaw dropping at the sight of four winged people spinning a net around Cipher and then vanishing in a spray of what he could only describe as anti-light, an oily black plume that seemed to have a life of its own.

And when it cleared, Cipher was gone.

"No," Hawkyn shouted. "*No!*"

Declan had no idea what that was about, and right now all that mattered was Suzanne. Ignoring his multitude of aches and pains, he rushed, limping, to her side.

"Did we win?" Suzanne's voice, thin and reedy, called out as he dropped to his knees next to her.

"Morroc's dead." He wanted to gather her in his arms, but her body was beyond broken, and his medic training kicked in. He didn't have enough hands to plug all her wounds, but with help from everyone—

"Back up, Declan." Hawkyn kneeled across from him, clearly still shaken by whatever had happened to Cipher, and Sexy joined him.

"Fuck off, dickhead," Dec snapped. "If you think I'm going to—"

"Sexy can help her," Hawkyn said in a shockingly calm voice. "But you can't be touching her."

"Oh." Feeling a little chagrined, Dec backed up as Sexy laid her hands on Suzanne's abdomen.

"This won't heal her as much as she needs, but it'll stabilize her so we can get her to Underworld General."

As Declan watched, the streams of blood pouring out of Suzanne's wounds slowed and flesh began to knit together. As a former medic, he couldn't help but be fascinated. If only humans could do that.

He reconsidered his wish. Humans could screw up anything.

"She's going to be okay, right?" He looked up at Hawkyn, who nodded, but worry lingered in his expression.

"If she survives, it's because of you," Hawkyn said, his voice rough with emotion. "You know that, right?"

If she survives? Declan wasn't much for praying, but that was before he found out that Heaven was real, and he sent up a silent "Please let her be okay" to anyone who was listening.

Unable to think about Suzanne dying, he looked over to the spot where he'd last seen the tech-savvy Unfallen angel who'd disappeared in a poof of evil. "What happened to Cipher?"

"Fallen angels." Hawkyn's body sagged, his head hanging from hunched shoulders. "They took him to Sheoul."

Oh, shit. He remembered what Suzanne had said about that. It was bad. Really, really bad.

Journey limped over, his right thigh a mass of mangled flesh that didn't seem to bother him all that much. Must be nice. Dec had seen humans keel over from a paper cut.

"I called Idess. She'll get the ER staff prepped for Suzanne's arrival." Journey tapped Declan's shoulder. "Yo, D. What's up with your wings? I thought you were a measly human."

"Excuse me?" Declan blinked, so focused on Cipher and Suzanne that he only heard half of what Journey said. The crazy half. "Wings?"

"You flew. I saw some sort of wing-things flapping like a hummingbird on your back."

Hawkyn nodded. "I saw it too."

"I totally missed it," Maddox said, cradling his clearly broken arm. "Can you do it again?"

"I don't even know how I did it the first time."

"Your tattoo," Suzanne rasped. Her eyes were closed, her face pale, but she was smiling. "It's like it came to life. Right out of a comic book."

"Okay, guys." Sexy said as she wiped her bloody hand on her jeans. "Let's get Suz to the hospital."

The hospital that was also right out of a comic book.

Chapter Twenty-Two

Suzanne woke up in a hospital bed with Declan and Hawkyn at her side. And they weren't trying to kill each other.

"You're awake," Hawk said, ever the observant one. "How do you feel?"

"Actually, I feel great." She sat up and checked herself out, surprised to see that she wasn't even wearing any bandages.

She was, however, wearing a pale pink hospital gown dotted with tiny gray kittens. It was adorable. She wanted pajama shorts made out of the print. But she couldn't imagine that demons were thrilled to have to wear this cuteness. Whoever ordered these things had a warped sense of humor.

But then, there were chains on the ceiling and shelves of hideous things in jars, demon skulls, and wicked tools she hoped weren't actively used in this medical facility, so warped appeared to be the natural order here.

Beneath the gown, red marks scored her skin, and her entire torso was a mass of healing scars, but aside from a little tenderness, she felt like she could run a marathon. "How long have I been in the hospital?"

Declan looked at his watch. "We're just coming up on the twenty-four-hour mark." He reached over and took her hand, and she swore her scars started healing faster at his touch. Her pulse was definitely beating faster. "You don't seem surprised to have woken up in a demon hospital."

"I heard you all talking when Sexy was healing me," she said, amused that Declan was casually discussing an underworld hospital as if he'd been doing it for years. He was adapting well. Now she just had to hope that he could keep his memory. No, she wasn't going to hope.

She was going to make certain. She'd fight every archangel in Heaven if she had to. She'd hide him in this hospital where Heavenly angels couldn't enter. Hawkyn should consider himself lucky that when he was promoted from out of the regular Memitim ranks that he hadn't lost his ability to access Underworld General.

Over the last few years since Idess had mated one of the brothers who ran the place, more than a few Memitim had sought medical treatment here, and a couple of her siblings had even consulted with the head doctor, Eidolon, on business related to their Primoris. And Sheoul-gra's resident healer, Darien, had even interned here.

Until he got fired for incompetence or something. He never said. But lack of competence was a safe bet.

She was lucky her siblings had brought her here instead of to him. "How did I heal so quickly? My wounds were nearly fatal."

"You're not going to believe this," Hawk said, taking a break from tossing a cotton ball into the air, "but our mother saved you."

"What?" She sat up straighter, and Declan's grip on her hand remained, more of a comfort than she could ever tell him. "How? She's not allowed to make contact with us except in Heaven."

"That's one of the rules I got changed," Hawkyn said, which was a shocker on its own. He'd sworn to make changes at the very top of the Memitim food chain in order to make all their lives better, and he'd lived up to his promise. "But it doesn't matter. She can't enter the hospital, so she wasn't even here. She gave me her blood. She's *vivificus*, remember?"

Declan frowned over at Hawk. "*Vivificus?*"

"Angels who give life," Hawkyn explained. "They're rare, and only a handful of our brothers and sisters inherited her gift."

"And even those who did got a diluted form of it," Suzanne said. Still, she envied those. Apparently Idess had been born with the ability to restore life, but Suzanne assumed she'd lost it when she gave up her Memitim status because, although she worked at Underworld General, she didn't do so in a medical capacity.

"Oh." Hawkyn held up his phone, and she forced herself to not make fun of him for the picture of Aurora as his background. She'd read in some magazine that teasing males about their tender moments ruined them for future tender moments. Or something. "Lilliana sends her love."

"How did she know I was here?"

"Apparently, nothing is secret in this place." Hawkyn lowered his voice as if someone was listening. Probably the skulls on the shelves. "Idess must have told Lore, who told his brothers, who told their mates, who told...fuck, I don't know. I swear, everyone here is related to the Horsemen, and I guess Lilliana is staying with War...or Ares...whatever his name is."

"So she hasn't gone back to Father yet?" He must be growing grumpier by the day.

"Nope." Hawkyn put away his phone. "He must have done something really, really bad."

Well, Azagoth *was* the Grim Reaper, so the doorway to "really, really bad" was wide open. But if he'd cheated on her... She sucked in a harsh breath. "Flail," she hissed. "That skank has been nosing around—"

A low, dangerous growl rattled in Hawkyn's chest, and damn if the temperature didn't drop. She'd never seen—or felt—Hawkyn do that before. It was straight out of Azagoth's hat of tricks. The ones that made you pray you weren't the target of his anger.

"She's gone," he growled in a voice that promised a lot of pain if he ever caught up with her. "She's the reason Cipher got taken."

"What are you talking about?" She jerked in surprise so hard the bed moved. "Cipher got taken? Taken where?" The moment she asked that last question, she knew the answer. Hell. Cipher had been taken to Hell. "Never mind," she croaked, leaning into Declan's powerful shoulder for support. She loved Cipher like another brother, and if she'd ever met an Unfallen who deserved to get his wings back, it was him. "What did you say about Flail? It was her fault? How do you know?"

Hawkyn's emerald eyes were as cold as the room. "I went to tell Father what happened to you. He's happy you're okay and he said he misses your 'dailies,' whatever that is."

She smiled despite the heartbreak over Cipher. During her human life, she'd made sure she either saw or talked to her father every day until she "went missing," and since moving to Sheoul-gra, she'd done the same thing with Azagoth. At first he'd seemed annoyed. And then tolerant. And then amused. Recently she thought he might have actually been looking forward to her brief visits or even just the hellos in passing.

"Anyway," Hawkyn said, bringing them back on topic. "While I was there, Razr said Flail took off. Packed all her shit and cleared out her room. Cleared out Cipher's too. She got his laptop. That's when I realized that she knew about the Siecher demons, and she knew where Ciph was going to be."

That *bitch*. "And you think she sent her fallen angel buddies to grab him."

"I'd bet my life on it." Hawkyn looked over at Declan. "Cipher was an Unfallen angel, which means he's not fully evil because he hasn't entered Hell yet. Fallen angels like Flail like to drag Unfallens to Hell and bring them over to their side."

"I know." Declan shifted just enough to press a tender kiss on top of Suzanne's head, and her heart gave a happy little thump. She knew he hadn't gotten much affection as a kid, so for him to show it as an adult, and to show it so openly, was remarkable. "There's an Unfallen in the *Demonica* comics named Reaver. I've been rooting for him to get his wings back."

Suzanne exchanged glances with Hawkyn. "Should we tell him, or make him wait until the comic comes out?"

Declan pulled away to hold up his hands. "No spoilers."

He was going to get spoiled on everything eventually, so she let it go. Besides, she was worried about Cipher and sad that he was gone, and it felt wrong to tease Declan about the fate of another Unfallen.

"We're going to get him back, right?" she practically begged her brother. "We'll save Cipher."

"Yeah, we will," Hawkyn promised, but his expression was understandably troubled. They might be able to find Ciph, but he wouldn't be the same. "Look, I need to tell you something, and now is as good a time as any."

She stiffened, and Declan did as well. "Is it bad news?"

"I spoke to the Council about you."

That wasn't a no. "And?"

"And you're in a lot of trouble. Most of the laws and rules you've broken wouldn't have come to the attention of the Council if it weren't for the house you blew up. It took fixers from Heaven's Rectification Bureau to make it look like a gas leak, and that triggered an investigation. Now they know you were not only living with your Primori, but that you told him the truth."

Oh, shit. She swallowed. "What else?"

"They don't know you've been...intimate, if that's what you're asking."

Yep, that was what she'd been asking. Mortified that her brother had figured it out and knowing there was no point in denying it, she awkwardly cleared her throat. "So what are they going to do to us?"

Hawkyn's leather jacket creaked as he stood. Her brother could never sit still for bad news. "They wanted to strip you of your powers and your Ascension and then relegate you to the human realm forever."

She waited to be torn apart by heartbreak. Or even mild sadness. But there was nothing. In fact, she was finding it hard to hold back a smile.

Until what he'd just said sunk in. "Wait. You said they *wanted* to do those things. They didn't?"

"I talked them out of it." He walked over to one of the creepy saw-looking instruments hanging on the wall, seeming pretty proud of himself, but her heart sank.

"You didn't." She swung her legs out of bed, prepared to shake some sense into her brother if she had to. "Hawkyn, I hate being a Memitim. I don't want this. Go tell them that! Tell them about me and Declan. Tell them—"

"Sis, stop." He swung around to her. "I know you're miserable. I didn't truly get that until today. But I couldn't let you lose Memitim status and all your powers. I couldn't stand to see you be vulnerable." He paused, and she wanted to cry. "So I convinced them to let you serve in another way."

She put crying on hold, but she held it in reserve.

"How?" she and Declan asked simultaneously.

"Suzanne will no longer protect Primori. Declan's already been assigned to Journey."

Startled, she turned her arm over, and sure enough, the *heraldi* was gone. Funny, but that bothered her far more than the possibility of losing her powers and her future wings. The *heraldi* was a connection to Declan, a physical monitor of his health and status. It was going to take some time to get used to not having it.

But she supposed if they were together, she'd know whether or not he was okay. Still, this was all so confusing.

"If I'm not guarding Primori, what will I do?"

"You'll do your cooking show."

He could have knocked her over with a feather, as her human mother used to say. "I'll do my cooking show." At his nod, she stared in disbelief. "Are you serious? How does that serve Memitim in any way?"

"It's not serving Memitim. It's serving Heaven." He raked his hand through his hair and blew out a long breath. "This is big, Suzanne. And it can't go beyond this room." He shot Declan a meaningful look, and Dec gave a brief nod. "The Archangel Council has given the go ahead to start revealing the truth to humans. Right now it's small-scale. People who can handle it, like Declan. But to prepare the rest of the population, they need friendly faces in place. And they think they can use your ability to infuse food with emotions to chill people out on a large scale or something. I'm not sure. The archangel I talked to wasn't filling in a lot of blanks."

Declan made a startled noise. "You talked to an archangel? Which one?"

"I was supposed to talk to Gabriel, but he canceled and sent Aramel instead."

"Wow." Suzanne was just glad it was her brother and not her who'd had to gab with an archangel. She'd have probably babbled like an idiot and gotten herself into more trouble. "Did he say when all humans will be fully aware?"

"It's going to be a super slow process. I got the impression it'll be a decade or so."

In angel time, a decade was like a mere second, but a decade for humans could bring about leaps in technology and huge societal shifts. Revealing the existence of their world over a period of ten or more years was probably a smart way to do it.

"There's just one problem with this plan of theirs," she said, thinking of Cipher. "The network execs who wanted to see me about my show canceled because I couldn't make it."

He grinned. "You're going to want to check your voicemail. The other deal fell through and they want to see you on Monday. You'll have the weekend to put together your pitch."

She wanted to scream with happiness. This was the best thing ever. But she couldn't be happy until she knew for sure that Declan's fate was not to be returned to a state of cluelessness. If she had to give up her cooking show to ensure he kept his memory, she would.

"What about Declan?" she demanded. "I mean, he knows the truth. They aren't going to erase his memory, are they?"

"Fuck that," Declan said. "They aren't getting anywhere close to my head again."

"They're not," Hawkyn assured him. "But there's a catch."

Oh, shit.

"They want you to work for a demonic activity response team. It's called DART. It's a unit that was formed after The Aegis broke apart."

Declan looked utterly put out. "They broke apart?"

"Oh, hey, sorry. Spoiler alert. Anyway, they'll be in touch soon. Oh, and you've been given immortality. I don't know what your importance is in the universe, and I don't know why you're Primori, but damn, you've won the Heavenly lotto. Now," Hawk said as he came to his feet, "I have to go tell our father about all of this. But something tells me he already knows. On the way out I'll let someone know you're awake."

"Hawkyn, wait." She leaped out of bed, not caring that her bare ass was open for everyone behind her to see. Good thing the "everyone behind her" was only Declan. "Thank you."

She threw herself into her brother's arms, grateful to him for so many things. He'd been there for her almost since the very beginning, first as her mentor, but always as her brother.

"Yeah, man," Declan said, extending his hand. "Thank you. For everything. You're not as much of a dick as I thought."

Hawkyn laughed. "Ditto." The two males shook, and then he left, leaving her alone with Declan. Finally.

"Now what?" she said.

He took her hand and led her back to the bed, where he sat down next to her. There wasn't much room, but that only made it better.

"It sounds like we don't have any restrictions on our relationship."

Her mouth went utterly, desperately dry. "Does that mean you want one? With me? For real? After everything that's happened?"

He looked at her like she'd lost her mind. "It's *because* of everything that's happened, Suzanne. I feel like I finally have a place in this world. All that shit with my family and the military and the tattoo... I'm cool with it. This feels like where I'm supposed to be. It's going to sound corny, but it's like I'm living in the comics I've loved my entire life. I mean, I basically just found out that The Avengers are real and they want me to join S.H.I.E.L.D. And the best part is that my girlfriend is a superhero."

Shifting so she was facing him, she placed her hand on his chest, over his heart. There was so much strength in there, beating against her palm. "You are too, you know. We'll get someone to work with you to understand your own powers. Jim Bob said the tattoo draws on what's inside you, and now we know you can use the wings to fly, so what else is in there?"

The slightest glint of doubt sparked in his eyes. "Maybe nothing."

"Oh, no," she assured him as she slid her hand down his chest to his abs, where she drew circles on his rock-hard abs. "I have a feeling the well inside you is very deep."

He didn't look convinced, but she figured there was time to get him on board. But for now she just wanted to get dressed and then go somewhere with Declan to celebrate.

Preferably a place with a bed.

* * * *

Declan took the next week off from work, spending some of it helping Suzanne look for an apartment in New York, where she'd be taping *Angel in the Kitchen.* The great thing about it was that the apartment was really for show. Since she could flash anywhere she wanted to go, she didn't have to actually live there.

Which meant they could live where they wanted to, and for now they'd decided on Dallas, where he had friends from McKay-Taggart, and she was developing a friendship with people from Top. His apartment was a true bachelor pad, so he was looking forward to finding a new place to live with Suzanne as long as it wasn't that damned angel mansion. He'd also be cool with a demon-detecting security system.

Turned out that this new world was a busy, dangerous place. And he had a lot of studying to do in order to catch up with everything he needed to know, right down to the gazillion types of demons he might encounter and the history of pretty much every important angel to have ever existed.

A representative from DART, a raspy-voiced guy named Kynan Morgan who was also a bearer of angelic DNA, had met him for an initial interview, and Declan would meet the local Dallas crew next week. And one of the local crew was a fucking *werewolf.*

Werewolves were *real.*

He still had a lot of holy shit moments.

And now he just had to figure out how to tell Tag that he was quitting McKay-Taggart.

He practiced his spiel as he sat in Tag's office, waiting for his boss to arrive. A couple minutes later, Tag slipped inside with an apology for being late. Well, it was as close as he ever came to an apology, anyway.

"Fucking jackass," he muttered on the way to the desk.

"Me? What did I do?"

"Not you." Tag sank down into his desk chair, and Dec couldn't help but watch for signs that he remembered, on even the deepest level, that he and Suzanne had come for the dagger. "So how'd the assignment go? I was surprised when Ms. D'Angelo said you were no longer needed."

"Stalker situation handled."

"Good. Because we need to talk about the D.C. assignment."

Declan groaned. "Not this again. Ian, Suzanne got a job in New York and I want to spend time with her there. That's why I'm here."

Tag sat back, mild surprise raising his brows. "Huh." And then he was all smiles. "It's about fucking time you got into the game. I was starting to worry about you."

"How nice that my sex life was cause for concern," Declan drawled. "So are we done with this D.C. nonsense? Because we need to talk."

"I wish I could say no. But there's someone here to see you." Tag got up and went to the door. "Says he's your uncle. Lawrence Cantor. He's the one who wanted to hire you for Senator McRory. Says he's McRory's aide or something. I checked his background, and he's not a lunatic, but if you don't want to see him, you don't have to. But the guy is insistent. And he's a world-class prick. I'll be happy to have security escort him out if you want."

It was tempting. Declan had only met his father's younger brother once, at one of the weekends out at the lake cabin. Uncle Larry had been an obnoxious braggart who had clearly hated "snot-nosed" kids. The guy was a world-class prick, all right.

"No, send him in," Declan told Tag. "I'm curious now." And he could give his notice later.

"You got it."

Tag left, and a moment later a balding, overweight man who was shorter and way less fit than Declan remembered came inside.

"Hi, Declan." He held out his meaty hand. "You've sure grown up."

Declan came to his feet, but he didn't offer his own hand. "Twenty years will do that to you."

Larry dropped his arm, looking a little perturbed. "I was hoping you'd come to Washington. I didn't want to fly out here. Never did like the heat much."

"And I never liked Washington much. What do you want, Larry? To apologize for hitting me in the head with your half-empty beer cans?"

And there were a lot of them. The bastard would laugh and laugh, and he'd then laugh harder when Declan complained about it.

Can't take a little joke, you crybaby pussy? Boo hoo. Life's tough. Get used to it.

Larry's perturbed look turned irritated. "That was a long time ago. We're both adults, so let's talk like it. I'm here to make sure you keep your mouth shut about your paternity."

Declan snorted. "Must be an election year."

"Your father is thinking about running for president," Larry said, leaving Declan too stunned to respond. "We'd like to offer you a tidy sum in exchange for your word, and a signed contract, of course, that you'll never reveal the truth about your father's identity."

Oh, hell, no. Declan's knowledge was the one thing he had that could make his father sweat. The guy had been looking over his shoulder for years, and with a presidential bid on the line, he'd be constantly paranoid. No amount of money could take that simple pleasure away from Declan.

"No." He gestured to the door. "Get out."

Ugly splotches of red colored Larry's cheeks and his fishy pale lips peeled back from his teeth. "Listen to me, you ungrateful piece of shit. We're offering six figures, more money than you've probably ever seen. I suggest you take it."

"Money doesn't mean jack shit."

"Says someone who doesn't have it."

Seriously, Declan wanted to punch this fuck. "You think money makes you better than me."

"I know it does." Larry's chest puffed out like he was a big, ridiculous rooster. "Did you go to an elite prep school? Did you get an advanced degree at an Ivy League college? Did you—"

"Did you serve your country in the military?" Declan took a step closer. "Have you ever put your hands inside a man to pinch off an artery and stop him from bleeding out? Ever even fucking stopped to help an elderly person cross a busy street?" Declan moved even closer, stalking him, enjoying the fact that he was much taller than this jerk off. "Tell me. What do you have besides your billions?"

"I have houses all over the world." Larry's voice was shrill with outrage that someone had dared to call him out on his self-importance. "Casinos. I own a goddamned private island resort. I can get anything I want with a phone call. Women beg to suck my dick."

"Yeah, okay. Who wouldn't love all of that? But I couldn't help but notice that you didn't say you have friends. A family who loves you. Self-respect. Did your Ivy League school teach you to survive? Not survive on Wall Street or in politics, but to *really* survive. You know, in the real world." He jammed his finger into Uncle Larry's sternum. "Take away your money, what have you got? In a lot of survival situations, money is worthless. Put you in a major disaster or real danger and you'll break like a twig. You'd lick my boots and beg for my help in a demon apocalypse. You're nothing, man. Waste of fucking air and a waste of my time."

He reached around Larry and opened the office door. "Get the fuck out, and tell my father to never make contact again."

"This isn't over, Declan," Larry said as he left. But it was. Because for the first time in his life, Declan was able to put the past where it belonged.

And also because Declan would make sure his father never sat in the Oval Office.

Assuming his father wasn't Primori and destined for it, of course. But even if he was, Declan was comfortable with the knowledge that there was a hell for people like him, and it was only a matter of time before his bad deeds—and the Grim Reaper—caught up with them.

In the meantime, Declan would enjoy his life.

And right now, his life was waiting for him at his apartment, and according to the text she'd just sent, she was cooking sexy food and wanted a taste tester. Obviously, he volunteered.

Not all heroes wore capes.

Chapter Twenty-Three

Six weeks after Suzanne signed the contract for the network cooking show, she filmed her first episode. She prepared sticky hot ribs with a celebration theme, and after they wrapped, the crew had eaten what she'd cooked. What followed had been a wild party she and Declan hadn't escaped from until well after midnight.

They were going to be late.

She flashed them to her apartment, where they spent about half their time lately. Declan's bachelor pad was adequate, but they needed to find a bigger place, and she liked the giant kitchen in her high-rise flat. Besides, it seemed like one of her brothers or sisters was always popping in, and her apartment had become an unofficial headquarters for leading the hunt to find Cipher.

So far...they'd found nothing. Flail had disappeared completely, leaving no leads, and Cipher, if he was still alive, hadn't shown his face anywhere, either. One thing was certain, though; they would never give up looking.

The moment they materialized in the living room, she rushed to the computer in the office, dragging Declan with her.

"He's going to be pissed that he had to wait," she muttered as she woke the screen, and sure enough, her father was trying to connect with her via Skype.

This was not the way she'd wanted Azagoth to meet Declan for the first time. Why the hell couldn't the Memitim Council make an exception to the rule that Primori couldn't enter Shoul-gra? They'd given permission to Hawkyn's mate, Aurora, after all.

Hawkyn had tried to explain that his situation was different because

Aurora wasn't Primori; the baby inside her was. Still, he was attempting to have the rule abolished. Aurora's skills as a Wytch and a massage therapist would be useful in Sheoul-gra, and being able to bring the baby to work would not only be great for them, but it would help ensure the child would stay safe. After all, what safer environment for a Primori than a realm full of Memitim?

"Hello, Father," she said as his face filled the screen. "I hope you didn't have to wait too long." She tugged Declan down beside her so he was in the frame. "This is Declan."

Declan nodded. "Mr...Reaper."

Azagoth grunted. "So you're the human who stole my daughter from me."

"I didn't steal her from you, sir." Declan wrapped his arm around her shoulder and held her tight against his big chest. "She'll always be your daughter. I'm just here to worship her."

Her heart pounded against her rib cage so forcefully she was sure her father could hear it.

She was positively gooey with love, but her father wasn't as enamored. "Suzanne is special to me," Azagoth said, his deep voice scraping gravel. "So worship her well and remember that my reach extends beyond my realm's borders."

Declan inclined his head respectfully. "Understood."

"Suzanne." Her father's expression softened when he looked at her. "I'll see you tomorrow?"

She nodded. "I'm volunteering to mentor one of the new arrivals. A thirteen-year-old."

The teen, a half-sister, had been orphaned recently in a civil war and was living in a refugee camp. Hopefully, learning she had another family and a new shot at life would help ease some of the pain, but Suzanne knew firsthand how long the pain of losing loved ones could last.

"Good," Azagoth said. "I'll see you tomorrow."

Grinning, she said good-bye. That was the first time he'd sounded like he was looking forward to their "dailies." She wondered if he was lonely. Lilliana hadn't returned to him yet, and he had to be desperate for her.

"See?" she said to Declan. "That wasn't so bad."

"For you, maybe. I thought he was going to reach through the screen and strangle me." He let out a sigh of relief and beelined straight for the kitchen. "I'm going to get a beer or ten. Want anything?"

"No," she said, taking a seat on one of the barstools at the island. "I just want to watch you."

He shot her a sly grin as he bent to grab a sparkling water from the fridge. "Yeah? Then what?"

"Then I'm going to peel off all your clothes and take advantage of you. Maybe in the shower." She reached up and unbuttoned the first two buttons on her blouse. "Or right here."

Straightening, he set the bottle on the counter. "I don't think I'm thirsty anymore."

"No?"

"No." His eyes darkened and his voice went low. "Now I'm hungry."

"You're insatiable," she purred. "I love it. I love *you*."

He came around the island and gripped her thighs, spreading them with gentle pressure. His mouth came down on hers as he stepped between her legs, his erection pressing into her core through their pants.

"I love you too, Suzanne. Every day I thank Fate that you were my guardian angel."

Every day she did the same. But the truth wasn't quite that simple. She'd been assigned to protect him, but in the end, it was he who had saved her life. It was he who had allowed her to break away from a life path she would have hated. It was he who had helped her to fulfill the dreams she'd had since the first time she'd baked cookies with her grandma.

So yes, she'd been assigned to keep him safe, but in the end, it was he who was the real guardian. He was, truly, her guardian angel.

<<<<>>>>

Discover the Lexi Blake Crossover Collection
Available now!

Close Cover by Lexi Blake

Remy Guidry doesn't do relationships. He tried the marriage thing once, back in Louisiana, and learned the hard way that all he really needs in life is a cold beer, some good friends, and the occasional hookup. His job as a bodyguard with McKay-Taggart gives him purpose and lovely perks, like access to Sanctum. The last thing he needs in his life is a woman with stars in her eyes and babies in her future.

Lisa Daley's life is going in the right direction. She has graduated from college after years of putting herself through school. She's got a new job at an accounting firm and she's finished her Sanctum training. Finally on her own and having fun, her life seems pretty perfect. Except she's lonely and the one man she wants won't give her a second look.

There is one other little glitch. Apparently, her new firm is really a front for the mob and now they want her dead. Assassins can really ruin a fun girls' night out. Suddenly strapped to the very same six-foot-five-inch hunk of a bodyguard who makes her heart pound, Lisa can't decide if this situation is a blessing or a curse.

As the mob closes in, Remy takes his tempting new charge back to the safest place he knows—his home in the bayou. Surrounded by his past, he can't help wondering if Lisa is his future. To answer that question, he just has to keep her alive.

* * * *

Her Guardian Angel by Larissa Ione

After a difficult childhood and a turbulent stint in the military, Declan Burke finally got his act together. Now he's a battle-hardened professional bodyguard who takes his job at McKay-Taggart seriously and his playtime – and his play*mates* – just as seriously. One thing he never does, however, is mix business with pleasure. But when the mysterious, gorgeous Suzanne D'Angelo needs his protection from a stalker, his desire for her burns out of control, tempting him to break all the rules...even as he's drawn into a dark, dangerous world he didn't know existed.

Suzanne is an earthbound angel on her critical first mission: protecting Declan from an emerging supernatural threat at all costs. To keep him close, she hires him as her bodyguard. It doesn't take long for her to realize that she's in over her head, defenseless against this devastatingly sexy human who makes her crave his forbidden touch.

Together they'll have to draw on every ounce of their collective training to resist each other as the enemy closes in, but soon it becomes apparent that nothing could have prepared them for the menace to their lives...or their hearts.

* * * *

Justify Me by J. Kenner

McKay-Taggart operative Riley Blade has no intention of returning to Los Angeles after his brief stint as a consultant on mega-star Lyle Tarpin's latest action flick. Not even for Natasha Black, Tarpin's sexy personal assistant who'd gotten under his skin. Why would he, when Tasha made it absolutely clear that—attraction or not—she wasn't interested in a fling, much less a relationship.

But when Riley learns that someone is stalking her, he races to her side. Determined to not only protect her, but to convince her that—no matter what has hurt her in the past—he's not only going to fight for her, he's going to win her heart. Forever.

* * * *

Say You Won't Let Go by Corinne Michaels

I've had two goals my entire life:
1. Make it big in country music.
2. Get the hell out of Bell Buckle.
I was doing it. I was on my way, until Cooper Townsend landed backstage at my show in Dallas.
This gorgeous, rugged, man of few words was one cowboy I couldn't afford to let distract me. But with his slow smile and rough hands, I just

couldn't keep away.

Now, there are outside forces conspiring against us. Maybe we should've known better? Maybe not. Even with the protection from Wade Rycroft, bodyguard for McKay-Taggart, I still don't feel safe. I won't let him get hurt because of me. All I know is that I want to hold on, but know the right thing to do is to let go...

* * * *

His to Protect by Carly Phillips

Talia Shaw has spent her adult life working as a scientist for a big pharmaceutical company. She's focused on saving lives, not living life. When her lab is broken into and it's clear someone is after the top secret formula she's working on, she turns to the one man she can trust. The same irresistible man she turned away years earlier because she was too young and naive to believe a sexy guy like Shane Landon could want *her*.

Shane Landon's bodyguard work for McKay-Taggart is the one thing that brings him satisfaction in his life. Relationships come in second to the job. Always. Then little brainiac Talia Shaw shows up in his backyard, frightened and on the run, and his world is turned upside down. And not just because she's found him naked in his outdoor shower, either.

With Talia's life in danger, Shane has to get her out of town and to her eccentric, hermit mentor who has the final piece of the formula she's been working on, while keeping her safe from the men who are after her. Guarding Talia's body certainly isn't any hardship, but he never expects to fall hard and fast for his best friend's little sister and the only woman who's ever really gotten under his skin.

* * * *

Rescuing Sadie by Susan Stoker

Sadie Jennings was used to being protected. As the niece of Sean Taggart, and the receptionist at McKay-Taggart Group, she was constantly surrounded by Alpha men more than capable, and willing, to lay down their life for her. But when she visits her friend in San Antonio, and acts on suspicious activity at Milena's workplace, Sadie puts both of them in the crosshairs of a madman. After several harrowing weeks, her friend is now safe, but for Sadie, the repercussions of her rash act linger on.

Chase Jackson, no stranger to dangerous situations as a captain in the US Army, has volunteered himself as Sadie's bodyguard. He fell head over heels for the beautiful woman the first time he laid eyes on her. With a Delta Force team at his back, he reassures the Taggart's that Sadie will be safe. But when the situation in San Antonio catches up with her, Chase has to use everything he's learned over his career to keep his promise...and to keep Sadie alive long enough to officially make her his.

About Larissa Ione

Air Force veteran Larissa Ione traded in a career as a meteorologist to pursue her passion of writing. She has since published dozens of books, hit several bestseller lists, including the New York Times and USA Today, and has been nominated for a RITA award. She now spends her days in pajamas with her computer, strong coffee, and fictional worlds. She believes in celebrating everything, and would never be caught without a bottle of Champagne chilling in the fridge…just in case. After a dozen moves all over the country with her now-retired U.S. Coast Guard spouse, she is now settled in Wisconsin with her husband, her teenage son, a rescue cat named Vegas, and her very own hellhounds, a King Shepherd named Hexe, and a Belgian Malinois named Duvel.

For more information about Larissa, visit www.larissaione.com.

Hawkyn

A Demonica Novella
By Larissa Ione
Now Available

From New York Times and USA Today bestselling author Larissa Ione comes a new story in her Demonica Underworld series...

As a special class of earthbound guardian angel called Memitim, Hawkyn is charged with protecting those whose lives are woven into the fabric of the future. His success is legendary, so when he's given a serial killer to watch over, he sees no reason for that to change. But Hawkyn's own future is jeopardized after he breaks the rules and rescues a beautiful woman from the killer's clutches, setting off an explosive, demonic game of cat and mouse that pits brother against brother and that won't end until someone dies.

Aurora Mercer is the half-wytch lone survivor of a psychopath who gets off on the sadistic torture of his victims. A psychopath whose obsessive psyche won't let him move on until he kills her. Now she's marked for death, her fate tied to that of a murderer...and to a sexy angel who makes her blood burn with desire...

* * * *

A blast of heat roared through the house, and the temperature shot up at least twenty degrees. Aurora always kept the house at a sixty-five degrees at this time of year, so the instant jump to summer temps was like stepping into a dry sauna.

"How the is he doing this?" Hawkyn's raw curse bounced off the walls. "He's going to force heat exhaustion and then take you while you're too weak to fight back. We need to get you out of here *now*." He slid one warm hand down, his fingers skimming lightly over her jaw and lower, to the sensitive skin on her neck. "With your permission."

Blinking, momentarily confused, she watched him flick the pink tip of his tongue across a fang. Oh, right. He could feed from her to recharge. Take her blood with those huge, gleaming canines.

She waited for the revulsion to kick in, but something else happened.

Something…hot. Hotter than the serial-killer induced heat that was testing the limits of her deodorant.

There's a serial killer outside.

The sudden thought came with a blast of memories, of Drayger with the scalpel that made tiny, stinging cuts. Of sharp things and his laughter and pain—

"Will it hurt?" she blurted.

"I'll make it feel good, I promise." A fresh blast of heat drove up the number on the thermostat near the door to 103. "But we need to hurry."

She nodded, and his emerald eyes darkened, holding her gaze prisoner as he lowered his head. Gently, he tilted her face to the side and opened his mouth over her throat, and she shuddered with a mix of anticipation and trepidation.

She'd only dated a handful of men in her twenty-six years, wasting most of them on her high school sweetheart, a human who had never known the truth about her. If he had, he might not have cheated on her during their junior year in college. Then again, maybe he enjoyed her curse of flatulence he came down with every time he kissed a girl.

The other guys had come after the breakup, mostly rebound dates she'd used for sex. Wytches needed to discharge their energy often, either with sex or magic, and she'd gone through an extended anti-magic phase for a while. But not one of those men had made her nervous the way Hawkyn did.

Granted, none of them had fangs. Nor had they been supernatural beings, let alone angels. And none of them had looked like Hawkyn, with his six and a half foot, thickly muscled build, a cocky smile that radiated confidence, and intelligent eyes that she doubted missed anything.

Hawkyn's breath whispered over her skin, and she shivered as her anxiety became excitement. As his tongue flicked across her vein, she even had to hold back a moan of pleasure. When his fangs sank into her flesh, the mild pinprick gave way to a shocking spear of ecstasy that went straight to her core.

His arm slipped around her, bracing her body against his big one as he disengaged his teeth and repositioned his mouth. She let herself go, sinking into him as he swept her up and then settled them both on the couch so she was straddling his lap.

He took slow, easy draws, one hand holding her head in place, the other gripping her waist, settled tamely above her hipbone. His pinky finger wedged between her waistband and her sweater, and consciously or subconsciously he was stroking skin, his touch adding to the heat that was building inside and out.

A drop of sweat trickled down her temple, and she glanced at the thermometer. 115 now.

Shifting slightly, Hawkyn let out a groan and swept his tongue over the punctures in her throat. She felt no pain, only a pinch and tingle that told her the holes were sealing themselves.

"Are we done?" she whispered, making no move to climb off him. She wasn't even sure she could. Her bones felt like noodles and her muscles like water.

"Yeah," he said roughly, tucking her head into the crook of his neck and shoulder. "I just need a minute to clear the fog."

"I get that," she murmured into his shoulder. "Because I feel like I drank a couple of Long Island Ice Teas spiked with some kind of super-aphrodisiac." Reluctantly, she pushed herself up, just in time for another heatwave.

125.

"Come on," he said, lifting her off him. "We're going someplace much cooler."

"And where's that?"

He grinned as he flipped the duffel into the air with his foot and caught it in his hand in one easy motion. "Hell," he said, taking her hand. "We're literally going to hell."

A Special Note from Larissa

I hope you enjoyed this journey between worlds, which includes not only the Demonica and Masters and Mercenaries universes, but the very tasty universe of Suzanne Johnson as well. See, for those who don't know, my inspiration for Suzanne D'Angelo was a very dear friend, USA Today bestselling cookbook author Suzanne Johnson. An amazing cook, Suzanne has also teamed up with Lexi Blake to create recipes and stories from the Masters and Mercenaries world, so be sure to check out those works. And if the dishes in Her Guardian Angel tempted you, hold onto your halos and horns, folks, because we have a *very* special treat coming for you in the winter of 2018! Stay tuned!

Southern Bits & Bites
Southern Kid Bits & Mom Bites
Southern Bits & Bites: Our 150 Favorite Recipes

Writing with Lexi Blake
Master Bits & Mercenary Bites~The Secret Recipes of Topped
Master Bits & Mercenary Bites~Girls Night

Writing with J. Kenner
Bar Bites: A Man of the Month Cookbook, Coming May 15, 2018

On behalf of 1001 Dark Nights,

Liz Berry and M.J. Rose would like to thank ~

Steve Berry
Doug Scofield
Kim Guidroz
Jillian Stein
InkSlinger PR
Dan Slater
Asha Hossain
Chris Graham
Fedora Chen
Kasi Alexander
Jessica Johns
Dylan Stockton
Richard Blake
BookTrib After Dark
and Simon Lipskar

Made in the USA
Middletown, DE
03 July 2018